Praise for *Wish You Weren't Here* (The Rooks, Book 1):

'The **new classics of the genre** offer a wider range of effects than merely the delicious shiver ... *Wish You Weren't Here* sees a quarrelling family of professional ghost hunters tackle a seaside town ravaged by the undead. **Exuberantly satirical**, it's the first in a series of Rook family adventures.'
Financial Times

Praise for Gabby Hutchinson Crouch's Darkwood series:

'Gabby is **one of the funniest writers I know**.' Sarah Millican

'Very funny. **If you like Terry Pratchett, or think gothic fairytales should have more LOLs, 'tis the book for ye**.'
Greg Jenner

'I have read this and it is great. **Pratchetty fun for all the family**.' Lucy Porter

'**Magical, surprising and funny**.' Jan Ravens

Out of Service

THE ROOKS
BOOK TWO

GABBY
HUTCHINSON CROUCH

This edition published in 2022 by Farrago,
an imprint of Duckworth Books Ltd
1 Golden Court, Richmond, TW9 1EU, United Kingdom

www.farragobooks.com

Print ISBN: 9781788424035
Ebook ISBN: 9781788424042

For my Mum, who is not a Brenda, either in temperament or in name. Her name is Rory, which I know is confusing.

Contents

CHAPTER ONE

Don't Even Talk To Me Until I've Had My Coffee

T hink about home. What is home to you? Where you grew up? Where you live now? A little of both? Maybe they're the same place. Maybe they're on opposite sides of the world.

I have no home. Not any more. I used to. I grew up somewhere. I had a flat, with my husband and my daughter. Home. I can't remember. I can't remember where I used to live. Perhaps I used to look out of a window at a little garden, or rolling fields, or a busy street. Perhaps bright early morning sunlight used to stream through into the kitchen and play upon my husband's face as he held our daughter up to the window, while I poured the coffee. Did our daughter excitedly press pudgy, sticky fingers against the glass, steaming the window with hot little huffs of baby breath? Did my husband turn to smile at me, dark eyes twinkling in the golden light? Did we even drink coffee?

I can't remember. It's all gone. It was taken from me. Everything was taken from me, when I died. When I was killed by a Demon. My husband was killed too, but my daughter lived on, in the arms of the family who were supposed to be our friends

1

– supposed to be our protectors. They allowed us to be killed and took our baby, to raise as their own. And so I followed them, in death, watching my daughter, my princess, my Charity... watching them all.

Charity doesn't remember the little flat any better than I do. She doesn't remember the kitchen, doesn't remember my husband's eyes, doesn't remember whether we used to drink coffee. Her baby brain retained nothing of that life, or of us. She's a woman now – thirty-one. Older than I will ever be. Growing up wiped our home out of her mind, just as death wiped it all from mine.

Charity has a living mother, who is not me. Her mother's name is Brenda Rook. She has a living father, who is not the husband I watched die. Her father's name is Richard Rook. She has always known that she was adopted as an orphaned baby, and up until very recently, that had been enough information for her. So many of the great heroes of her favourite stories were orphaned young. We simply became a part of that narrative for her as far as she was concerned, which turned out to be very convenient for Brenda and Richard... until, as I say, very recently.

Charity also has an older brother, called Darryl Rook. Darryl is happily married to an accountant named Janusz and, less happily, has issues regarding his own parentage. It makes the story of how Charity came to be adopted by the Rook family seem pedestrian by comparison and he found out about it very recently. When I say 'very recently', I mean 'yesterday'. There was a considerable incident yesterday. As a result, partial details about Charity's adoption and Darryl's birth came to light. Brenda and Richard promised to tell their children more, once they had escaped, found a hotel to crash at overnight, showered and rested. They managed to do all of these things last night, but still haven't given their children any more information, citing 'tiredness' as an excuse. I have watched the Rooks long enough to know that there will always be an excuse. It has made for a very awkward breakfast buffet, and an even more awkward train journey home.

They've had to take the train back because the family car was destroyed during the incident. Even if the car had survived, they wouldn't all be able to fit in it any more, since during the course of the incident, they have picked up a mystery priest. The priest is a small, middle-aged woman named Grace Barry – or at least, she's pretty sure she is, anyway. That's all she remembers – or thinks she remembers – about herself. Quite a feat to have an even worse memory than me. There's something very wrong about the priest, that much I can tell.

I should probably tell you about the nature of yesterday's unpleasant incident – a hole in the sky to multiple dimensions beyond the realm of the living opened up, flooding a haunted island with Demons, and then a powerful otherworldly being calling itself the Manager tried to end the world. It was a whole thing. My Charity was able to close the hole using her psychic powers and, in the end, the only thing that was destroyed – at least, for now – was the haunted island.

I should probably have told you first that my Charity has psychic powers. So do Brenda and Darryl, although theirs are different to Charity's. Richard also had supernatural powers, right up until – you guessed it – yesterday. As I say, it was a whole thing.

And so, wearily they trudge back from the train station, in the awkward silence of their own creation. They saved the world yesterday. All of it. They saved the peeling billboard over there, advertising a gambling website. They saved the bus stop shelter just here, with the bench deliberately designed to be so uncomfortable that nobody will be able to sleep on it when it's raining, with the ancient cigarette scorch marks and the hard grey clumps of last year's chewing gum and the crude penis scrawled onto the face of a woman cheerfully advising bus users to 'order a new sofa now in time for Christmas', so as not to look like some sort of old-sofa-owning pauper on Christmas Day. They saved that soggy homeless

3

guy who Grace and Janusz give a pound each to while the rest of the family hang back, looking awkward. They saved the Wine Warehouse, and the sign outside the Wine Warehouse telling wine lovers like Brenda to treat themselves to six bottles of wine, 'since it's Christmas'. It's early November. At some point in the thirty years since I died, early November started counting as Christmas.

Brenda notices the sign advertising the special offer on six bottles of wine, and pauses briefly, but after a moment she makes the decision not to go into the shop. I suppose some people could call that progress. Brenda was recently given a pamphlet on problem drinking, and for once she hasn't immediately thrown it away.

They reach a comfortable enough but fairly nondescript three bedroom semi-detached house, on a nice enough but fairly nondescript street an inconveniently long walk away from the train station. It is their house. Their home. They get to go home, and I get to follow them, and tell their story, because their mistakes have left me with nothing else to do with my personal eternity.

My name is Constance, and this is not my story, and yet here I am, telling it anyway. Don't judge me – ghosts aren't exactly known for making rational decisions. Lingering spirits have done far stranger things on impulse than hanging around narrating other people's lives for three decades. And goodness me, you'd better believe there are lots of other lingering spirits. That's the Rooks' whole business. That's why they made sure they were the ones to raise my daughter. That's what paid for this deeply unimpressive house.

Brenda unlocks the deeply unimpressive door. They are home.

They were home. Well. Most of them were home. Grace was not home. The Clergy House where Grace used to live had been destroyed the day before, along with the whole of the island off the East Midlands coast where she'd been stationed. She had no idea where else to go, so she was here.

'What a lovely home,' Grace declared on impulse, and in fairness it *was* nice. Ish.

'It's a little pokey for five adults,' sniffed Brenda, 'but my two won't move out…'

'You're the one who keeps telling us how much cheaper it is to stay,' interrupted Darryl, 'and reminding us how impossible it is to save for a deposit on our wages – wages which you and Dad set in the first place.'

'Instead,' continued Brenda, 'Darryl just brought another one in.'

'You love having me around,' beamed Janusz. 'I'm the son you never had.'

'*I'm* her son,' Darryl exclaimed. 'I'm not being usurped by my own husband.'

'Yes. You're the son she *did* have, I'm the son she *didn't*. The one who's good at spreadsheets and speaks four languages.' Janusz kissed his husband on the forehead and dumped his laptop in Darryl's arms in one slick movement. 'I'll put on the kettle.'

'The good news is there's three loos,' said Brenda, taking off her shoes, 'upstairs, downstairs and ensuite…'

'You never let anyone except you and Dad actually use the ensuite, though,' said Charity.

'Well, obviously not, our bedroom is not a hallway for the rest of you. The bad news, Reverend, is that due to my very large, adult chicks refusing to fly the nest…'

'We can't afford to leave, Mum!'

'…we don't have a spare room for you, so the sofa will have to suffice.'

'The sofa's absolutely wonderful, thank you!' Grace gave Brenda a smile that she worried might have come across as a little too manic.

The priest was trying to stay calm and count her blessings. She had been rescued from a very haunted island by this family, who were providing her with a roof over her head, a sofa to sleep on and a choice of toilets. Those were all wonderful things, for which she really was grateful. However, it was still troubling her more than a little bit that she'd needed to be rescued in the first place, that the island where she'd lived had been so very haunted that all of the ghostly misery had become so condensed that it had punched a hole in reality, and that huge, insect-like Demons, along with the terrifying entity of eyes and fire that called itself the Manager had come out of that hole to attack them and try to end the world. She was worried that it made a mockery of her faith in all things bright and beautiful, and in the Lord God who made them all. She was also still pretty upset by having borne witness to the island folding in on itself and vanishing – and not merely physically, but historically. No matter how much she tried to search for Coldbay island on her phone, there was no mention of it ever having existed – no maps, not even a terrible Trip Advisor review. Coldbay had been real! She remembered it! There had been a pier and a pub and a Tesco. Coldbay *had* to have been real, because it was pretty much all she *could* remember.

While Grace was counting her worries, there was another one. She still couldn't remember a thing about her life before being Coldbay's resident priest. She couldn't remember any family, or romantic partners, or friends. Her phone had no photos and no contacts, and she had no idea why that might be, or why she had only just noticed.

Also, the sofa which would be her bed was made out of leather. Grace wasn't sure that she approved of leather upholstery, but she certainly wasn't going to say that, now was she?

'You've had a tough couple of days, Grace,' said Richard, quietly. It was the first thing Richard had said in several hours. 'If you need a rest or a nap or anything…'

'I'm fine,' replied Grace, quickly. She really was fine, honest. Yes, she was worried about a few things, but other people had had it far worse – one of those people being Richard.

'Are *you* OK?' Grace asked Richard.

Richard nodded, wordlessly, casting his eyes away. Richard was very definitely not OK.

Grace was given a quick tour of the house. The living room she had already seen, the downstairs loo, the kitchen – where Janusz was merrily milling about making several mugs of tea – which was also part-dining room and part-office since it was, Grace was told as if being let in to a state secret, where the WiFi was strongest. Upstairs was a family bathroom, Charity's small bedroom, which contained a *lot* of plastic figurines for the decor of a woman in her thirties, the cramped double room that comprised Darryl and Janusz's sole private space as a married couple, and finally Brenda and Richard's master bedroom with ensuite, neither of which Grace was to enter. The entire 'tour' took around ninety seconds. By the time she came back into the living room, Janusz was setting tea and biscuits out on the coffee table. He smiled at her and she was struck again by the man's handsomeness. It was a very specific handsomeness, slightly worn-in, like the handsomeness of an actor who does well on Sunday night telly but never quite cracked Hollywood, or a school run dad who's always a bit baffled by how popular he is with the mums. Handsome like a knitwear model for a mid-range menswear store. Without wanting to sound uncharitable towards Darryl, they were not the sort of pair that you would automatically place together.

Obviously, Grace would never say that out loud. She felt bad enough just thinking it to herself.

With his Knitwear Model Smile, Janusz indicated towards one of the mugs on the coffee table. It had a cartoon of a grumpy-looking kitten on it, along with the warning 'Don't even talk to me until I've had my coffee'.

'This one's yours,' he announced.

Grace picked it up and drank, aware that he likely didn't just mean the tea. Janusz and Darryl were already holding matching 'Mr & Mr' mugs, Brenda had an elegant Wedgwood affair, Charity's cup declared her to be 'Plus Ultra' and Richard sat cradling a mug that professed him to be the World's Best Dad. These were *their* mugs. And now, the kitten who didn't want to talk until she'd finished her coffee was Grace's mug. She had her own mug now. It was a weird, ugly looking kitten, and, being a chatty type who energetically embraced early mornings, Grace certainly didn't agree with the sentiment, but the idea that she had her own mug now hit her like a sack of feathers to the heart.

They sat – or at least, most of them sat. Grace perched on an armrest so that the others would have room – and they drank – or at least, most of them drank. Richard mostly just held his cup and gazed down at the gently trembling liquid within.

'So,' said Charity, after a while. 'You were going to tell me what happened with my birth parents.'

Brenda flutters her eyes up, very briefly, to meet my gaze. Yes. Hello, Brenda. I'm still here. Darryl notices, and follows her eyeline. He squints in my direction. I've faded a little since he saw me on the island, but I might still just about be visible to him. He can't see the dead as clearly as his mother can, but he's just about enough of a clairvoyant to make out my shape, as a smear or a shadow against their living room wall. Darryl doesn't know who I am. He doesn't

remember, he was only little when it happened. Brenda, though –
oh, Brenda remembers. She turns her eyes away from me, to look
at Charity instead.

Brenda sighed. 'They were our best friends. Constance and
Harry.'

His name was Harry! I try to remember his face. I can't.

'Actually,' added Brenda after a brief pause, 'it was probably
more that Constance and I were best friends. You got on
well enough with Harry, didn't you, dear, but you were never
particularly close…'

'Harry didn't trust me,' Richard said into his cup, his voice little
more than a whisper, 'because of You Know Who. Poor fellow.'

'We were rivals at first,' continued Brenda, 'but Constance
had the same abilities as you, Charity, so we decided it would be
better if we teamed up, especially with Darryl still so little and
Constance being pregnant with you. And it did work out, for
quite a while. Working together, pooling childcare. But then
came The Longest Night. It was…' She trailed off, lost in the
horrible memory.

Brenda's leg jiggles. I can tell how much she wants a drink far
stronger than tea, right now. She glances at me, again, her face
etched with guilt, regret and a longing for a hit of self-medication.

'We were able to save you, my princess,' Brenda told Charity.
'That was the one silver lining.'

'And you kept me,' added Charity.

'Kept you and adored you,' Brenda replied, emphatically.
'We couldn't just send you off to an orphanage knowing how

9

special…' Brenda cut herself off in mid flow, and tried a different tack. 'Certainly not after we'd promised Constance and Harry that we'd protect all of you as much as we possibly could—'

'But they still died,' said Charity. 'How? Why? Why weren't they protected by… by You Know Who… and, how long are we supposed to not mention You Know Who, or what just happened with him?'

'Princess—' breathed Richard in a pleading tone.

Charity steamrollered on over him. 'Because I know Dad's still sad about it and all that, but it's a pretty massive Demonic elephant in the room, or, y'know, not in the room any more.'

'Princess,' begged Richard, again.

'I have pictures,' said Brenda, suddenly. She got up, and went over to a bookshelf full of files. 'Of Constance and Harry, I mean.' She pulled out a slim photo album.

'And you never showed me?' said Charity.

'You never asked, princess. Quite the opposite – in fact I seem to recall you calling any reference to the early years of our marriage "annoying squishy stuff in embarrassing olden times outfits".' Brenda sat next to Charity and opened the album. She turned to a rather faded photograph.

The photo isn't of Harry and me, it's of me with Brenda. I must be pregnant, there. Harry is behind us in the background, out of focus, I still can't see his face, still have no image of my husband's face. Brenda's arm, around mine. Our arms, intertwined. Yes. I do believe we loved each other, once, Brenda and me. The memory of love hits, and with it, the gut punch of disappointment and betrayal.

Darryl frowned at the photo. 'I recognise her.'

'Well,' said Charity, 'she looks like me, so.'

'No,' said Darryl. 'I've seen her, really recently. She was on that island. And then, watching us after we escaped.' He looked across at his mother. 'Right, Mum? If I saw her, you must have seen her.'

Brenda met her son's eyes unflinchingly, and, with a steady, calm voice, lied her arse off. 'No,' she said. 'Must have just been someone who looked like her.'

'But—'

'No, Darryl. I would recognise my best friend.'

I glare at her. It does no good. It's been many decades since Brenda was last intimidated by an outraged spirit of the dead, even the one who was abandoned to die when an ancient Demon made the selfish decision to prioritise Brenda, Richard and Darryl's safety over everyone else's.

That Demon's name was Murzzzz. He used to possess Richard's body – two consciousnesses in one space like a meaty timeshare. Yesterday he was ripped out of Richard and dragged back to Hell or whatever dimension it is that Demons come from. I hope you don't expect me to feel any sympathy for him. Even if ghosts did feel sympathy for others – and in my years of being dead, I've had no cause to believe that we do – he was a stinking Demon who betrayed me. Besides, one could say that being dragged into Hell was an occupational hazard for the Rooks' line of work – as is having your house haunted by your dead best friend.

The Rooks, you see, are professional ghost hunters and they are some of the best in the world. They're certainly the real deal, unlike flashier, showier rivals like Aurora Tavistock, who has been on GMTV and everything, despite not even really being psychic. And, following yesterday's event, they are in huge trouble. I mean – all of you living people are in huge trouble, following yesterday. Even Aurora Tavistock is in big trouble, not that she knows it, the big fraud.

The Rooks, however, are probably in the biggest trouble of all. Because they know what's coming, and they know it's down to them to stop it.

CHAPTER TWO

World's Best Dad

'**M**um,' said Darryl, the next morning, 'I think the house is haunted again.'

His mother groaned from the other side of her closed bedroom door. 'Yes,' came her sleepy voice after a moment, 'well, it usually is – occupational hazard. Leave it a few weeks, if it doesn't sort itself out I'll have your sister fix it.'

'You think someone might have followed us back from the island?' asked Darryl. 'Maybe that woman you keep saying definitely *isn't* Constance Xu?'

'Darryl, it's barely nine in the morning, it's too early for this nonsense. If a ghost is bothering you, do one of your happy clappy snowflake seances and politely ask it to leave, since apparently that's how we operate nowadays.'

On his side of the bedroom door, Darryl rolled his eyes. So, his mother was still sulking about the family's request to try expelling ghosts a bit more humanely than their previous method of just popping them out of the living realm without a by-your-leave. Darryl hadn't even got to his main reason for knocking on his parents' bedroom door, yet. He tried again.

'Also,' he said, 'both toilets are occupied, can I use the ensuite?'

'Number one or two?' asked his mother.

He hesitated. It was all the answer Brenda needed.

'Darryl, you know how I feel about number twos in the ensuite.'

'I'm your son!'

'Irrelevant! It's right next to where I sleep. The rule applies to everyone, even your father.'

'Yeah, I think that's why downstairs is in use.'

'Just hold it. I'm going back to sleep.'

'Speaking of Dad,' attempted Darryl.

'I'm going back to sleep, I said!'

Darryl sighed, and went back to his own bedroom, which didn't have an ensuite, but at least currently had a Janusz in it.

'That didn't sound productive,' muttered Janusz.

Darryl's husband was sleep creased and in need of a shower and a shave. He was propped up on his side of the bed, his ever-present laptop open on his lap, frowning over some admin. As Darryl got back into bed, he found his husband was also very warm, and soft in all the places Darryl liked softness, and bristly in all the places Darryl liked bristle.

'Yeah, the house is definitely haunted,' Darryl told him, deciding to warm his cold feet on Janusz.

'Did you tread in a ghost on the landing?' Janusz asked. 'Your feet are freezing.'

Darryl glanced at the spreadsheet on Janusz's computer. It made no sense to him at all. 'How's the admin?'

'Not great,' admitted Janusz. 'I'm trying to reschedule the Aldwych booking, but we've had so many emails since Coldbay.

Twenty just last night. Usually when we get a lot of requests I sort them by urgency, but so many of these seem really bad. I still need to factor in rest time, you and your sister need your strength back after exhausting yourself on that island, and Richard… how is Richard?'

Darryl shrugged. 'Still not talking.'

'This is another issue,' added Janusz. 'We need to think about who will offer protection now that Richard's lost You Know Who.' He folded the laptop closed and set it carefully on the floor, which Darryl knew was an indicator that his husband was about to initiate either something sexy or a serious talk about their relationship, and considering most of the household was already awake, it was unlikely to be the former. 'We need to talk about the Demon thing,' said Janusz.

'No,' groaned Darryl.

'Yes.' Janusz rested his hand on Darryl's. '*Zabko*. I love you. Always. All of you. Even the bit of you that—'

'The bit of me that's part Demon?' asked Darryl. 'Because a Demon was possessing my dad at the moment of my conception, and I only found this out the other day when we were attacked and I turned into one of those disgusting things? You mean that? You love *that*?'

'So, you're still taking this badly then, yes?'

'Yes, I'm "taking it badly"! My parents lied to me and I turned into a Demon! I'm amazed you're *not* taking it badly, you're the one married to this mess.'

'I always knew I was marrying a mess. The Demon thing is just icing on the mess.' Janusz squeezed Darryl's hand a little. 'I already knew about Murzzzz. He's…' Janusz corrected himself. 'He *was* part of the family. So you're Murzzzz's son as well as Richard's. So what? It could even help us…'

'No.'

'Because we still sort of need a Murzzzz.'

'No!'

'And Murzzzz is gone.'

'I don't want to be a Demon!'

'But you are, a little bit. The universe doesn't really care about what you want.' Janusz gave him a little smile. 'If it helps, you actually looked pretty cute when you turned into a Demon. Or half-Demon, or whatever it was. You probably didn't notice because you were fighting for our lives at the time.'

Darryl scowled, but didn't pull his hand away from his husband's. 'Demons aren't "cute".'

'You were.' Janusz leaned into him. 'You know in *The Lion King* when Simba is still a baby lion and does his little baby lion roar? It was like that. Like a little baby kitten Demon.'

Darryl shook his head, refusing to believe it.

'This is why you should try to transform again in a controlled environment,' Janusz continued, 'so we can see your Demon abilities without you being attacked. And so you can see your cute little Demon face.'

'Janusz, I transformed as a *reaction* to being attacked and I hated it. I can't just do it at will…'

'How do you know until you try?'

'And I don't want to. I'm not going to.'

'You could try to do it right now, there's only me watching.'

'I'm not turning into a Demon in bed with my husband!'

Janusz cocked an eyebrow, suggestively.

'Put that eyebrow down, mister.'

Janusz did as he was told. 'I'm only teasing a little. I do still think you should try embracing and harnessing the Demon thing. And it genuinely was cute. And a tiny bit hot.'

Somebody banged on their bedroom door. 'Stop having sex in there, you two,' called Charity.

'We weren't,' said Darryl.

'Good,' replied Charity. 'Don't want to be put off my breakfast.'

'Well, in that case, maybe we should.'

'Ew,' shouted his sister. 'Bathroom's free, Bee Tee Double-U.'

'Oh, good.' Darryl sprang out of bed, and made no attempt to remind his sister that verbally, 'BTW' didn't work as a shorthand for 'by the way', since it actually took longer to say. He'd given up trying to get her to stop doing that years ago.

Janusz sighed and went back to his laptop. 'Another three emails,' he said. 'At this rate, maybe we *could* earn enough for a deposit.'

Darryl wasn't sure whether Janusz was joking. It wasn't as if they hadn't talked a lot about getting a place of their own, it just never really seemed to happen, and after all, living with his family wasn't *that* bad, was it…?

He stepped out onto the upstairs landing just in time to see Grace disappear into the upstairs bathroom with considerable urgency and lock the door. Bugger.

Richard Rook decided that he would make breakfast for the family and their guest. It was a decision that he made alone, as he had time to kill and eggs to use up. He was not used to making decisions alone. He'd spent the vast majority of his life sharing his body with a Demon. A real Demon – and quite a high ranking one too, from what he'd been able to gather. Ancient and powerful. And yes, sometimes annoying and sometimes morally questionable, but for the most part, Richard had found Murzzzz to be a surprisingly nice guy. They'd made it work. And now, Murzzzz was gone. And Richard felt as if he'd had his insides ripped out.

Still. No point in making a big song and dance about it. Grace and the rest of the family had enough to worry about

17

without adding his feelings to the mix. He would make them breakfast, stop moping about and crack on with things. He couldn't bring Murzzzz back... could he? No. No, he couldn't. He had to stop even entertaining that thought. Murzzzz had been dragged by twenty Demons through a hole in reality back to the dimension from whence he came. No, Richard couldn't bring Murzzzz back, but he could do other stuff. Useful stuff. He could finish off the insurance paperwork on the old car – and hope that the car being thrown at them by a furious otherworldly entity on a haunted island that was folding on itself and vanishing into the void didn't count as an 'act of God', since they weren't covered for that. A slight worry nagged at him that it may have literally been an act of the closest thing there was to a 'God'. Was that what the Manager was? Probably wasn't a great idea to go around annoying deities – if religious texts were to be taken even slightly seriously because they rarely stopped at just smiting one's Ford Focus. Also, due to said smiting, he now had to look for a new car. Maybe a people carrier, to fit the reverend in. Something like a Citroen Berlingo. The thought made him feel nervous. He'd never bought a French car before and he didn't know if he had the charisma to pull it off.

Grace Barry wandered into the kitchen just as the toast popped. 'Vicar!'

'Just "Grace", please, I'm not a vicar.' Grace poked at her phone with her usual expression of quiet anxiety. 'Technically I'm a rector. I think...'

'Should I get a Citroen?'

'Are you asking me that as an ethical question?' Grace asked. 'Because mechanically speaking I don't know anything about cars.' She put her phone away and regarded Richard sympathetically. 'I really am so sorry about everything that happened on Coldbay. Your poor car. Poor Murzzzz...'

'Yes, well,' replied Richard, briskly, 'not to be helped. You weren't to know that terrors from the realms beyond were going to throw my car at us to try to keep us from escaping. And, in fairness, they did throw your entire church at us, too.'

'But it's still my fault you ended up there in the first place,' said Grace, buttering the freshly popped toast even though Richard hadn't actually asked her to do that and it would make the toast go soggy if she did it now. He decided not to complain about it. She was only trying to help. 'I was the one who emailed you lot for help. And I still can't get hold of my higher-ups. I'm sure I used to have a number for the diocese, or an email address or something…'

Richard turned away from the rapidly cooling, soggy toast and began to scramble the eggs. 'Well, where were they based? I'm not big on religious hierarchies myself, that was more…' He stopped himself. Murzzzz had been the one fascinated by human faiths. He scrambled the eggs a little harder. Take that, eggs. 'Isn't there usually a bishop or something?' he asked. 'At a cathedral? Can't be that hard to check all the cathedrals, can it? I don't think there's too many of them because they were such a faff to build.'

'Right,' said Grace, blankly. 'Of course.' She wandered off again, leaving in her wake a pile of damp toast and a nagging worry in Richard's mind.

Grace had been the only person alive on Coldbay island. There was something off about her. For starters, he was becoming increasingly doubtful that she was really a priest. In fact, he couldn't be sure that she was who she said she was at all. And now here she was, under his roof, with his precious wife and children, ruining his toast.

*

Three days passed. Charity continued to look at photos of Constance and Harry, but gave up on asking for more details about The Longest Night and how her biological parents died after the second day of vague answers from Brenda and troubled silence from Richard. A sort of hot, itchy feeling was growing inside her stomach about the whole thing, and Charity didn't like feeling it.

Janusz continued to worry about the vastly increased volume of emails, but only mentioned them to Darryl. This time was, Janusz insisted silently to himself, a necessary period of rest and recuperation, as well as a chance for his husband to discover more about his semi-Demonic powers. Although Darryl continued to refuse to try out his semi-Demonic powers – not even in the garden shed with Janusz promising he'd stand guard outside to make sure nobody looked at him.

Richard tried and failed not to think about the desperate emptiness of Murzzzz's absence. He didn't talk about it. Instead, he spent an hour Photoshopping his head and shoulders into the driver's seat of various people carriers to see which one suited him more.

Grace continued to stare at her phone a lot with a vaguely worried expression. To be fair that is the expression many people have when staring at their phones, but in her case, it was because she still had amnesia, not that she was checking the news.

Brenda continued to refuse access to the ensuite.

The household did at least get heavily into the second series of The Big British Metalwork Contest on the telly, which helped them to spend those three days avoiding any unpleasantly meaningful conversations, and limit communication to comparative soldering techniques instead. On the third day of not discussing any problems more important than whether Greg or Melita had metalworked the better patio set, or whether Ravi's early eviction from the contest over a poorly constructed weathervane was 'a total set up', something changed. Richard left the house in a taxi and came back two hours later with a grimly determined expression and a seven seater car.

'Ooh la la!' Brenda regarded the car from the doorway, coffee in hand. 'This is a flamboyant turn, dear. I rather like it.'

'You think so?' Richard got out of the car and took a good look at its exterior. 'It was the only option, really. Although, the biting point is too high and the thingie for the windscreen wipers is in entirely the wrong place.'

'I'm sure you'll get used to it.'

'And it's French.'

'I noticed. Very cosmopolitan.'

'And *red*.'

'I noticed that, as well. Quite the diversion from your usual silvers and greys.'

'It was the only one they had with the sort of mileage that made it worth the asking price.' The determination of Richard's expression wavered. 'It's too much, isn't it? It's too out-there.'

'It's fine, dear. We can all fit in it and it'll get us from A to B...' Brenda paused, giving the new car one last look. 'It does look a *little* bit like a postman's van.'

'What?'

'But I'm sure it'll be fine and nobody will ask if we've got their parcel whenever you try to park. At least, I'm sure they won't if you're not wearing a red polo shirt and cargo shorts.' She patted her husband on the back, directing him into the house.

'I do have a red polo shirt and cargo shorts,' noted Richard, his expression now far away from grim determination and residing in a world of self-doubt and worry.

'I know you do, dear, and they make you look like a postman. I've said so before.'

'What? Really?'

'Are we talking about Dad's postman outfit?' asked Charity as she made her way past the open front door. 'Ooh! New car!'

'It's just a comfortable summer outfit,' said Richard, 'it's good for walking…'

'It certainly is, dear, which is why so many people wear it when they have to spend the day walking around an entire neighbourhood delivering their mail.'

In the house, Janusz poured the last of his cafetiere of 'proper coffee' into the 'World's Best Dad' mug and handed it to Richard.

'Fine,' sighed Richard, 'I'll just throw a perfectly good outfit out, then, shall I?'

Nobody replied to that, because they all knew he wasn't going to throw his favourite polo shirt and shorts away. By the time shorts weather rolled around again, he'd have likely forgotten all about this conversation. Or perhaps by then they'd all be dead. Shorts weather was months away. Were they going to make it that far, considering what had happened at Coldbay? Would anybody? Would the world?

The Rooks had not permanently stopped the apocalypse at Coldbay, they'd merely postponed it. The terrifying, burning creature that called itself the Manager had made it very clear that it was fully capable of destroying the mortal world, and intended to do so as soon as one outstanding celestial matter – what it called the 'Red Sticker Issue' – had been resolved. Unfortunately, none of the Rooks had any idea what that Red Sticker Issue actually was. It had turned out that the Red Sticker Issue wasn't Murzzzz, as they'd assumed at the time. You can imagine the family's surprise when their friendly Demon was pulled through a hole in reality, and the world didn't end after all. Grace believed that there was a new Red Sticker Issue keeping the Manager from signing off on the apocalypse, only she didn't know what that new issue was, because of all her amnesia.

It's one thing being in a race against time. It's another being in a race against time when you don't know what the time limit is. Or where the race begins and ends. Or what kind of race it is. And when you're racing against ancient Demons and huge creatures made out of impossible rings of flaming eyeballs. And you're just six human beings with a laptop and a second-hand Citroen.

With the cafetiere empty, Janusz made instant coffee for himself and his husband and joined the rest of the family in the living room. The family decided to put on the semi-final of the metalworking show, but something had changed – Janusz could feel it. He'd grown accustomed to shifts in the family's energy. Both Charity and Darryl were listless and distracted, even in the face of the supposedly gripping semi-final. Brenda barely looked at the screen – her gaze kept getting drawn to something in a far corner of the room. Darryl was right – the house was definitely haunted again. Richard kept glancing out of the window at the new car.

The new car had been the start of it. The gears were already in motion. The family just knew, deep down, that their rest and recuperation was over and they needed to get back to work saving the world – even though actually how they were supposed to manage that was still beyond them.

Even Grace seemed to be attuned to the shift in the atmosphere. 'Is it me,' she asked, halfway through the episode, 'or is this... boring?'

'You can already tell Greg's going to win the whole thing,' sighed Charity. 'Foregone conclusion, now.'

'Ravi was robbed,' grunted Darryl. 'Kind of lost interest after that…'

'After they booted the best-looking man from the show, you mean?' asked Charity.

'It's not like that!'

'No, no, it's fine,' replied Charity. 'I feel the same. And Ravi *was* the best-looking one, that's not sexist, it's just science.'

There was a pause. Charity looked at her phone. Darryl played with his wedding ring. Brenda looked at whatever or whoever was in the corner. Richard looked at the car. On TV, an amateur metalworker named Greg crafted a boringly good coffee table out of salvaged aluminium. Quietly, Janusz opened his laptop and pulled up a shortlist of urgent jobs the family should attend.

'Edendale,' said Grace, suddenly.

'Pardon?' asked Richard.

'My higher-ups.' Grace frowned, clouded with confusion, like a sleeptalker trying to make sense of their own ramblings. 'My diocese, you asked about a cathedral. Edendale. I think…'

'Where *is* Edendale?' Brenda asked. 'I've heard of it, obviously,' she added, defensively, 'just I've never been.'

'North,' replied Grace, vaguely. 'I think.'

Janusz had also, obviously, heard of Edendale before, but had never been nor was quite sure where it was, so he looked it up. 'Yes! Few hours north by car.' He showed them the map, pleased with himself.

And here they were, with a new car.

There was no point watching the rest of the metalworking show. They all knew who was going to win, anyway. Perhaps the next series would have more good-looking semi-finalist contestants. For that, there needed to be another series. And for that to happen, the world needed to survive another year. And for that to happen, the Rooks were going to have to get back to work.

The Rooks were going to save the world. Competitive metalworking shows and all.

CHAPTER THREE

Edendale, Interrupted

'Everyone comfortable?' Richard checked his mirror and his seatbelt. 'Kids?'

'Yes,' chorused the 'kids', comprising of his two adult children, both in their thirties, his thirty-eight-year-old son-in-law and a middle-aged priest.

Richard checked his mirror again, and adjusted it slightly. 'And you boys are OK in the back-back?' he asked the married couple in the rear seats.

'We're fine,' said Darryl.

In her seat next to Grace in the middle row, Charity turned backwards to face her brother. 'No snogging back there.'

'We're married, we'll snog if we want to.'

'Not if it obscures the rear windshield.' Richard readjusted the mirror so that it was back at its original angle, and started the car. After a very slight jolt – with Richard apologising profusely for having 'completely messed that manoeuvre up' – they were away.

Janusz and Darryl didn't snog in the back-back after all, although Janusz did take the opportunity to give Darryl's knee a quick squeeze before getting back to his laptop.

'So. Edendale Cathedral first, get some answers for Grace…'

'How is the old amnesia now, Reverend?' asked Brenda. 'Any other memories jogged along with Edendale?'

Grace shook her head. 'It's something though at least,' she said, 'isn't it?'

'I suppose.' Brenda turned to gaze blankly out of the car window. 'Maybe in another three days you'll have a second memory come to you.'

'Or perhaps they'll have all her files and stuff at the cathedral,' said Charity. 'Maybe amnesia is an occupational hazard when you get posted to an incredibly haunted island. Maybe her bosses made contingency plans for it.' Her eyes lit up. 'Maybe *they* wiped her memory to protect their operation from the Demons and stuff. Maybe she was a spy!'

'Um,' muttered Grace. 'I really don't think so. And they're not my "bosses" as such, they're just, you know… bishops and stuff. But hopefully they'll be able to shed some light on… well… anything. Also, they should be able to pay off your invoice for clearing my old church of ghosts.'

'That would be nice,' Janusz agreed.

'You did do a really good job on that, even though the church got thrown at you and the island vanished,' Grace added.

'Now, there's a glowing testimonial,' said Richard. 'You should put that one on the website, Janusz.'

'I might,' replied Janusz, cheerfully. 'Hey, after we drop Grace off, there are three urgent bookings in the north-west we should see to while we're up there.'

'Wait,' said Charity, 'we're just dropping the reverend off and leaving her on her own?'

'Not forever,' said Janusz. 'I thought she'd be OK. It's a cathedral! Priests like cathedrals, don't they?'

'We can't just leave her,' Charity argued, 'look at the poor little thing, all tiny and scared.'

'I'm not *that* little,' Grace protested, in a little voice, 'I'm not a child.'

'So, did you want us to go with you?' asked Janusz, in exactly the tone one would use with a small child.

'No. No! That would be ridiculous! I can meet with my superiors by myself, I survived on my own in Coldbay all that time.' Grace was sounding less and less sure of her own convictions. 'I'm a grown woman. I'm forty… something… probably.'

Janusz sighed softly, and made some alterations to his spreadsheet. 'We will go with you.'

'That's unnecessary, but OK,' said Grace, quietly. 'Thank you.'

'But after that,' said Janusz, 'house calls. We have extreme… *zaległości w pracy…*' He looked at Darryl, trying to think of the English term. 'Job Constipation. Does that make sense…?'

Darryl nodded. 'Job Constipation. I get you.'

'I think it's called a backlog—' attempted Grace.

'It's called Job Constipation, Vicar,' Charity told her, emphatically.

The streets widened, houses turned into industrial estates and then litter strewn hedgerow sidings as they went from town to the string of A-road tributaries that eventually deposited them into the flow of the motorway.

Brenda put her chill-out playlist on the car stereo at a distinctly un-chill volume. Darryl and Janusz listened to the same podcast together using an earbud each. Charity ate three bags of crisps before anybody else could get a look in.

Around an hour passed before Charity asked, 'How much further?'

'Maybe a couple of hours?' said Richard.

Janusz checked his phone. 'Three hours,' he told everyone.

Another hour passed. Charity had finished all the cans of Coke. Janusz and Darryl were told off for laughing too much at the 'Real Life Paranormal Investigation' podcast and put on an audiobook instead.

'Can't be much longer now,' announced Brenda.

Janusz checked his phone again. 'Three hours,' he said.

'Right,' sighed Brenda. She went back to listening to her chill-out mix with her eyes closed.

'Wait a minute,' said Darryl.

'We could play a game to pass the time,' Charity said, over her brother. 'I've got a good game – it's called "How Did Constance And Harry Actually Die?" Mum, Dad, you go first.'

Brenda rubbed her forehead. 'Now really isn't the time, princess.'

'No, I know. "The time" was when I first asked you – or before that, even, when I was little so I'd just know about them and not keep having to ask.'

'You never used to ask!'

'Well, I'm asking now!'

'It was three hours to Edendale an hour ago,' said Darryl. 'Bit weird.'

'Maybe the satnav can see something ahead that's going to slow us down,' suggested Grace, vaguely. 'Accidents, roadworks, that sort of thing.'

'An hour's worth of roadworks that just popped up while we were driving?' Darryl furrowed his brow. 'What if… what if Edendale doesn't want us to find it?'

Charity turned in her seat to face him, her mocking expression set to Peak Little Sister. 'You think a whole city is running away from us?'

'Only four days ago, we were trapped on an island that kept moving its bridge so we couldn't escape,' Janusz reminded her, gently. 'And then it ate itself and was deleted from history. We annoyed something that gets to play with reality. Why not a city trying to run away? Or maybe there's just an hour's delay because of an accident ahead or something. *Zabko*, can you rewind the audiobook for me? We missed a bit because we were talking.'

'Speaking of accidents on the road,' muttered Brenda, 'have you noticed, Darryl? No motorway ghosts at all.'

'Oh yeah,' replied Darryl, with the tone of mild surprise one would use if it was pointed out that the cardigan one had been wearing all day was on inside-out.

'Is that good or bad?' asked Grace.

'It's odd,' Brenda told her. 'Motorways are usually teeming with the buggers. Combination of sudden, violent death and being lost miles from home. Road death spirits can almost never move on, and there are *so* many road deaths. People drive like maniacs. But I haven't seen one for a few miles, now.' She cast a quick, guilty glance at the empty space on the middle seat between Charity and Grace. 'At least, not on the roads.'

'A coincidence, maybe?' asked Grace.

The rest of the family gave one another knowing glances. Grace may as well have barged into a brain surgeon's symposium and loudly asked if any of them had simply tried a combination of homeopathy and trepanning.

'Or maybe,' continued Grace, reading their expressions, 'it's all connected? You don't think Edendale could be another Coldbay, could you? That would be... oh, Lord. Edendale's much bigger than Coldbay, we're talking tens of thousands of people. They tortured the souls of Coldbay! They wouldn't do that to a whole city…?'

'I suppose we'll find out,' replied Brenda, 'once we eventually get th— OH MY CLATTERING SHIT!!'

'Dear?' asked Richard in alarm. He struggled to keep control of the steering wheel as his wife clutched at his sleeve urgently.

'Pull over! Pull over!'

'Here?' Richard tried to indicate left and turned the windscreen wipers on by mistake instead.

'Not on the hard shoulder!' Brenda shouted.

Richard tried the indicator again and got it right the second time. 'Good, because we're only supposed to stop on the hard shoulder if it's a mechanical emergency.'

'The services!' Brenda pointed at a service station just about visible, half a mile or so ahead.

'No need to be so dramatic about needing a toilet break, Mum,' said Charity. 'I've been holding in three cans of Coke for the past half hour. Bladder of steel.'

'Don't you see it?' Brenda turned to Darryl. 'Darryl! Tell me you see that.'

Darryl craned his head to see out in front. He took out his one ear bud. He hissed, with a noise that wasn't quite human, and for a moment, his eyes turned a colour that wasn't quite visible on the human spectrum. He blinked hard, and they went back to their usual builder's tea-brown.

'Hell Hole,' he said, in a voice that was ever so slightly off. He cleared his throat, and said in a much more Darrylish tone, 'above the services.'

Charity looked more offended than surprised. 'Another one?'

'Another one,' sighed Brenda. 'Turn off here, Richard dear.'

'But we only just shut one down,' cried Charity, appalled. 'Just the other day! It was knackering!'

'We know, princess.' Richard joined the slip road signposted towards Helsbury Services. 'We were there.'

CHAPTER FOUR
The Sandwich of Hope

It wasn't the same as the Hell Hole they had encountered above Coldbay. The hole in the sky above Helsbury Services was still small and cosmically subtle enough to only be visible to Brenda and Darryl's clairvoyance. It was a 'well, we're glad we caught this when we did' sized hole, rather than Coldbay's 'shit on a biscuit, where do we even start?' sized hole. It was, however, still very definitely a swirling void in the sky which, recent experience had taught them, would already be acting as a portal between the living world, the Demon realm and multiple other celestial dimensions. It was also, like the Coldbay Hell Hole, likely created by concentrating hundreds of tormented ghosts in one spot, a sinkhole of misery that even the fabric of reality could not help collapsing into. Like the Coldbay Hell Hole, it could only get bigger with time and, like the Coldbay Hell Hole, it was almost certainly going to be used by an officious immortal nightmare creature of swirling fire and eyes to try to bring about the end of the world. And it was still really, really, *really* bad news, for the Rooks and Grace, for Helsbury Services and for the continuation of life on Earth in general.

Richard parked, frowned at how close he was to the SUV next to him, pulled out, found a different spot with more space and parked again. They got out and surveyed the car park.

Helsbury was a smaller, older service station, with a squat building on either side of the motorway, connected by a covered footbridge. Clearly built at some time in the sixties, the blocky design and oddly slanted roofs must have once been the pinnacle of modernist luxury for drivers in brown flared suits and bright Rayon dresses to stop their Ford Cortinas and have an egg sandwich, a smoke and read deeply worrying newspaper articles about how the Cold War was going. Sadly for Helsbury, its golden age of nicotine stains and the threat of imminent thermonuclear war had long since passed, and what must once have been cutting edge municipal design had gone beyond retro chic and was now just shabby and sad. Algae crept up its once proud brutalist columns, moss gathered in the folds of its once daring, space age roof.

A handful of soggy picnic benches mottled with bird droppings lined the grass sidings, but nobody had taken the opportunity to sit having a lovely picnic on a chilly, damp November day, even with the offer of a seat with stunning views of a medium-sized car park. Nobody bustled in with the urgency of one who had waited slightly too long for their toilet break. Nobody poked at their phones under the concrete veranda while listlessly sipping a cardboard cup of coffee. In fact, the only signs that Helsbury was in use at all, and hadn't been completely abandoned to the gradual inevitability of the weeds, were the overflowing bins and a number of neatly parked cars.

There was nobody actually inside any of the cars, Janusz noticed as they made their way towards the service station.

This in itself was odd. Usually on a cold day there'd be people in cars, waiting for the one passenger who needed the toilet to come back, or sharing a lunch that some thrifty family member had packed in advance to avoid the costs of a takeaway, or even cheerfully digging into greasy bags of burgers and fries, filling their own vehicle with the heady, lingering scents of chip oil and vinegar rather than sharing the service station's lounge area with other travellers' fussy babies and pent-up arguments.

Janusz continued to look in through every car window as the family slowly made their way towards the service station's main building. Nobody. Nobody at all. He couldn't help comparing the car park to Coldbay. When they had arrived at Coldbay Island, it had already been emptied of all human life with the sole exception of Reverend Grace Barry. Food had been left to rot in shops; houses, once bright and noisy, were now dark, silent shells; seafront fish and chip shops stood shuttered and forbidding, in spite of their colourful facades featuring anthropomorphic fish who seemed very cheerful at the prospect of being eaten. The lost souls of the inhabitants that the Rooks had eventually found had very definitely not been cheerful at having had their lives eaten up by the Hell Hole.

And now here – according to his husband, whose clairvoyance Janusz trusted absolutely – was a new Hell Hole. Also here, according to Janusz's own eyes and innate sense for lurking danger, was a new desolation, a new uncanny emptiness of a human space that ought to be full. Janusz felt that same ball of worry establish itself in his core. He craned his head to look inside a deserted Vauxhall Astra and saw one thing that reassured him, just the tiniest bit. It was only a sandwich, but still. Sometimes, Janusz told himself, a sandwich was not merely a sandwich. Sometimes, it was a sandwich of hope, to hold to one's heart – metaphorically speaking, since the sandwich in question was locked inside a small family car at the time.

He pressed the image of the sandwich of hope against his growing worry, as a balm. It didn't make the worry go away, but it just made it a little more bearable.

Janusz took Darryl's hand. 'Any ghosts yet?' he asked.

'None in the car park,' noted Darryl.

'Is that usual?' asked Grace.

'It's not,' said Brenda, 'for car parks this old. Back when this place was built, some people would think nothing about knocking back a bourbon before hopping back in the driver's seat.' Brenda smacked her lips a little at the word 'bourbon', even though she had been the one who'd brought it up.

'It's a miracle any of us made it out of the twentieth century in one piece,' said Richard quietly, in spite of the fact that he personally had spent much of the twentieth century as the host body to a Demon.

They got to the door – a manual push–pull affair of painted steel and advert-covered glass. The handle and frame had probably once been blue, but it had since faded to a sort of off-grey. Brenda tried the handle. The door wasn't locked, but it was stiff and heavy. It opened slowly as she pushed it. It even creaked a little. It would have seemed every bit the traditionally foreboding door to a haunted house, were it not for the mid-century modern accents and the cheery visual plastered onto the glass, encouraging them to experience the uniquely festive thrill of drinking a flavoured latte out of a red disposable cup.

Brenda paused, the door ajar, her hand still on the handle.

'I have a feeling this might be quite bad,' she said.

'Worse than Coldbay?' asked Grace, fingers playing nervously over one another.

'I don't know,' replied Brenda. 'Probably worse than Clapham Junction.'

'Oh,' replied Grace soberly, even though she hadn't even been there for the Clapham Junction job.

'*Jasna cholera*,' said Janusz, who *had* been there for the Clapham Junction job.

'I take it that's not good?' asked Grace, her fingers growing even more fidgety.

'It might not be so bad,' Janusz told the others, hopefully. 'There was this sandwich…' He trailed off, feeling self-conscious.

'That a Polish idiom or something?' asked Charity.

'No,' replied Janusz, awkwardly. 'It was just a sandwich. But it was still fresh, you see, in the front seat of a car. In Coldbay, everyone there had been killed, so all the food had gone rotten. A fresh sandwich means, this isn't another Coldbay.'

'Well, that's encouraging, at least,' replied Brenda. 'Although if this place is full of the living, we'll have to exercise a little covertness.'

'Like we did at Clapham Junction,' noted Charity.

'Maybe I can split away and see if there's one of those little Marks and Sparks that does tiny wines,' added Brenda, 'you know, to blend in.'

'Like you did at Clapham Junction,' said Charity.

Janusz didn't mention that Brenda had now had her hand on the main entrance door for almost a full minute, and if a motorway service station was indeed still full of the living, surely somebody would have pulled the door from the other side and walked into her by now. Still, he clung to the hope represented by that fresh sandwich, even though the sick feeling was creeping back with every second that passed that nobody bumped into his mother-in-law.

Brenda opened the door fully, at long last, and they stepped into the service station's food hall.

The sight in front of Janusz caused the ball of worry in his core to swell, pushing all the breath out of him in a distressed sigh.

In the centre of the hall was a large, partially sunken octagonal space, full of dining tables, booths and fake ficuses. Half-full cups, plates and take-away containers sat on most of the tables, with disposable cutlery and chopsticks left either in the partially eaten meals or in dollops of their own grease by the side. All of the little shops and kiosks lining the sides of the octagonal hall were bright, cheerful and open. The coffee stand by the door displayed rows of croissants and gingerbread men, beneath a stacked triangle of festive disposable red cups. The smell of the baked goods wafted over – not rotten or stale, but sweet and tempting.

From somewhere near the ceiling, a long-dead man sang gently, but there was nothing paranormal about a dead man's voice echoing around the hall; they'd just reached the time of year when all of the music piped into any public space needed to be at least thirty years old, for reasons that Janusz never quite understood. The long-gone crooner was singing that he was dreaming of the sort of Christmas where treetops glisten, oblivious in his death that Christmas was still a very long way away and the only thing that the trees outside glistened with was rain and the gleam of digital advert displays.

All of the individual elements of the scene were normal for a British motorway service station in early November. What *wasn't* normal for a British motorway service station in early November was that, besides their own party in the doorway, it was completely deserted.

'No way,' breathed Darryl.

'There's… nobody,' said Janusz. 'Nobody dead, even.'

Janusz had been worried that they would find a food court full of dead bodies – that the formative Hell Hole might have sucked the life right out of the owners of all those parked cars, and that he would be hit with the sight of hundreds of corpses slumped face down in their katsu curries – but that wasn't the case. There were no bodies. There were just half-eaten dinners, half-drunk coffees, and… and now that he looked closer, a lot of coats hanging off the backs of chairs, and handbags nestled in the corners of dining booths.

'Oh, there's dead people in here.' Darryl's eyes were wide, and danced with horror. Janusz had seen his clairvoyant husband look at what seemed to be an empty room in grim trepidation before, but in all their years together, Janusz had never seen Darryl look at an apparently deserted space with quite so much alarm.

Darryl let out a shaky breath. 'There's… *so many* dead people.'

Brenda turned around. Her expression was a mirror of Darryl's. Janusz had seen that expression on her once previously – when she'd been treated by a paramedic for a concussion obtained during a job, and had been told to avoid alcohol for at least a week.

'One moment.' Brenda's voice trembled a little. She walked steadily but speedily back out of the main door, wearing that 'no alcohol for a week' expression all the way.

'Uh oh,' muttered Richard.

The rest of the family stayed put, still gazing out at what seemed to be a hastily abandoned food hall.

'It's like the *Rosie Lee*,' murmured Charity.

'The what?' asked Janusz.

'The *Rosie Lee*. Henry the Eighth's ship, it was found all empty except for the dinners.'

'You mean the *Mary Rose*?' asked Darryl, quietly.

'Yeah,' replied Charity, 'vaguely. That's what I said.'

'I think,' said Grace, politely, 'you're both getting a bit muddled up about the *Mary Celeste*?'

Charity tutted. 'What do you know? You've got amnesia.'

'The reverend's right, actually,' replied Richard.

'Don't take her side, Dad,' grumbled Charity. 'So she can't remember when her birthday is but she can remember old boats?'

'I don't get to control how the amnesia affects me,' replied Grace, in apologetic tones.

The main door opened again, and Brenda came back in, looking slightly more composed.

'Good grief,' she said, 'it's heaving. It's like a Boxing Day sale in here.'

'It's really that bad?' Janusz asked his husband.

'You remember when we had to get to Highgate during that tube strike?' Darryl asked him.

Yes, Janusz remembered that. 'When the whole of London was all trying to get on the same bus...' he replied.

'It's a bit like that,' Darryl said, 'but instead of stressed commuters, it's stressed ghosts.'

'Yikes,' interjected Charity, unhelpfully.

Janusz took a long, deep breath, and looked around the food court. Like the sandwich of false hope in the car park, none of the food that had been left out was rotten yet. In fact... In fact, there was one red cup on the counter of the coffee stand next to him that caught his eye. It was sitting forlornly in the serving section of the counter, and it was full. He took a couple of steps over to it, to inspect it more closely.

'Careful,' Darryl told him, nodding at the empty space inside the stand. 'Ghost Barista. From what I can lipread, she *really* wants to know if there's a Yasmina here.'

Indeed, the word 'Yasmina' was scrawled in marker on the side of the cup.

'She can tell you're not a Yasmina,' said Darryl, eyeing the serving area nervously. 'That's not your order and she's getting quite angry about it.'

The milk in the coffee had not congealed. Janusz gingerly dipped the tip of his pinky finger into the drink, in spite of his husband's urgent advice that he should stop. The coffee was still lukewarm. Whatever had happened, it hadn't been weeks or days ago, or even hours. It had been minutes.

'Babe,' warned Darryl, slightly too late. The cup tipped over violently, splashing Janusz's good jumper with harmlessly cool but smelly coffee. Janusz sighed. That was going to stain and his good jumper was cold wash only.

'Whatever killed all these people,' said Janusz, 'did it maybe a half hour ago.'

'What?' breathed Richard, his eyes wide. 'What could have done…' he paused. 'Bother,' he muttered. 'That was a question for Murzzzz. Did it on impulse. Sorry.'

'Well,' said Brenda, 'all the more reason to get to the new Hell Hole and shut it down, soon as. Right, Charity?'

Charity gnawed at her lower lip. It was unusual to see Charity looking less than completely confident at the prospect of just blindly muscling her way through any supernatural problem, using her considerable psychic powers. Janusz reminded himself that the events of Coldbay were still fresh, and had given all of them a new perspective on ghost hunting. Still, it was unsettling to see his sister-in-law hesitate like this. Darryl would often compare Charity to the small cartoon puppy Scrappy Doo, and he'd once spent an hour making Janusz watch the cartoon in question to prove his point – 'You see the resemblance, right?' And, to be fair, in spite of the fact that Charity was a thirty-one-year-old woman with streaks of prematurely silver hair and not a small cartoon puppy at all, Janusz had agreed that they had a similar vibe. He had never seen an episode where Scrappy Doo had looked worried and unsure. It would be, he realised now with a sickening sensation, too upsetting to see Scrappy Doo hesitate. And *this* was upsetting. He wanted Charity to stop pulling that face and run in to try to punch a ghost in the nuts or something.

'Did you pack black velvet and smelly candles?' she asked Janusz.

Janusz nodded. Of course he'd packed black velvet and smelly candles. He always did – they were ghost hunting staples.

'Then,' said Charity, 'we should talk to these poor sods, find out what happened.'

Janusz nodded again, solemnly. Charity was right. Something this serious called for a seance.

CHAPTER FIVE

Soy Macchiato

*S*eances are nonsense. Take it from a ghost. They aren't based on *any sort of ancient mystic paranormal science. There's nothing about them at their most fundamental level that particularly compels the spirits to communicate, or to leave a place. Frustratingly though, when performed a certain way, they do tend to actually work. The Rook family developed this method while hunting ghosts and performing paranormal clearances, and it was easily altered to make it more about communicating with ghosts than fighting them – because seances have nothing to do with substance, and everything to do with style.*

The trick to getting a seance to work is annoyingly simple. For a seance to work, it merely has to look *like a seance. The cheesier and more cliché, the better. Most ghosts float adrift through the world, with what little shreds of memory and self they have left fading like last night's dream at breakfast time. They need strong images and memories to latch on to. So, since the explosion of Victorian Spiritualism, if a ghost sees a room draped in dark velvet, dotted with moody candles and chalked sigils, with a crystal ball in the centre of a table, there is a very good chance that the trite imagery will resonate in what's left of their minds – 'Oh, this looks like a seance, to summon a ghost.' Next thing they know, there they are – summoned. It's an automatic reaction. A few are able to make a further link in the ravaged remains of their last-night's-dream minds: 'I have been summoned to a seance, seances are for summoning the dead, therefore I must be dead. Oh dear.' Often, this just causes further problems. For example, what is a ghost who's just realised they're a ghost even supposed to do about it? Many times, the penny still doesn't drop that they're dead – they're too far gone, the dream has been completely forgotten.*

Yes, the Rooks have got the art of making any room look superficially like a seance down to a tee. It's patronising, it panders to stereotypes and I'm pretty sure it's offensive, which is why it frustrates me so much that it works.

Brenda kept herself pressed against the wall as her family dressed a booth table with black and purple velvet, silver charms, chalk runes and pentagrams, thirteen red candles and a plastic 'crystal ball' Richard had got from a fancy dress shop years ago. She really didn't like this new area of ghost hunting and psychic clearances that the rest of the family had decided to explore. It was namby-pamby, and horribly naff. After all, she thought – just look at the state of it. The 'seance table' looked like a bad Halloween display. It looked like the sort of nonsense that fraud Aurora Tavistock would pose with on the front of *Take a Break* magazine. She briefly caught the eye of the ghost who had been following them closely ever since Coldbay. Constance looked just as disapproving about the seance table as Brenda felt. Brenda deliberately looked away again.

Richard started lighting the candles and a sweet, chemical smell wafted over to her. Janusz had a habit of bulk-buying the coloured candles they needed for their work in the January sales, so every job they did tended to have a cloying Christmassy scent of cranberries or cinnamon. This time, it was a vaguely woody smell with jarring notes of clove and vanilla that the candle company had grandly declared was the fragrance of 'Festive Magic'. Brenda just hoped that the dead had no sense of smell – she didn't want to upset them any further.

To most of the family, the food hall was an eerily empty space of abandoned cups and plates. To Brenda, it was anything but. The food hall heaved with ghosts. It was like being in the first service station after a three-hour traffic jam, only the people milling about were even more disorientated, tired and aimlessly angry than they would usually be, on account of them all being dead – and, for the most part, very recently so. Every fast food concession stand now had ghost staff, doomed now to spend eternity in spectral corporate polo shirts with their names displayed on incorporeal shiny name tags. Some were still going through the motions of their jobs. Others had worked out that something was wrong, but hadn't yet been able to process what that actually was. A young man at the hot bento place was silently screaming in rage at his sudden inability to put the lid back on his now rapidly cooling noodles. A woman in a cleaner's tabard was slumped near a bin, her face covered with her hands, a spilled mop and bucket on the floor a few feet away, impossible now for her to pick up. It wasn't often, noted Brenda, that one saw a ghost wearing rubber gloves.

It *was* much more common in Brenda's line of work to see ghosts wearing winter coats, given the number of lingering spirits she was called to deal with who had died outside their homes. Most of the ghosts in the food hall were dressed suitably for a brisk walk across a car park on a grey November day. Many of the women carried handbags, and some of those who didn't were trying to get handbags off the floor, or the chairs where they'd been placed for safekeeping. Some people were still trying to eat and drink and were becoming distressed as they found they could no longer grasp their forks and cups. Children wandered lost. Two elderly people who might have been a couple stood less than a metre from one another, frantically looking about, unable to see each other.

Every occupant of the couple of hundred cars parked outside had to be here and possibly an extra coachload or two, to boot. Even that didn't account for just how many ghosts there were in the food court. Indeed, as Brenda looked, she could see that some of the ghosts were dressed in older trends. She could make out enough flared trouser suits, power jackets, wet-look perms and low-riding bootcut jeans to be convinced that at least some of the ghosts had been gradually collecting since the place was built in the sixties. Whatever had made the Hell Hole over Helsbury Services had been in the process of going about it using the same method that had been used in Coldbay – layering years and years' worth of human misery and loss in one spot – but something, very, very recently, had caused it to throw its whole schedule out of the window, and do something hitherto unheard of.

Supernatural forces didn't simply wipe out an entire motorway service station's worth of people. Certainly not without an explosion or a freak meteor or something else to cover it up. Yes, sometimes a particularly mischievous set of Demons might delight in picking off the entire crew of a ship on open waters, leaving it eerily adrift. They'd even been known to snatch the odd plane out of the sky, but they always ensured that it was conceivable there could be a rational, earthly explanation for what had occurred – that was part of the game for Demons. It wasn't like Demons to do something so flagrant, or so sudden as what had happened here. Besides, if it *was* Demons, there would be more mess. There wasn't any mess here, at all. In fact… in fact, there was something else wrong here… what *was* it? It was on the tip of her tongue…

'Where are all the bodies?' Darryl said, quietly.

Brenda blinked across at her son. Darryl's brow was furrowed in concentration. He didn't see the dead as easily as Brenda did, so she had assumed that the poor boy would need a while to take in the sheer horrific magnitude of the haunted food court, but bless him, it had taken someone with a far, far, far less gifted clairvoyant eye than hers to point out the simplicity of what was missing, right under her nose. A few hundred of the ghosts were very freshly dead. And so the food court should have been piled high with still-cooling bodies, but Brenda couldn't see a single corpse. It was as if all these people's earthly bodies had just been ripped away from them, transported to another place – perhaps another plane of being entirely – where these poor ghosts couldn't find them and where their surviving families wouldn't be able to bury or cremate them. They were just… gone.

This had to be the work of something powerful *and* organised. There was the suddenness of it, the stomach-churning clinical cleanness of it, and the fact that it had only just happened – less than an hour ago. The Rooks would have already been on the road when all these people were wrenched from their lives. Brenda thought back. An hour ago, they were already having trouble getting to Edendale. An hour ago, something was already messing with them.

It *knew* Brenda was coming here.

It just killed hundreds of people *because* it knew Brenda was coming here.

'Perhaps the ghosts will know what happened to their bodies,' suggested Janusz, sounding unsure. The expressions of the rest of the family did nothing to encourage him. The dead rarely knew much about anything. Only Grace nodded in quiet agreement at him, and – no offence meant to the little priest – she wasn't exactly an expert on these matters.

Still, they'd gone to all the trouble of covering one of the tables inside the closest booth in velvet and candles, so Janusz felt that they really should give it their best shot anyway. Grace sat at the newly decorated seance table with them and gestured for Darryl and Charity to hold his hands. They all waited for Brenda to slowly and reluctantly pick her way through whatever unseen horrors filled the food court from her corner by the door to their booth. Richard waited, a hand outstretched towards her, as she approached. Once Brenda finally got close enough to accept her husband's hand, it was as if he'd just pulled her out of invisible quicksand. Brenda's demeanour lightened at his touch, and her step quickened. They walked together to join the others at the table as if breezily meeting them for brunch.

'Let's get this nonsense over with then,' huffed Brenda, sliding into the booth and taking Grace's free hand and closing the seance circle.

The family had only pulled off one decent seance so far, at Coldbay, and, crucially, that time they'd had access to information about the ghosts they were trying to contact – their names, their photos. It had helped. Many of the dead had been so relieved at hearing their names spoken aloud by living voices that it had made them immediately warmer and more cooperative. This time, the family had nothing. Janusz wondered vaguely whether they should go through some of the abandoned handbags and find at least some forms of ID of the vanished, but the family were already sitting down. If they took a break now to raid bags and purses, they'd have to start all over again, and Brenda would complain. It was probably not the best practice to base so much of their method around whether or not Brenda would complain about something, but whenever they were deep in the chaos of a haunted house or shop or church or factory or, in this case, motorway service station, Janusz really found it best to follow the path of least resistance, when it came to Brenda. She could certainly cause a *lot* of resistance, when she wanted to – and, sometimes, when she didn't want to, but couldn't quite help herself. Janusz hadn't seen many ghosts. The first and worst had been the top half of a long-dead pirate in a ghost gibbet jutting out of the kitchen lino in his flat. In the months before he'd called the Rook family out to rid him of said pirate ghost, he'd been tormented, terrified and deprived of sleep. That had just been one ghost. Brenda saw ghosts all the time – had done since she was little. Janusz could only imagine how much that must have messed with her. He didn't like to think about it too much. Also, whenever he thought about his kitchen ghost, he'd find himself harking back to flirting with the young man who had come to clear his flat of the malingering spirit. It had been very unprofessional of Darryl. Even now, as a married man, the memories would make him feel very warm about the neck, and he'd get distracted.

Where was he…? Oh, yes! Seance time.

With no names to call out, Janusz opted to go with the most cliché seance opening he could think of, in the hope it would resonate with some of the dead.

'Is anyone there?'

At his side, Janusz's husband tensed briefly, before suddenly going limp. Janusz kept a tight hold of Darryl's slack hand, and bolstered him a little with his shoulder to keep him slumped with his back against the padded corner of the booth seat instead of drooping onto Janusz or the table. Darryl's eyes were rolled back, his jaw lax. A thin line of drool escaped the corner of his mouth.

Somebody *was* there, of course.

In the past week, Janusz had learned two new things about his husband. One was that, due to his unusual conception, Darryl could take on the form of an itty-bitty Demon in moments of overwhelming supernatural stress. The other thing was, possibly also due to the whole conception thing, Darryl could channel the voices of the dead. Actually, thought Janusz to himself, "channel the voices of the dead" made it sound much more gentle and controlled than the reality. What happened in reality was, the dead were able to enter Darryl, through his face, or his brain, or... somehow. Janusz still wasn't entirely sure how that bit worked, but the ghosts could push Darryl's consciousness to the back. If it was just one, fairly lucid ghost, Darryl could remain largely functional. But when it was lots of spirits all at the same time, like here, he would become overwhelmed, and collapse like a broken doll. The dead didn't seem to be able to control the movements of his body, thankfully, once he was in his half-asleep state. But they could speak through him, using his mouth as a transmitter to the living world.

Of these two new supernatural phenomena presenting in Darryl, Janusz found the latter one the hardest to watch. He didn't mind seeing Darryl's Demon form so much – he'd spent years around Murzzzz, so Demons in themselves held no particular terror or mystique for him any more, and when Darryl was Demon Darryl, at least he was still himself, he was still in charge of his body. Also – and Janusz had mentioned this a couple of times but still didn't feel like they were talking about it enough – Demon Darryl was adorable. Demon Darryl looked like a monster in a cartoon for pre-schoolers that made most of its profits selling stuffed toy tie-ins. Darryl didn't look cute now, sagging helplessly against the padded booth seat. He looked vulnerable, and Janusz didn't like it.

A voice came out of Darryl's face.

'Soy macchiato?' called the voice. It was female, young and already very close to completely losing its temper. 'Soy macchiato for Yasmina?'

The barista from the coffee stand. It made sense, Janusz supposed – the coffee concession was physically not far from the booth, and the family had already annoyed her… Well. Janusz had already annoyed her. His jumper still smelled of the soy macchiato that the ghost barista was still trying to find the customer for.

'I think Yasmina's gone,' Grace told the ghost, gently.

'Yasmina,' called the barista again, testily. 'Soy macchiato! Yasmina!'

'Think the macchiato's gone as well now, mate,' added Charity. She jerked her head in Janusz's direction. 'You threw it all over this one's jumper.'

'Yasmina!'

'Can you tell me your name?' Janusz attempted.

There was a pause. Janusz wondered hopefully whether the barista remembered how angry he'd made her only minutes before, and if that might snap her into the here and now. He then wondered with concern that remembering how angry he'd made her would cause her to get angry all over again. He really didn't want that while she was in possession of his husband.

'It's not for you,' said the barista after a moment, 'it's for Yasmina. If you want to order—'

Janusz tried again. 'Can you tell me your name?'

Another pause. 'If you want to speak to management—'

Brenda snorted a joyless laugh. 'Young lady, you have no idea of the management level we want to speak to.'

'You'll have to phone customer support,' replied the barista in harassed tones, 'or use the website.'

'Can you tell me your name?'

'No,' said the voice, defensively. There was another brief pause, and the voice replied 'no' again, but this time it was weighted with a sense of realisation. This wasn't just a person who didn't *want* to give her name. This was someone whose mind had been so scourged that she had no name to give besides that of her final customer. A whole life, a whole identity, reduced to nothing but a coffee order from a stranger who would never collect. The cruelty of it hit Janusz hard. How Darryl and Brenda could bear to see people in this sort of condition day in, day out, was beyond him.

'It's OK,' said Grace, in her most priestly of tones. 'I think you've realised something's gone wrong, haven't you?'

'I can't remember,' admitted the voice. It sounded more lost than angry, now.

'Did something bad happen here?' Grace asked. 'It might have been quite recent…'

'I can't remember,' repeated the voice, and, oh, the anger was coming back.

'It's OK,' soothed Grace, 'we're here to help. We recently helped some people who were a lot like you, and—'

'Look,' said the voice, 'did you order a soy macchiato or not?'

'Would it make you feel better,' tried Grace, 'if I told you that I did order a soy macchiato?'

Another pause, and the voice came back angrier than ever. 'You're not Yasmina!'

'I know, but—'

A new voice spoke, lovely and well-spoken and of indeterminate gender. 'You're not Yasmina, you're Grace Barry and you shouldn't be here.'

'Yes, I know, but... wait, what?'

'Hello?' said a third voice, from Darryl.

'Someone knew my name,' said Grace. 'We didn't tell anyone my name, did we?'

'Hello?' came a fourth voice from Darryl, distressingly young.

'You all heard that, right?' Grace asked the family. 'They knew my name.'

'I'm lost,' said the young child's voice.

'Hello, little one,' said Richard, 'maybe we can help you.'

'I shouldn't talk to strangers...' began the voice. A fifth voice sounded, so soon after that of the frightened child that it cut the bewildered little voice off. The fifth voice was old and worried. 'Sangita?' it asked. 'Sangita? Are you here? Please, my wife, she has dementia, she shouldn't be alone.' Before anyone could reply, a sixth voice cut in. 'Hello?'

'We can't help these poor people,' whispered Janusz. 'There's so many of them and they're so lost.'

'Told you so,' murmured Brenda.

'OK, but could someone bring that second voice back, please?' Grace asked. 'I have questions.'

Janusz knew that there was no chance of bringing the second voice back, or indeed of controlling anything about this seance, now. The whole thing had spiralled into chaos. Voice after voice tumbled out of Darryl, speaking over one another, sometimes even calling out at the same time. A multitude of accents, a few speaking other languages – two in Polish, one in Russian and four speaking a language Janusz understood to probably be Japanese but couldn't interpret. Old, young, children... a couple of babies cried, lonely and scared. The family didn't have the chance to so much as get a word in edgeways to ask for names, or ask how they could help, or find out who or what had attacked all these people.

'There's so many of them,' Charity murmured, over the cacophony of terrified voices.

'*Told* you,' repeated Brenda. 'But none of you listened to Muggins, here.'

'What do we do, Mum?'

'You could try popping some of them away, princess.'

Charity shook her head. 'I'm not going to do that, any more. I'm not sending the dead off to who-knows-where without their permission. That's not the superhero way. Wonder Woman would never.'

If anybody else in the group had any answers on what to do about the increasingly crowded seance, they had no opportunity to air them, because at Charity's invocation of her favourite Amazonian superhero, the situation resolved itself in a less than ideal way.

A multitude of voices tried to speak from Darryl at the same time, and suddenly stopped short. Darryl began to choke, and shake.

'*Zabko!*' Janusz broke the circle of hands and grabbed Darryl by both shoulders. He'd choked at the end of the first seance they had conducted. Janusz had hoped that it had just been because Darryl wasn't used to channelling the dead and that it would be better the next time, but it was even worse, now. This time the choking was prolonged, and it felt more violent. 'They're hurting him!'

'I don't think they're doing it on purpose,' said Brenda.

'Dear,' warned Richard, scooting over to help Janusz with Darryl.

'Right, right,' sighed Brenda. 'Besides the point, I suppose.'

'What do I do?' asked Janusz. He tried shaking Darryl a little. 'Do I Heimlich him? Can one Heimlich out a ghost?'

'Charity, princess,' said Richard, 'I know you said it's not the superhero way, but if there's a ghost stuck in your brother's throat...'

Grace came around the table and joined Janusz and Richard in helplessly shaking Darryl's shoulder.

'Get out of him,' Grace demanded, in a rather woeful attempt at a commanding tone. 'By the power of Christ, or Buddha, or Stephen Fry... or whatever it is you believe in.'

Darryl was still choking, his lips taking on a worryingly blueish tinge. Grace's expression altered. It wasn't exactly a glaring change, but it also certainly wasn't subtle.

'Please?' she said. 'Let's keep things civil.'

Janusz couldn't find a way to describe it to himself in any of the languages he spoke, except to say that there was something to Grace's new demeanour that hurt his face, and he had no idea why. Darryl coughed, inhaled, blinked and focused his eyes on Janusz.

'Well, that wasn't fun,' he croaked. 'Did any of them say anything useful?'

'Not really,' Charity told him, 'except that the drink that got thrown on your husband's good jumper was definitely a soy macchiato.'

CHAPTER SIX

Not A Vicar

'What a waste of time and breath.' Brenda remained seated in the booth while the rest of the family tidied up the seance things.

'I could have done with more breaths, certainly,' noted Darryl, as he packed away the Festive Magic scented candles.

'Is that going to be a thing every time, now?' Janusz asked. 'The not being able to breathe?'

Darryl shrugged at his husband, helplessly. Janusz turned to Richard. 'Should we get him an emergency inhaler or something?'

It was Richard's turn to shrug apologetically at Janusz. Richard honestly didn't know. He was out of his depth, here. His son's newly discovered psychic powers were bewildering. Richard had no idea why they'd only just manifested in Darryl after thirty-five years, what he now was capable of, or what dangers this could bring to his boy, and the rest of his family. He had nobody to ask, any more. For the first time in decades, there was no guiding voice within him, nobody to whisper the ancient secrets of the mortal and Demon realms. It was so quiet inside Richard. So quiet and so lonely. He felt like an abandoned ship, bobbing, all forlorn on the open sea, drifting along with the current. Richard put the fake crystal ball back into its little velvet pouch, and said nothing.

Charity heaved a disappointed sigh. 'Maybe if we close this new Hell Hole first, it'll make it easier to help all the ghosts.' She looked to her parents for validation. 'Sound like a plan?'

Richard shrugged again. It wasn't as if he had an alternative plan of his own.

'Worth a try,' replied Brenda, wearily. 'Hell Hole's on the other side of the motorway, though, and whatever did this knew we were coming, so get ready for some nasty surprises.'

Charity nodded. 'I'm going to have to carb-load in advance, aren't I?'

'Oh gracious,' replied Brenda, 'that goes without saying, princess.'

Richard didn't say anything. Brenda was right. Charity's psychic powers burned through energy at the best of times. The psychic effort of closing the Hell Hole at Coldbay had caused blood to pour out of her face, and that was after eating three bags of crisps – not individual sized bags, either, but the big packs you get to fill serving bowls with at parties. Richard didn't want to think about what might happen to his princess if she ever became overwhelmed and out of energy…

His mind's eye flashed, unbidden, back to The Longest Night. Terrible. Terrible. The blood. The eyes, staring and unspoken blame frozen on those two dead faces. Little Darryl sobbing, terrified. The baby, screaming. The baby, still alive. Brenda, taking the baby out of Constance's dead arms. Darryl staring with streaming eyes at a spot where Constance's face would be, were she now standing next to her own dead body. Murzzzz's voice deep within Richard, like a rhythm, like a heartbeat. '**I'm sorry. I'm sorry. I'm sorry. I'm sorry.**'

'Janusz my lovely, if you could take your husband as a little spy for us to scope out the state of the footbridge to the other side?' he heard Brenda ask. 'Check for unexpected Demons and whatnot.' Richard blinked, and forced himself to concentrate back on the matter in hand 'Don't let him fight any big beasties alone,' continued Brenda, 'not with those diddy little kitten fangs.'

'OK, why does everyone keep describing my horrible cursed Demon manifestation thing like that?' asked Darryl.

'Darryl, have you *seen* it?' Charity asked.

'No, I have not. It's horrible and cursed.'

'It's adorable,' said Charity.

'*Right?*' added Janusz, in enthusiastic tones of agreement. 'I've said this to him; he doesn't believe me.'

'Demon Darryl looks like a sort of sharp Ewok.'

'I was thinking Baby Simba on hind legs.'

'Yeah,' Charity nodded. 'I can see that.'

Darryl rolled his eyes. 'I hope a massive Demon *does* attack me, if I've got nothing but this to look forward to for the rest of my life.'

'Love you,' replied Janusz with a smile that could destroy burgeoning marital complaints with a single twinkle.

Darryl kissed his husband's cheek, the argument-in-waiting swiftly slain by Sir Janusz and his smile of wonder. 'Fine, I'll go and look at the footbridge.'

'How kind of you to do your job,' trilled Brenda. 'Vicar…'

'Just "Grace",' said Grace, for the umpteenth time. 'I'm not actually a vicar.'

'Vicar,' continued Brenda, unabashed, 'you can help Charity get croissants and I'll pop over to pick up the other necessary staples.'

Richard's heart sank. Ah. Speaking of marital arguments that never quite happened. He knew what his wife meant by 'necessary staples', and it wasn't bottled water or a first aid kit. She meant booze. He'd tried talking to his wife about the drinking several times, back in the early days of their relationship. Even Darryl and Charity had attempted the talk, when they'd been younger and rather more naive about the power that a child's concern could have over an addiction. All that any of the interventions had achieved had been to make Brenda hostile and paranoid until they'd given up. But then, this week, Grace had tried and, perhaps simply due to a happy coincidence of timing, things had gone a lot better than usual. Brenda had cut down – only had a few glasses per evening. Richard had actually allowed himself to believe that perhaps his wife could simply drink in moderation from now on, and there wouldn't need to be any sort of a fuss. He did allow himself to think some terribly silly, lovely things from time to time. It only made it all the worse when reality came crashing in, as it always did.

He'd known the truth of it, deep down. He had done all week, but especially when they'd come into the food hall and Brenda's eyes had flitted between gazing at the clamouring, invisible dead and searching for an off-licence. He'd tried to ignore it, and continued to hope for the best. Even now, he knew that if he mentioned it she'd keep up the pretence that it was just for the task in hand. Unfortunately, strong alcohol was a genuinely useful weapon against Demons. There was something about its chemistry that burned Demons like acid. It had been a well-known tool of the trade for ghost hunters for well over a century now. Some of the more churchy types liked to use consecrated wine, but that was just for show – what mattered wasn't the prayers, it was the alcohol content and the stronger the better. There was nothing in the living world,

Richard had been reliably informed, that a Demon feared more than absinthe.

To an outsider, the ghost hunter community's discovery of such a potent weapon could seem like a tremendous bonus for all involved. Outsiders, Richard was grimly aware, tended not to know just how many clairvoyants responded to the horrors they were constantly forced to see with some serious self-medication. The Demon-fighting properties of alcohol gave clairvoyants a rational reason to always have booze around. Even if a ghost hunting clairvoyant wanted to quit drinking, it was incredibly hard when there were always a few bottles of Smirnoff to hand. Most clairvoyants didn't even want to quit drinking. For a lot of clairvoyants, trying to get to sleep sober was an impossibility. Richard tried not to judge. Yes, he'd slept soundly for over forty years with a Demon inside him, but he'd never tried nodding off as a burned child hung over his bed, silently screaming in eternal terror. That kid had followed Brenda around for a fortnight. So, no – he tried not to judge the methods she used to cope with what she saw. He just tried to be grateful that Darryl didn't drink much. For now. Darryl's comparative sobriety had always made sense to him as Darryl didn't have anywhere near the clairvoyant abilities of his mother. But, all of a sudden, things were so different now. Richard had no idea which paths his son's new abilities might lead him down.

Richard really wished he could talk to Murzzzz about it – or about anything. Demon culture, or ancient wisdoms, or just what Murzzzz wanted for breakfast – anything. Just one more time. Without Murzzzz, Richard's mind was like a house with all the furniture taken out – all wrong, all wrong.

*

Brenda got up, smoothed down her skirt. Then, to Richard's surprise, she clacked over to the coffee stand and squinted. 'Your name tag says "Olivia", dear.'

'What?' asked Richard.

'The barista. She was getting upset that she didn't know her name, which is daft because it's right there on her top.'

'You helped her,' said Grace, proudly.

She had. Well, that was Brenda, thought Richard. Maybe this time it *could* be different.

'Don't be daft,' replied Brenda, striding back over to the others, 'I just wanted her to stop whining and chucking macchiato at our knitwear. Right – we'll see you in ten minutes next to that rack over there selling novelty neck pillows and, for some reason, wetsuits. Dear, will you join me?'

'Of course.' Richard deflated, yet again. He was always going to go with her. Just… he really wished that for once their journey wasn't straight over to the nearest place that stocked booze.

Obviously, Brenda went straight over to the nearest place that stocked booze. It was a very small Marks & Spencers – the kind that mostly sold sandwiches, flowers, own brand fizzy pop and big bags of sweets shaped like pigs. The strong liquor was in a sliding door cabinet behind the tills, so that you had to ask the cashier to fetch it for you, as you did cigarettes, lotto tickets and stamps, in some sort of attempt to curb the British's four main vices – drinking, smoking, gambling and sending one another letters. In this case, Brenda didn't have to ask the cashier to fetch her two bottles of vodka and a rum chaser, because the cashier was dead. The cabinet had thankfully been left unlocked, so Brenda just walked to the other side of the till, ignored the silent protests of the ghost cashier and took a few bottles for herself.

She glanced at Richard. He looked worried. He'd been looking worried since Coldbay, but it was getting progressively worse. These past few days, Brenda contemplated, had been the first time she had ever been with Richard without Murzzzz. The Demon and man double act had already been in their symbiotic arrangement for a couple of years before she met them. She tried not to think about what that said about her marriage, that Murzzzz had been there when they'd married… That Murzzzz had been there every time Richard had said 'I love you'… No. The loss of Murzzzz wasn't about her. It was about Richard. It was also a little bit about her, she conceded to herself, in that if Richard was off his game on this job it could mean big problems for the whole family, which included her.

'Did you want to talk about it?' she asked.

Richard looked taken aback. 'Do you?'

'If it helps.'

'Oh. OK.' Richard shuffled and looked down at his feet, awkwardly. 'Just, after Grace gave you that leaflet on problem drinking, I sort of hoped you might—'

Brenda bristled. 'Not about that!'

'Ah.' Richard looked even more awkward and miserable.

Brenda hastily put the bottles into her handbag. Honestly – the alcohol was just for the job! For warding off Demons and such. Well, maybe she'd treat herself to a little bit of it. Why should Demons get all the vodka? They were Demons and they didn't even like the stuff.

'I meant, about You Know Who,' said Brenda. 'I know you miss him. We all do. In a way. He was part of the family.'

Richard sighed. 'It's not that. It *is* that. But… Oh, sweetheart, what are we going to do?'

'We're going to carry on.' Brenda decided to take a bottle of brandy as well – for good luck.

'How? Without Murzzzz what good am I to you? I'm just an old man, getting in the way.'

'You will stop that nonsense right this moment, Richard Rook. Do you ever catch Janusz moping about just because he doesn't have a Demon in him?'

'Murzzzz was the muscle, the bodyguard. If we don't have him any more… You know this place is almost certainly a trap, don't you?'

'Oh, definitely,' replied Brenda, blithely. 'That's why we're all stocking up and scouting out, while we have the chance.'

'What if this place is like Coldbay, or worse? What if something happens, and nobody's there to protect us?'

'*You're* here to protect us.'

'I can't! Not like Murzzzz.' Richard no longer just looked miserable, lonely and awkward any more. He now looked actively panicked. 'And on this sort of job, we *know* what can happen without Murzzzz's protection.'

Richard's voice was becoming strained. Brenda was used to him getting stressed like this, but usually, it would mean he was about to let Murzzzz take over for a bit while he calmed down. He didn't have that option any more. He was going to have to deal with it by himself. Brenda half-considered offering him a drink to help him, but she decided she didn't want to.

Yes. She knew what could happen to mortals on big jobs like this, when they didn't have a Demon's full protection. She'd had enough reminders of it, recently, not that she had ever forgotten after…

'The Longest Night,' blurted Richard.

OK, well Richard really didn't need to say it out loud like that, even if he *was* all of a tizzy.

'Constance and Harry,' continued Richard. 'Murzzzz didn't help them, I still don't understand why he didn't help them, and they just... they just *died*. They were just mown down by shards of glass like they were nothing, and...'

Brenda flicked a guilty glance up at the ghost beckoning from the little shop's doorway.

Hello again, Brenda. Nice to know you're both still thinking of me, at least. But if you could just pop your head around this door and take a quick look...? No...?

'...and,' stammered Richard, 'what if that happens again, this time? With Grace? Or you, my love, or... oh God, or the kids – Brenda, the kids! I couldn't... I couldn't go on. It's too much. We should leave.'

Brenda stepped over to Richard and laid a gentle hand on his shoulder. 'My darling, I love you with my whole heart but you are talking absolute arse gravy right now, and I think you know it.'

'But—'

'No, dear. Our son, as you may have noticed, has rather inherited the "muscle" role from Murzzzz.'

'He's nowhere near as strong as Murzzzz. And he looks so sweet in Demon form, honestly, I'm worried the other Demons are just going to laugh at him.'

'Also, Charity closed a whole Hell Hole the other day—'

'With help from Darryl and Grace. And it nearly wiped her out.'

'And, yes, now that you mention Grace... there's something off about that vicar,' Brenda confided in her husband. 'I take it you've noticed, too?'

Richard hesitated, glancing about to make sure Grace wasn't in hearing range. 'I sort of assumed I was just being paranoid.'

'Oh come on, darling, I know you're having a bad week but there really is no such thing as "just being paranoid" about somebody's vibes in this line of work. How does a priest end up wandering around a deserted, cursed island with no memory whatsoever, unless for nefarious reasons? And then there's the way she sometimes makes my face hurt.'

'You feel that too?' asked Richard, surprised. 'Like at the seance earlier?'

Brenda nodded. 'A burning in the eyes, whether you're looking at her or not. It's definitely her doing it and I'm not sure if she knows.'

'It happened when Darryl was choking,' Richard recalled. 'Do you think she's dangerous?'

'Not sure. Edendale could give us answers, if we make it out of *here* alive.' Brenda gave Richard an encouraging little smile. 'You never know, she might just be dangerous to Demons.'

This, unsurprisingly, didn't seem to do much to set Richard's mind at rest. Oh, well. At least they weren't talking about The Longest Night any more. Or the vodka in Brenda's bag.

'Charity'll be fine alone with her, right?'

'They're hardly "alone". They're right over there, getting pastries.' Brenda nodded at the coffee concessionary stand at the other side of the food court where Charity and Grace were gathering all of the muffins that had been abandoned in the perspex display case. 'That ghost barista's less stroppy now she knows her name so it seems safe enough for now. We can allow Charity time for a bit of cake and a girl chat.'

'...Blade, Miles Morales and then my top two are interchangeable between Captain Marvel and Doctor Strange,' said Charity, through a mouthful of double choc-chip muffin. 'Now, I know what you're thinking – why no X-Men in my top

Marvel heroes? Thing is, I just have too many favourite X-Men, so I decided to do a separate top ten for them, even though I know there's a load of crossover I thought I might as well, so I have a top ten for DC, Marvel, X-Men, anime superheroes and, I know it's a little bit of a tangent, but witches and wizards are kind of superpower-adjacent, so that's another one.'

'You really like superheroes, don't you?'

'Well… yeah,' replied Charity. 'That's the whole point of all my top tens.'

'I never really got into all of that,' Grace told her. At least, she thought to herself, she didn't *think* she ever had.

'Yeah, well,' said Charity, still eating, 'superheroes make sense, don't they? Maybe not the fashion. I tried wearing a leotard once when I was seventeen – never again. But, the general thrust of superheroes, you know? Great power, great responsibility and all that. Makes everything nice and simple. It doesn't do to overcomplicate things when you're dancing on the veil between the living world and the realms beyond, or you'd end up all panicky – like Darryl, and where would we be with two Darryls? In a right old sweaty state, is where.'

'So…' Grace frowned, faintly. 'So, you basically take your understanding of the mysteries of Heaven and Earth, as well as your spiritual and moral guidance, from comic books and action movies?'

Charity nodded, matter of factly, still chewing. 'And fantasy novels and anime. Yep.'

'And you don't think that's at all…' Grace faltered. She didn't want to say something as impolite as 'childish', or 'asinine'. In the end, she settled on 'unusual'.

'I *am* unusual.' Charity shoved the last of her muffin into her mouth, and kept on talking through the crumbs. 'That's the point.'

'Yes, but you're also thirty.'

'Thirty-one,' Charity corrected her, unabashed and chocolatey. 'And you're, what, mid to late forties?'

Again, Grace didn't know for sure, but that seemed the right ballpark. Grace half-nodded, half-shrugged.

'And you,' continued Charity, 'take your understanding of the mysteries of Heaven and Earth, as well as your spiritual and moral guidance, from a set of ancient myths that have been translated and edited by powerful blokes for thousands of years.'

Grace set her face, defensively. 'I wouldn't dismiss the Bible as "myths".'

'I know you wouldn't, because you take it seriously. To the point that you made yourself a priest. I take my stuff seriously to the point that I made myself a superhero.'

Did Charity have a point? Grace wasn't sure. Unfortunately, Charity spoke with such conviction that Grace felt like she *must* have a point. Grace found herself faltering again, uncertain of herself and more than a little bit jealous of Charity's confidence in her own argument.

'Maybe,' Grace replied in as dignified a manner as she could muster, 'a higher power decided to make me a priest.'

'Maybe a higher power decided to make me a superhero,' countered Charity. She swallowed the last of her muffin and immediately picked up a croissant. 'Often the way, with Chosen Ones. You don't choose to become a Chosen One yourself – you're too humble.' She tore into her stolen croissant. 'Wonder if I've got time for a wee between carb-loads,' she added, through the pastry, 'I could do with one, especially before saving the world again.'

From Charity's tone, the conversation was over. Grace was quite relieved. Talking to Charity about superhero stuff was a bit like standing in front of a tsunami, asking if it had any interesting saltwater to show you. Grace pointed out where the ladies' loos were, and continued to fill a couple of paper carrier bags with the rest of the muffins and pastries. She couldn't shake the thought that Olivia the angry barista was probably still standing right there with them. She really didn't like to imagine just how affronted the ghost must be at them just taking all of the products from her stand.

'Sorry, Olivia,' Grace murmured in the direction of the till. 'It would only have gone off, otherwise.' She looked across at Charity. 'Would it help if we left some money?'

Charity shook her head. 'The ghost can't pick it up, can she? Even if she could, what would she do with it? Can't take it with you – John Lennon wrote that.'

Grace wanted to say that she really didn't think the ill-fated Beatle had actually coined that one, and that besides, she knew of a *certain other* bearded peace-lover who had far better quotes about wealth and the afterlife, but she was fast learning that, as with Brenda, it was better to let things go when it came to Charity.

Something else was still upsetting Grace. 'One of the ghosts during the seance knew my name. Is that normal? For them to know your name like that?'

Charity swallowed a piece of croissant. 'No, that's a bit weird.'

'Just, they knew my *full* name, and I'm pretty sure you guys have only been calling me "Grace" or "Reverend" in here. Or "Vicar", even though I'm a rector, not a vicar.' Grace thought back. 'Sometimes your mum calls me "you, there".'

'Even with that,' replied Charity, 'ghosts don't often listen when the living are talking amongst themselves. They usually don't care.' Charity gave her croissant another, more thoughtful, munch. 'The Manager called you by your full name, didn't it?'

'Of course it did. The Manager's an all-seeing nightmare of burning eyeballs in another dimension that's trying to destroy the world. Of course it knew my full name – the Manager knows all. Probably.'

'Yeah,' said Charity, 'probably.'

'So why bring it up?'

Charity regarded Grace, with an odd expression. Was Grace panicking? It felt like maybe she was panicking. It felt like there was a bit too much of Grace. The too-much-ness crackled like static, like a hijacked analogue TV station.

'Just thinking out loud,' replied Charity after an uncomfortable moment.

'You don't suppose the Manager is here as well, do you?' Grace asked. 'That maybe it's controlling all this mess?'

'Do I think that an incredibly powerful being which used the misery of the dead to open a portal in the sky a few days ago, and is now really annoyed with us, might be what is behind all these very recently dead people and the portal that started opening up right as we were driving past? It's a possibility, Vicar.'

Grace frowned worriedly in the direction of the footbridge, even though she could see nothing beyond the empty foodhall, food cooling and congealing on plates and in serving tureens and a cheerful display of novelty personalised kids drinks bottles in the doorway of the abandoned WHSmith. 'I'm not a vicar,' she said, automatically.

CHAPTER SEVEN

The Bridge

The footbridge had clearly once been a gleaming testament to hyper-modernity. Decades ago, people who wore hats to the office and smoked at their desks would have drafted the designs and dreamed that in the twenty-first century, families in vibrant unitards with floating hoops for skirts would enjoy the view from over the motorway as one would enjoy standing on a bridge to watch the river below. Perhaps they pictured little boys with atom models instead of bobbles on their hats, pointing at the sleek hovercars as they streamed in a graceful flow beneath the glass-lined bridge.

The twenty-first century had brought no such space age glory to the footbridge. For a feature designed to be all about looking out at a landscape as vast and promising as the future, everything about it in reality felt horribly claustrophobic. The inside had been cleaned that day, but the outside of the glass was grubby with many years' worth of algae, mixed with the streaked grey of exhaust fumes, general motorway grot and old stains of rain. The daylight outside remained steadfastly Novemberish and the colour of a smoker's teeth, so, if anything, it just added to the darkness of the glass corridor.

Outside the services, the world was carrying on as usual, for now. The sight of the cars and lorries as they trundled along below brought no comfort to Darryl – their drivers blissfully unaware of anything untoward about the service station as they passed it at a mile a minute. Kids in the backs of Subarus hit each other and played on their phones until they felt sick, with no idea that an apocalyptic portal was in the process of being carved out of the sky. Lorry drivers tried to stay awake for their sixteenth hour on the road with no comprehension that hundreds of lives had just been snuffed out, only metres away. True, these things had no bearing on one another, but it still didn't seem fair, considering.

Also, the walkway was full of ghosts. That was rather adding to Darryl's downer on the bridge in general. Overall, he was not a fan.

Darryl stopped in the middle of the footbridge and glumly watched a large dead man in a shell suit trying to hit the glass with ghost hands and scream for help with a silent mouth. Janusz stood by Darryl's side, unaware he was only a few inches from the mute and panicking ghost.

'How is it?' asked Janusz.

'Bad,' said Darryl, quietly, 'but no Demons. It won't be pleasant, getting to the other side, but it should be doable without any of us getting our heads stoved in.'

'Well, that's something,' replied Janusz, sapped of his usual easy cheer. 'I do prefer for my head to be this shape.'

'Assuming it's not a trap. And I think probably it's a trap.'

'Yes,' sighed Janusz, glumly, 'me too. But what options do we have?'

Darryl found Janusz's hand with his, as he continued to keep an eye on the ghosts. 'You bummed out about the seance?' Then

71

he remembered, a little too late, about his husband's occasional issues translating English idioms. 'I mean, are you still upset that—'

'I know what "bummed out" means, you explained that one to me before.'

'Oh, yes.' Darryl remembered the mix up over that one now, which had resulted in Janusz thinking Darryl was coming on to him when he was feeling down. Luckily in that case, Janusz's bad mood had only been over Poland being knocked out of the World Cup. Things could have been much more awkward, had Darryl used that phrase only a few months earlier when Janusz's grandmother had died.

'I thought we could fix it,' sighed Janusz, 'if we listened and talked. I thought the seances could be a breakthrough, and now it's only going to be harder to get your mother to agree to them.'

'Don't write Mum off just yet.'

'*Zabko*, you know I love your mother. But she's very… Brenda. Which is a good thing, a great thing! Until, it's not.'

'It was only one bad seance, babe. No one was hurt, we live, we learn, we…' he frowned, his attention grabbed by one ghost in the listless crowd. 'We try again another day…'

'They were all so lost and upset,' sighed Janusz.

'Well,' replied Darryl, still distracted, 'that's ghosts for you.' The ghost who'd caught his eye was standing still and gazing at him, as other ghosts shuffled aimlessly about or tried to press spectral hands against the murky glass. She was a young woman. Her clothes were practical rather than fashionable so a time of death was a little harder to pin down, but the cut of her jeans and jumper coupled with the style of her trainers suggested she'd died around the late eighties or early nineties. He'd seen her before – on the island, near the van after they'd escaped, and in photos at home... and in the face of his little sister, every day.

'I *knew* it,' Darryl exclaimed. 'She *is* following us!'

'Who?' asked Janusz.

Darryl pointed at the ghost, even though his husband couldn't see her. 'Constance Xu. She must have come with us in the car.'

'But your mum said—'

'I know what Mum said. Mum lied. She does it all the time.'

'Brenda being Brenda,' muttered Janusz, resignedly.

As Darryl watched, the ghost of Constance Xu raised a hand. He raised his own hand in response, impressed. Constance seemed lucid and controlled. She seemed to recognise him, and now she appeared to be trying to communicate, in a friendly, calm manner. This was considerably more rational behaviour than the vast majority of ghosts. Could it be due to being a former ghost hunter herself, he wondered, or her proximity to Charity? Or maybe it was the Hell Hole...? The one on Coldbay had made ghosts and Demons alike more powerful, the closer they got to it. Maybe it was having an effect on her.

Constance maintained eye contact with him, and waved her upheld hand.

'Hello, Constance,' he said, in a light, warm tone, hoping this might help the ghost further. 'Are you here for Charity?'

Constance gazed intensely at him, and waved harder. She was mouthing something, but Darryl couldn't make out what it was.

'Would you like to speak with her?' he asked, still waving. 'I can help you, if you like...'

Constance started waving with both hands. She bounced a little on the balls of her feet, urgently. Her expression didn't look calm or friendly any more. There was something desperate

73

about it. Whatever it was she was trying to tell them, she was growing increasingly agitated about not being understood.

Look behind you, you idiot! Behind you! The Demons are here!

I'm not going to be a dick about the whole 'Harry and me were left to die, while they took my baby and raised them as their own' thing. As I mentioned before, the sadness of death swamps everything else, even the anger. Mostly. Maybe I'm still a little bit bitter. Pissed off. I'm allowed to be pissed off. Just a little. In a way, it's all a part of the sadness, it just tastes a bit different.

But I'm definitely not the kind of ghost who wants to wreak vengeance. Honestly. From what I've seen of other ghosts, not many of us are. We're too tired. So, when the shadows on the ceilings start to solidify into pulsating, squirming shapes behind Darryl and Janusz, I try to wave a warning. When I check the shop where Brenda and Richard are still getting alcohol and contemplating a couple of bags of pig-shaped sweets, I see dark patches outside the shop door taking on Demonic shapes. I try to get Brenda to come and look, but she's still pretending not to see me. See? I'm not being a dick about it at all, if anything I'm actively trying to help them. Still! After all the help they didn't give me! And Brenda's just ignoring me. If I were still alive, I'd be putting serious thought into ending our friendship over this nonsense.

The Demons creep, unseen. It's a trap, it's a trap! Obviously, it's a trap. They all know that, don't they? Perhaps the problem isn't so much that it's a trap, it's that they haven't quite worked out yet what the trap is for.

Charity! Charity's still cheerfully eating, over by the coffee kiosk, with Grace Barry.

Grace Barry, who is, by her own admission, not a vicar. Grace Barry, who doesn't know what she is.

I'm not sure what she is, either.

Whatever Grace Barry is, she can't see or sense the Demonic shapes, slithering and creeping and hovering slowly towards the coffee stand – some squirming like huge, fat maggots, some held aloft by buzzy wings like flies. Neither can my Charity. Without Brenda or Darryl nearby, she has nobody to warn her.

Charity!

Charity!!

She can't see me, can't hear me. My Charity! My princess!

Help. Please. Somebody!

Death is too sad, too sad, I wouldn't wish it on anyone. I don't want my Charity to die. Not here, not now, not so young, not like this. I don't want the Rooks to die here either. I don't even wish it on Grace Barry, even though I really don't trust her.

Like I say – I'm not being a dick.

I'm going to have to find a way to help, aren't I? Even after what happened. Like some sort of mug. Urgh. Brilliant.

In the shop, Brenda frowned at the doorway. Constance was behaving erratically. Ghosts often behaved in an erratic manner, that was ghosts for you, but since following them back from Coldbay, Constance had mostly kept to lingering quietly, making Darryl feel all haunted, giving Brenda dirty looks, wafting sadly around Charity and generally laying on the guilt with a trowel. Even when they'd arrived at the service station, Constance had just been moping in corners. Now, she seemed to be actively seeking attention. She flickered into sight in the shop's doorway, pointed urgently at something hidden behind the shop's walls, and flickered away again. It was the second time she'd done it.

'Dear,' muttered Brenda, quietly. She put one more bottle in her bag – violet-flavoured gin, as a treat – and started moving cautiously towards the door.

'You see something?' Richard followed her closely, as if he still had the supernatural ability to protect her from the undead in any way.

'Sort of,' replied Brenda.

'What do you mean, "sort of"?'

Constance flickered into Brenda's second sight again, right in front of her this time, which made her jump. The dead woman waved her arms wildly and mouthed furiously at Brenda. Brenda had spent a lifetime of being forced to see the dead, and had always counted it as a mercy that the vast majority of the time, she couldn't hear them. Most ghosts were, to her, silently wailing smears of misery, and while that was still not exactly her idea of a good time, at least she could close her eyes and get to sleep without hearing some poor dead kid screaming for its mummy all night long. The unfortunate flipside of this was that, right now, she had no idea what Constance was trying to tell her. Brenda couldn't even lip-read. And she'd never tried to learn because, to quote herself, she 'couldn't be arsed'. She could tell that whatever it was Constance was trying to say, it was urgent. Urgent enough to make her temporarily overcome her strop over the whole 'dying' thing.

Richard noticed Brenda's automatic flinch at the point when Constance suddenly appeared nose-to-nose with her. He put a hand on his wife's elbow.

'It's OK,' Brenda told him, quietly.

Constance vanished again. Warily, Brenda walked to the shop's doorway, one hand clasping a bottle of cheap vodka, the other hand wrapped around her husband's. She stopped in the doorway and peered around outside the door. She saw the shapes pressed against the wall.

And saw that it wasn't OK, at all.

*

On the footbridge, Darryl frowned at the ghost of Constance Xu as she appeared yet again, waving frantically once more. He waved back, which just made Constance pull an expression of over-the-top exasperation.

'What?' he sighed. 'I can see you. Hello. Do you have a message, or...?'

Constance made a very unkind gesture at him.

'Rude.'

Undeterred, she went from waving to pointing, urgently, at a spot just behind Darryl's head.

Darryl had lived with a younger sister for as long as he could remember, and his experience of such didn't make him automatically inclined to look behind him when somebody told him to do so – especially when the person doing the telling was a young woman who looked remarkably like his little sister. Nevertheless, in a 'haunted glass bridge' situation like this it was generally a good idea to heed warnings from beyond the grave, so he turned and looked.

Oh, no. He *really* ought, he told himself, to look behind himself more often when in very haunted buildings.

CHAPTER EIGHT

She Just Really Liked Kitty Cats

At the coffee cart, neither Grace or Charity saw Constance, just as they didn't see the ghost of the barista whose name, she had just rediscovered, was Olivia.

Olivia had finally stopped worrying about getting the spilled soy macchiato to its rightful owner. She didn't know it, but this was excellent progress considering she hadn't even been dead for an hour yet. Some ghosts ended up in terrible loops, obsessively performing their final act over and over again for decades, even centuries, and here she was – she'd snapped out of it in less time than it took to watch an episode of *Love Island*. Unfortunately, with this new sense of awareness came the realisation that a dozen or so creatures – dark and fuzzy as shadows, big as bears and shaped like bloated insects – were silently creeping towards her coffee stand. She wasn't worried that they were going to steal from the stand. She wasn't even that concerned any more about the large quantity of pastries the two women standing next to her had taken from her little display case.

Sod the coffee stand, said a voice in Olivia's head, and she was surprised to recognise the voice as her own. *Those buggers only paid you nine pounds fifty an hour anyway. On a zero hours contract. And they wouldn't even let you join a union. Didn't you want to have your own café? Didn't you want to buy that little shop on Halifax Road and sell ethically sourced single origin coffees and Narin's baklava? Sod the croissants. They're just bog standard mass produced rubbish. You hate those croissants. The monsters are coming, Olivia. The monsters are coming, get out of there, leave the soy macchiato, leave the croissants, get out of there!*

But Olivia couldn't get out of there. She wanted to get away. The monsters were coming! But she couldn't leave the coffee stand. Narin would be home from her shift soon. She wanted to get home to Narin, and watch her silly reality shows and complain about them and talk about the shop on Halifax Road. But she couldn't move. And the monsters were coming!

The monsters are coming, for my Charity. Ten… no, twelve… no, thirteen. And five waiting to ambush Brenda and Richard at the shop entrance. And eight creeping up on Darryl and Janusz. Why so many going for my Charity? Why so many more than they sent after a clairvoyant and a part Demon? Charity, get out of there! Charity, please listen, please hear me…

Grace turned, a bewildered frown on her face. 'I think your mother's calling you?'

'What?' asked Charity.

Grace opened her mouth, unsure, then pivoted violently forwards, as if suddenly having her ankles yanked upwards from behind, hit her head on the coffee stand's till and flew backwards several feet into a table. Grace didn't usually do that sort of thing.

Fortunately – or unfortunately, depending on how you looked at it, this was behaviour that Charity was used to – it just normally happened to her brother. Maybe it was happening to her brother too, over on the footbridge. There was a telltale smash from the direction of the shop where her parents had gone. Ah. So her mother was having to fight a Demonic ambush of her own, and wouldn't be able to come over to the coffee stand to help. Charity was going to have to do this without any clairvoyant guidance at all. Bums. You see, the thing about fighting Demons – your actual monstrous, ancient, possibly immortal shadow beings from an unknowable realm beyond the living world – was that it was really difficult.

Charity ran full-tilt towards Grace as she slumped, winded and bruised, against the table she'd been thrown into with superhuman force. Whatever had thrown her couldn't be far away. She opened her arms wide and grasping, like a deeply unpicky child playing kiss-chase.

Because the thing about fighting an unknown number of Demons when you couldn't actually *see* any of the Demons was, it was really, *really* difficult. Occasionally, Charity could see Demons, but those occasions were more down to the situation or the Demons themselves than they were about her own psychic skills. She could see very powerful, high-ranking Demons like Murzzzz. Or if the Demons were all charged up with the supernatural energy of a large nearby Hell Hole, she could just about make them out, but in those situations, Janusz had been able to see Demons too, and Janusz didn't have a psychic bone in his body – bless him. No disrespect to her favourite brother-in-law, but if Janusz could see something supernatural, pretty much anyone could. Clearly, the burgeoning Hell Hole above the service station was still too small and new to give this wave of clamouring Demons whatever extra energy they needed to appear as greasy smears in Charity's vision. And, being invisible didn't make them any less capable of inflicting serious damage to squishy, mortal bodies. All in all, this was not ideal.

There was one thing working in Charity's favour, however – and here it came – she caught something cold, wet and unseeable in one of her outstretched hands. She turned on it fast, grasping with her second hand as well, focusing all of her attention on the barely solid something in her hands. It was difficult to keep a grasp of – it felt like a trifle that had been dropped in the rain. This was what a Demon felt like. She had done this before, many times. The invisible wet trifle thing moved suddenly and violently, trying to free itself from her grip. She had to grit her teeth hard and focus intently on it to keep a hold of it. A sharp pain was already manifesting in spots above her eyes. Just because she'd done this a lot, it didn't make it any easier.

Charity could catch hold of ghosts and Demons, contain them briefly in one spot, and then – the real work – she could send them out of the world of the living. She didn't want to do it to ghosts without an I-beg-your-pardon any more. She'd realised that they were just sad dead people and she still wasn't entirely sure where she was sending them when she popped them away. Demons, on the other hand, could sod off. All she ever did was send them packing to their own plane of existence so she was pretty sure they'd be completely fine. They'd just stop throwing people around and generally making a mess for a while.

She focused some more. The pain in her head got sharper, and she felt the familiar warm wetness of a nosebleed on her top lip. She mentally applied pressure to the invisible trifle thing, then more, and more. She felt the pressure against her hands, the resistance as she pushed, and then something in the fabric of reality very briefly gave way, the tiniest rip, and the invisible Demon in her grasp was pushed through it.

As she let go, reality sucked at her fingers again, fixing itself immediately.

And there it was – her superpower. She was aware that to an outsider, it might not look all that impressive. Just some woman grabbing at air and getting nosebleeds. But, this was the superpower that had already saved the world once this week, and now it was saving a weird priest. Not all heroes wore capes, Charity told herself, proudly – some wore She Hulk socks and kittycat jumpers. The leggings were a bit like superhero spandex, she supposed. And she probably did deserve a cape. If she ever wanted one, she could probably get one cheap off eBay.

There was a low moan from the table. Grace was still in trouble. More invisible claws were dragging her up into the air, again. Well, a superpowered Demon hunter's work was never done, Charity supposed. It certainly wasn't done after getting rid of just one Demon in a haunted food hall during what was almost certainly a triple-fronted ambush. She thrust her hands towards the stricken priest, with the aim of both stopping Grace from being hurt again, and catching a hold of whatever had grabbed her. She found the telltale wet jelly sensation around Grace's left elbow – there was a sting to it, this time, which Murzzzz had informed her long ago meant she'd caught hold of a Demon's claw.

Murzzzz…

She was aware of the sounds of a struggle over by the shop. Her mum and dad would be trying to tackle the Demons attacking them over there, armed with nothing but Brenda's clairvoyance and a few bottles of schnapps. That couldn't be good. They could really do with Murzzzz. She really couldn't spare the time or the concentration to stop and think about Murzzzz right now, but she found her mind turning to him, anyway. Not just for the Demonic assistance he provided – Charity couldn't help but wonder if maybe she missed the ancient horror that used to reside in her adopted father. She'd known the big fella since she was a baby— since, she reminded herself, Murzzzz had messed up somehow and got her birth parents killed.

She concentrated hard, and felt the pressure build around the Demon claw clasped in her hands. Reality gave way a smidge again. Just as she felt the little push-suck of the Demon being sent into its own dimension, something invisible shoved into Charity's back and threw her to the tiled floor. She managed to break her fall with her forearms, and protect her face at least, but now her back, elbows and palms were flooded with pain. Yeah. So Murzzzz had made a mistake – a deadly mistake as far as Constance and Harry were concerned – but he would have been all over these Demons right now, and she wouldn't be sprawled on scuffed tiles, trying to fight them all off, blind and alone.

Something that felt like jellyfish stingers grabbed at her scalp. Charity pulled a face. She hated it when they messed with her hair. She reached up with both hands, grabbed at the unseen Demon and tried to flip it to the floor.

At least they still had Darryl, right, Charity thought as she struggled. He could help fill the vacuum Murzzzz had left, now that they knew he was an itty-bitty part-Demon. Right? True, he didn't look that scary as a Demon – he looked like he'd come from a Halloween range at Build-A-Bear – but the important thing was, there was some of Murzzzz's Demon DNA, or slugs, snails and puppy dog's tails or whatever it was little Demons were made of, inside her brother. So surely, *surely* he'd be able to help. Surely he'd come bounding back down the stairs from the footbridge any second now, cute little fangs bared and wet with Demon blood, and stop this horrible bugger from pulling her by the hair.

Any second now, surely. Any second now.

*

Darryl was not bounding down from the footbridge, a triumphant dervish of fangs and claws. Darryl was frozen to the spot in the middle of the footbridge, an extremely worried collection of uncooperative knees and elbows.

'Babe,' he whispered, watching the menacing shapes crawling across the ceiling towards them, 'get behind me.'

'It's a trap?' asked Janusz.

Of course it was a trap! They knew it was a trap, didn't they? And yet here they were.

'It's a trap.'

'If it's a trap,' murmured Janusz, 'wouldn't it make sense that they'd also be approaching from the other direction? You know – to trap us.'

Darryl dared a glance over his shoulder. Right. Yes. Demons had also begun sneaking towards them from the other side of the footbridge, closing in on him and Janusz in the middle.

'Sake.'

'This always happens when we split into groups,' sighed Janusz. 'You think we'd learn.'

Darryl tried, without luck, to shield his husband from both the front and the rear as the Demonic pincer attack crawled ever closer. He could just about make out the sounds of struggle coming from the side of the bridge where he'd left the rest of his family. So, they were in trouble too. Calling for help was going to get him nowhere.

Suddenly, one of the Demons lunged. It launched itself off the ceiling and barrelled into Darryl, knocking him against the reinforced glass wall of the footbridge with an upsetting, hollow sound.

'Janusz, run,' wheezed Darryl, 'it's me they're going after.'

Janusz didn't run. 'I'm not leaving you here.'

'You can't fight them!' The Demon struck Darryl again, hitting his head against the window. 'Ow! Go, get Grace out of here, wait by the car.'

'I don't want to wait by the car, I'm not a dog.' He grabbed Darryl's hand and pulled him away from the window. 'We'll get out of here together.'

'No you can't!' Darryl was really panicking, now. There were eight Demons crowding around them. 'You'll only get—'

One of the Demons grabbed Janusz by the face and threw him several feet along the bridge.

'Janusz!' Darryl tried to run to his husband, but was held back by Demonic hands.

Janusz propped himself up, wincing in pain but mercifully free from any serious injuries. He tried to get to his feet, but unfortunately in doing so went through the incorporeal form of one of the ghosts already on the footbridge. Going through a ghost could be a very unpleasant experience even for those with no psychic powers, especially if the ghost in question is upset, and this ghost was very agitated at the sudden appearance of an a cappella choir's worth of Demons on the footbridge. Janusz gagged at the sensation.

'This is why I said to run,' added Darryl, urgently.

'We are not having an argument about this now,' managed Janusz through dry heaves, 'so please don't patronise me.'

'I don't patronise you!'

'I said we don't have time for an argument!' Janusz got to his feet and was knocked straight back down again.

Darryl struggled against the Demons holding him back from helping his husband. 'Babe, get *out* of here! Crawl, I don't care.'

'I'm not going to crawl.' He tried to get up again and, yet again, was knocked back down.

'Oh my God!' Darryl still couldn't free himself from the Demons' grasp. 'What has got into you? Is this all because the seance didn't work?'

Janusz tried crawling towards Darryl. 'I thought we could change things – talk more to the ghosts, fight less. Because we can't—' Another Demon grabbed Janusz by the leg and started dragging him towards the group of Demons that still had Darryl.

'We can't fight them without Murzzzz,' managed Janusz.

Amazingly, Janusz still managed to keep talking even while being dragged, wounded, by a horror from beyond. It was a skill that Darryl hugely admired in him.

The Demon dragging him by the leg hauled him up and threw him into Darryl. Darryl couldn't free his arms to catch his husband, he just had to brace himself for them bonking heads. Janusz looked Darryl in the eyes, and – oh, Darryl hated seeing that expression on his husband's face so much.

'I can't do *anything*,' said Janusz.

'Babe, that's not—' began Darryl, but he was thrown, face first against the window before he could finish that thought. He landed spreadeagled, leaving a Darryl-shaped grease stain on the glass, like a confused bird. Next to him, the ghost that had been banging on the window spared him a silent glance that was actually a bit sympathetic. Darryl wondered briefly what all of this must look like to the traffic flowing steadily beneath, before he was peeled off the window and thrown backwards straight into the window on the other side. Yeah, he thought to himself dreamily, through the pain, this must look *so* weird to any kids in the back of a car playing I spy.

Janusz was thrown at the glass next to him. Darryl reached to clasp his hand. 'You can do loads,' Darryl managed, winded.

'OK? And we *can* make the seances work, just not with Demons—' Another Demon grabbed Janusz's waist and tried to pull him away from Darryl.

'No,' wheezed Darryl, still desperately grasping Janusz's hands, 'no no no, we're trying to have a heart to heart.'

'Homophobes!' added Janusz, struggling to keep a hold of his husband.

Darryl had no idea whether Demons were actually homophobes, they tended to be dicks to everyone, regardless. With an almighty yank, Janusz's hands were wrenched out of Darryl's.

'No, no, no…'

Four of the Demons held Darryl fast while the other four clamoured around Janusz, a Demon to a limb.

'No no no no no…'

The Demons started carrying Janusz off along the footbridge, towards the other side of the services. The side that had unknown horrors lurking. The side that had a Hell Hole growing over it.

'Darryl?' Janusz, unsurprisingly, sounded hugely worried.

'No no no!' Darryl struggled against the Demonic claws. 'Put him down! Leave him alone!' He wasn't just scared – he was angry. Furious. Deep within his chest, something very cold manifested itself.

'*Zabko!*'

Darryl hated that tone of Janusz's voice, hated that look in his eye, hated that this place and its stupid Hell Hole and its stupid Demons had made his lovely Janusz feel that way. The coldness swelled swiftly in his chest. There was a sting to it, a jellyfish sting.

They were trying to take his Janusz away! Again! Why did they keep doing that?

'Leave him be,' he snarled, and his voice suddenly had something of big cats and wild dogs about it, and his mouth was full of sharp. 'It's me you're after.'

'Darryl??'

Janusz was almost at the stairwell that led to the other side of the services, about to be dragged down out of Darryl's view. No. No! The coldness was everywhere, the sting, the crackle, his anger was all fangs and nails.

'No!'

It wasn't a human cry at all – it was a roar.

A teeny itty-bitty baby Simba of a roar.

'Oh good,' gasped Brenda, 'that's something, at least.'

She was gasping because she was running, dragging her husband behind her by the wrist. She was running to get away from the Demons that had snuck up on them while they were in the shop. She had managed to clear a narrow path for themselves by hurling a bottle of vodka at a large Demon that had blocked their way entirely, leering down at them like a giant sea cucumber with an angler fish underbite. The alcohol had burned the Demon, causing it to squeal, let off a considerable amount of sulphurous smoke and disappear back to its dimension for a Demonic cold compress or whatever was going to make it feel better.

That had given Brenda the vital seconds she'd needed to grab Richard and make a dash for it, but it wasn't ideal. There were still four Demons right on their heels, and she was already down a whole bottle of vodka.

She really should have paid attention to Constance when she had the chance. There was probably some introspection to be done about why she still couldn't bring herself to fully acknowledge the ghost of her dead best friend, but honestly, now wasn't the time.

'What's good?' asked Richard, breathlessly.

'Either someone's keeping a baby lion on the footbridge, or our son just went Demony again.'

'Doesn't that mean he's in trouble, though?'

Brenda tried to dart towards the coffee stand, but one of the Demons blocked her way. She feinted in the other direction, hoping to get around to Charity the long way.

'Safe to say we're all in trouble, dear, we're just a little bit better armed for it, now. Probably.'

'Pardon?'

'I said...' Brenda faltered. They had come to a sudden, and very noisy, dead end in an enclave that was at the same time both too dark and too bright. Gaudy colours flashed at them in the gloom, all baying loudly for attention in tinny electronic yelps, like a set of aggressive Casio keyboards, all on a slightly different demo setting. One was playing a faintly out of tune loop of *The Simpsons* theme. They were in the service station's Casino Corner.

Honestly, Brenda had forgotten that services even had gambling areas any more. She avoided casinos, arcades and betting shops in general since her life already had enough bleakness and unpredictability about it, but also because she'd always hated their vibe. The ghosts of people who'd died there tended to be particularly upset, and when you're in an enclosed space with a deeply distressed ghost, dark corners and little flashing lights do nothing to make that situation any less disquieting. Brenda could see eight ghosts, packed into the miserable little corner. Three looked new, but the others had clothes that ran a fashion gamut of the past fifty years or so. Their Naf Naf sweaters, lumberjack shirts and frustrated expressions flashed eerily out of the darkness in flickers of yellow and pink as the fruit machines wailed for more money.

This was, Brenda was pretty sure, what a panic attack would look like, if panic attacks could self-actualise. This was really bad. *And* she was sober, *and* she wasn't sure yet whether she could spare one of her precious booze bottles to numb the awfulness of it all.

And, here came the Demons. Her day *could* get worse, after all.

CHAPTER NINE

This Is Fine

Charity's scalp hurt. She desperately tried to prise the Demon off herself without it pulling out too much of her hair with it. She could practically hear her parents nagging her to tie it back for work since she insisted on keeping it long, but come on, her hair was great. When one has supernatural powers *and* a prematurely silver streak flashing through one's raven locks like a sexy witch or a member of the X-Men or something, one does *not* scrape it back into a severe bun because of health and safety or whatever.

'Get *off*,' she demanded of the Demon, as if that ever worked. 'I'll get my big brother on you! Darryl! Where is he??'

There was another faint little cub roar from the direction of the footbridge, and more distant crashing. It sounded even further away than the first baby roar she'd heard, which wasn't promising.

'Darryl!' Argh, she was going to lose some hair, she just knew it.

A couple of yards away, Grace pulled herself painfully up off the bolted-down table, and approached Charity, with the wobbly walk of the recently-bashed-in-the-head.

'Get back, Reverend!' The top half of Charity was pulled painfully up off the floor by the hair. 'Fetch Darryl and then go and wait in the car park or something, this is too…'

Grace's face contorted – or at least, Charity thought it did. In fairness, Charity was in the process of trying to wrench a Demon off her hair, so in her awkward position it was difficult to see. She just knew that something about Grace's demeanour changed. Something about it hurt Charity's face – but then something about Grace's demeanour hurting Charity's face was becoming a regular occurrence now. She had supposed it was because Grace was just one of those amnesiac priests who made your eyes feel like they were boiling whenever she got too intense. *Was that a thing?* Charity wondered. Probably not.

Grace lurched towards Charity in one, fast, unnatural movement, as if tugged forwards by the chest.

Oh yeah, thought Charity through her various different pains, *there's still a bunch of other Demons around.* She pulled at the Demon clawing her hair some more. She was just going to have to sacrifice some hair to rescue the priest from the Demon attack. But then, Grace moved, suddenly. Charity could still barely see but there was a bright blur and then Grace's fist was outstretched and, in a painful blink of the eye later, the stinging wet claws gripping Charity's hair went slack. With the strong invisible claws pulling her upwards suddenly gone, Charity fell, landing flat on her back. She grunted and coughed, automatically feeling her scalp. No bald patches, Charity noted. What a relief. With the most important matter checked, she propped herself up on her elbows and forced herself to take a reasonably controlled couple of breaths in spite of her spasming diaphragm. Charity tried to get a look at Grace's expression and discovered that she couldn't, it was like trying to gaze at the sun.

'Vicar?' croaked Charity, still winded.

Grace threw one more punch at nothing.

'No,' replied Grace, and Charity's ears were flooded with tinnitus.

Grace stood very still, her chest heaving, her arms tense, her hands trembling. Charity recognised that stance. When you force a ghost or a Demon out of this realm and nothing remains but your own adrenaline, and for a moment your body isn't sure what to do with it, where to put all that fight-or-flight juice when the fight is suddenly over.

Wait.

Was Grace… like Charity?

'I'm not a vicar,' said Grace, and the tinnitus was gone. The boiling pain in Charity's eyes disappeared as swiftly as it had arrived.

'No, I get that.' Charity hauled herself back up onto her feet. 'Mate, did you just do what I think you did?'

'What's that?'

'Punch a Demon.'

Grace furrowed her brow. 'I… think I might have actually punched a few of them.' She looked down at her trembling hands. 'I had no idea I could do that.'

'Yeah, no, you're definitely not supposed to be able to do that. Also, did you know sometimes your voice hurts?'

'What?'

'And your face.'

'My face?'

'Yeah, we need to talk about your face.' There was another smash from the other side of the food hall. Charity glanced over. Arsecheese! Her parents were trapped in an alcove with a bunch of fruit machines – her mum hated places like that. 'Later,' she added. 'First, I think we need you to get violent in a tiny little casino.'

*

93

Darryl's father always described his experience of being taken over by the Demon within as suddenly being pushed to the back of his own mind and body – like being gently yet firmly taken from the driver's seat and placed amongst some thoughtfully added cushions in a spacious boot. The experience was nothing like that for Darryl. He was still driving his body, it's just that his body had gone straight from a sensible hatchback to a monster truck with skulls and boobs painted on it. But then the Demon within his father had been Murzzzz – a separate personality; an eternal, immortal creature from a realm beyond the mortal ken, and also, Darryl still firmly believed, a dickhead. The Demon within Darryl was still Darryl, but just the bits of Darryl that were literally Demon Spawn. The other Demons had not been at all happy with Murzzzz for spawning a part-human offspring. Darryl, for once, found himself agreeing with the Demons on that one.

He hadn't meant to transform. He didn't want to transform. Ever. He'd spent thirty-five years not even knowing he could take this form and he'd quite happily spend however many decades he had left continuing through life in his usual human shape. But then, the Demons had grabbed his Janusz.

Nobody messed with his Janusz. Janusz wasn't a proper ghost hunter, he was the paperwork guy, he was supposed to be off limits, and… and… and *nobody* messed with his Janusz!

He sprang at the Demons who were still hauling the stricken Janusz to the far side of the services. Darryl wasn't sure why he'd decided that the other side of the bridge was such a red line, it just was. The Demons would not be taking his husband to the other side of the motorway, not while he had breath in his body.

He roared again, and again was vaguely embarrassed by how non-threatening it sounded. Maybe it sounded better from outside his head. One of the Demons looked up at his roar and sneered, mockingly. OK, so maybe it didn't sound better from outside his head – his human voice never did, after all. Why would his Demon voice sound any less cringey?

The Demons dragging his husband away weren't even slightly impressed by his transformation. He was going to have to take direct action. This wasn't ideal for Darryl. He was not one of life's fighters, at least in human form, and his one foray into attempting to battle Demons in this new form had resulted in him being swung around by the leg like a meaty, toothy club. Nevertheless, he was out of options. He was also really, really angry. His Demon form made his driving emotion rage, instead of the usual cocktail of fear, melancholy, inferiority and awkwardness. He was sure his sister would have some smug comparison to the Hulk if he told her about that.

There was one possible advantage for Darryl – these slug-like creatures were the most common Demon type and, according to Murzzz, amongst the lowest ranking. One time, Charity had asked how highly Murzzzz ranked, compared to other Demons. Murzzzz had chuckled – the sort of low, horrible chuckle that makes every nerve ending in the back of your neck panic – and had told the family that they didn't want to know. Darryl's swirling rage briefly eddied around the thought that whoever had arranged this ambush had not sent their best Demons to fight the spawn of Mur— no. He was *not* going to refer to himself as the 'spawn' of the Demon who had until recently resided in his father's body. His anger at Murzzzz now joined all the rest of the tornado of rage. It was a big rage, now, amalgamating lots of smaller squalls of frustration into one big fury storm.

He grabbed at one of the Demons holding his husband, and found its flesh to be wet and unpleasant, but solid enough to get a purchase on with his semi-Demonic claws. He was a little taken aback at his own strength in this form when he heaved to try to wrench the Demon away from Janusz and discovered quickly that he'd pulled far too hard. The Demon gave a shocked little screech and let go. Darryl lost his balance and tumbled backwards, still holding the Demon, only to barrel inelegantly into the two other Demons that had been behind him. It was like a cartoon character trying to open a stuck door and accidentally pulling off a whole side of the house.

He flipped himself up to his feet as quickly as he could, spinning to slash at the three Demons surrounding him with his claws, like he'd always seen Murzzzz do. His claws were tiny darning needles compared to Murzzzz's, and he likely only managed to give the Demons a little scratch, but they hissed and vanished anyway, in puffs of wounded sulphur.

Three down. Five to go. But if they were anything like the last three, this should be easy. He leaped at the five Demons surrounding Janusz, again surprised at the newfound power of his body in this form, as it cleared a good ten feet in a single bound. He landed on top of the group of Demons, his fangs bared and oh, no, it actually wasn't that easy trying to take five of them on in a single go after all. He was strong in this form but, as it turned out, not *that* strong. Long appendages emerged from the body of one of the Demons, like giant spider legs pushing through jelly. The wet appendages tried to grab him. He yelped, and was annoyed by how much the noise sounded like a frightened puppy.

He managed to twist as he resisted its grip and scratched another Demon. It deflated into nothing like a punctured dinghy, if punctured dinghies went to a different dimension instead of just sinking. Four down. Halfway there. He could do this.

He was grabbed then and thrown, hard, against the glass wall. *Ow*. Far from being deterred, Darryl's head colliding with the reinforced window yet again only served to make him angrier. He turned and scrabbled back towards the Demons. He tried just catching hold of two at the same time, instead of taking on all four. He was able to pull those two off Janusz, but unfortunately the Demons had also learned quite quickly that they could overpower Darryl if they worked together. As the Demons he'd grabbed were yanked backwards, the Demons left holding Janusz dropped him and jumped to attack Darryl instead.

Well, thought Darryl as the Demons descended on him, at least that meant Janusz was OK. For now. He struggled against the Demons. They were all over him. Darryl wondered if they were trying to crush him. There was an extreme weight on his… chest? Could you still call that area his chest, in this form? Thorax? Whatever it was, it felt as if there were a walrus on top of it. He snarled, and sank his teeth into some shadowy part of one of his Demon attackers that oozed and tasted absolutely disgusting. He really hoped it wasn't the bit of the Demon that he thought it might be.

Another Demon hiss, another slight shifting of reality as the dimensions opened just enough of a smidge to allow the bitten Demon back to its own world. So now it was only three against one. This was fine. This was actually going great. He still felt like there was a walrus on top of him, and there were those spider leg appendages again, clawing out to grab Darryl's head, and pull. Again – *ow*.

Darryl was quickly learning that this group of Demons – slug-like, common and low ranking though they were, were not all of the same strength level. These remaining three were strong. And heavy. And, one of them was definitely trying to rip

Darryl's head off at the neck. Darryl tried catching one of the arachnoid appendages with his fangs, but his head was held too firmly for him to manage. He tried to lash out with his claws, but his arms were pinned down. He struggled and hissed. He could still do this. Oh, no. He *couldn't* do this. He couldn't do this, actually. Oh no, oh no. And it wasn't as if Murzzzz could come and save him. Nobody was coming to save him.

There was a grunt from behind the Demons, and a liquid sound, followed by the hiss of corrosion and a sulphurous stink. A Demon squealed, above him, and then the Walrus on his chest vanished.

'Graa?' managed Darryl.

The sulphur cloud where the Demon had been, dispersed enough to reveal Janusz, standing at Darryl's feet, a grimly determined expression on his face and a silver flask in his hand.

'My *Babkaci* taught me a lot of things,' announced Janusz, his eyeline levelled not at Darryl but the rough area of where the attacking Demons were.

The Demon pulling Darryl's head stopped and looked at Janusz. Darryl supposed that, for low status Demons, used to slithering about unseen and attacking in silent secrecy, it was probably a real novelty for a human to try to address them. Stealth hunters aren't used to their prey turning around and going 'What are you playing at, mate?'

'This was from her, as a confirmation gift,' Janusz continued. He waved the flask in the general direction of the Demons. There was a cross etched onto it but both Darryl and Janusz knew that that wasn't going to do Janusz the slightest bit of good. Demons just thought human religions were funny things to mess with. Janusz went on, unabashed. 'She was the one who got me videos of UK comedies because I learned English better that way. And she helped me see that I didn't just like Edmund Blackadder and Arnold Rimmer because I found them funny. And she taught me I would always be loved, even when some of my family made me feel that wasn't true. Also, she worked as a spy in the war and killed five Nazis. And when my *Dziadek* got sick, she taught me about being there for your husband, even in the face of fear and change. And while you may think that's unconnected to anything, while I've kept you distracted talking about her I've managed to work out fairly accurately where both of you are from the way my husband is being held down, so I can do this without hurting him.'

As Janusz spoke, he tipped something from the flask onto his hand and wiped it with swift, expert precision onto the face of one of the two remaining Demons. Quite a feat, considering that to Janusz he was interacting with thin air.

The Demon screamed, clutched at its face with slithering tendrils, and vanished.

'She also taught me that Spirytus vodka is probably the strongest you can legally buy,' continued Janusz. 'I'm not a big drinker, but I like to carry some, anyway. Just in case.' He smiled over at the space where the Demon with the spider-arms was, still clutching Darryl's head. 'You're the last one left, aren't you? Want some vodka?'

With his arms freed again, Darryl was able to reach up and grab the Demon's appendages. The Demon struggled and snarled. It hissed at Darryl, then looked up again at Janusz, approaching it, flask still in hand. It threw back its head in a wordless expression that seemed to scream 'Oh for pity's sake', and disappeared through to another dimension.

Darryl sighed with relief, checking his sprained neck.

'All gone?' asked Janusz.

'Nnn,' grunted Darryl in the affirmative.

Janusz held out his hand to help Darryl up, but Darryl shook his head. He took a moment of concentration to force his body back into its human form.

'Aww,' complained Janusz, gently, 'I wanted to touch your little paws.'

'They weren't paws, they were claws,' replied Darryl.

'They were kitty cat paws,' smiled Janusz, his hand still extended. 'They were so fuzzy.'

Darryl accepted Janusz's hand now that he had his human fingers back. 'Was your first crush really Edmund Blackadder?'

Janusz hauled him upright. 'Not my first, but yes. I must like my men sarcastic, bony and English.'

'I liked him too. I think it was the tights.' Darryl watched as Janusz carefully screwed the top back on his confirmation flask and put it back in his pocket. 'Don't ever, *ever* let my mum know what's in that flask.'

'Don't worry. I decant it in secret, the bottles never even make it to the house.'

Darryl nodded gratefully. 'Bit sad we have to think about that, isn't it?'

Janusz shrugged. 'My family history's sadder. Did you not just hear all about my dead *Babci*?'

There was a crash, from the direction of the food hall. Darryl and Janusz looked at each other. Wordlessly, they ran back along the footbridge towards the stairs, leaving the ghosts to get back to standing around aimlessly or desperately smacking the glass windows as the traffic whizzed beneath, blissfully unaware of the miserable haunting that dragged on above their heads.

'Did you get it?' Richard asked Brenda.

Brenda looked at the patch of smoke over the smashed brandy bottle next to the brightly coloured *Simpsons* slot machine.

Richard caught a whiff of the sulphurous wafts and coughed a little. 'Smells like you got it.'

'Yes, I got it.'

So that was now two out of the five Demons sent on their not so merry way. However, Brenda was now down two bottles of good booze, and they were still surrounded by all sorts of horrors from beyond, in a grim little corner space of a casino. Really not ideal.

'Also, I'm not sure that fruit machine's official *Simpsons* merchandise.'

'Dear,' sighed Brenda.

'Lisa's dress is the wrong colour, see.'

'Not helpful, dear.'

'Sorry. I'm just not sure how I *am* supposed to help, now.'

Brenda offered him her handbag. 'You could hold my bag? It's pretty heavy.'

Richard took the handbag, awkwardly.

Out of the corner of her eye, Brenda saw two of the Demons closing in on them through the dancing neon lights.

'And pass me a bottle,' she said, quietly.

Richard set his face, and passed her the fancy violet gin. She pushed it back at him with the side of her hand.

'Not the nice one,' she whispered.

Richard gave a little eye flicker of understanding and switched bottles. She still didn't focus directly on the Demons. Instead, she was distracted by one of the dead in the casino. She opened the bottle.

'There's too many dead in here. Old dead, I mean, not counting whatever happened here today.'

'As you always say, dear, casinos are hotspots.' Richard watched her take a heavy, appreciative sniff of the brandy inside the opened bottle. 'Addictions, you know? Really not good for people's health.'

'Even for a casino,' said Brenda, ignoring her husband's rather ungraceful passive aggression. 'I think the powers that be have been working on this place for a while. Really layering the misery. Just like on that wretched island.'

'Hence the Hell Hole,' noted Richard.

'Well, quite.' The Demons were close enough, now. She turned swiftly, swinging the open bottle in a long, smooth arc, so that its delicious-smelling liquid splashed an elegant line in the path of the approaching Demons, like a swordswoman twirling to cut down two foes in a single move. She'd have been more pleased about it if it hadn't cost her the entire contents of another bottle. She also could no longer see the fifth Demon anywhere.

'Now,' she ordered, and ran out of the casino corner, her husband following close behind.

Yes, she thought – accidentally running through some poor woman in flared dungarees – all of the recently culled ghosts were upsetting enough, but there really were also too many old ghosts here, too, for a service station. Car parks and roads were one thing, but people didn't generally die *inside* service stations that much – they were temporary spaces, anonymous and functional. Even staff didn't stay there all that long as a matter of course. So, people didn't usually get trapped in them after death. But these people were trapped now, and there were so many of them. How had that come about? She knew now that the entities beyond the living realm created pressure points of human misery that they used to power doors between dimensions – entities like that nightmare of eyes that called itself the Manager, that spoke of humans as 'produce' and ghosts as 'waste'. But why a service station? How could the Manager even begin layering generations of human despair in the space of a service station in the middle of nowhere?

She ran through the ghost of a teenager in a Naf Naf jumper and felt bad for her – and annoyed at herself for feeling bad. More to the point, she thought to herself, why was she suddenly so concerned with the sadness of the dead? It was basically rule number one of ghost hunting to 'remain unaffected by dead people's feelings'… actually, that was more like rule number two – rule number one was always 'try your very best not to get killed'.

Through the thronging dead she could just about make out Charity and Grace, making a beeline for her and Richard. Brenda drew breath to shout a warning that one Demon remained at large. Obviously, that was when the Demon in question decided to make its appearance, rendering her warning pointless. Typical.

It squirmed out of the poster where it had been hiding. It was not a pleasant sight, especially since the poster was advertising a Christmassy family movie about a quaint English couple having a heart-warming adventure with a CGI Polar Bear. Brenda watched aghast as Ben Whishaw and Keira Knightley melted horribly into the once cute Polar Bear, turning it into a snarling, snapping, John Carpenter-style mess of flesh, teeth, dewy eyes and sculpted cheekbones. It peeled itself out of the poster and landed wetly on the tiled floor of the food court. Brenda really hoped it wouldn't keep its Whishaw-Knightley-Bear-Thing disguise now that it was out of the poster. That hope was in vain. It clearly quite liked being a terrible amalgamation of Hollywood Darlings and cartoon animal. It slithered at speed towards Charity and Grace.

Brenda broke into a sprint.

'Another bottle,' she demanded, her hand out towards Richard.

Richard handed her the violet gin like a baton in a relay. Brenda winced. She really didn't want to waste it. But she was going to have to. It was fine, she could get more, couldn't she? Her family wouldn't nag at her *that* much if she just went and got herself another one, surely. Especially if she'd sacrificed this bottle for the greater good. And after all, she was allowed to treat herself – it *was* nearly Christmas. Still running, she took aim and swung the gin bottle back over her head, to get a bit of momentum to her throw.

The terrible mass of undulating Film Star and Polar Bear reached out toned arms and CGI paws, and swiped at Grace. But Grace did something odd. The little priest didn't scream, didn't panic. Something flickered across Grace's expression that was unnatural in a way that Brenda couldn't put her finger on, and was gone again before Brenda had time to even try to think about it. The priest took a swing at the Demon, as if on autopilot, at the same moment that Brenda pitched the bottle back over her head and threw.

As the gin bottle span through the air, the priests' punch landed, right in the misshapen jaw of the Demon's wonky appropriation of Ben Whishaw's prettily melancholy face. But that was impossible, surely. Surely! The Demon fell sideways from the impact of the punch, just as the gin bottle smashed in the spot where it had been standing less than a second before. Sweet, floral-scented gin splashed in an impressive radius of wasted deliciousness, and still managed to miss the Demon completely.

Brenda watched aghast as the Demon, untouched by the gin, screeched in outrage out of all three mouths. It clutched at the spot where Grace's fist had made contact with it as it collapsed on the floor, apparently unconscious but still managing to avoid every drop of her good booze.

'Did you get it?' asked Richard.

'Ooh, is that Parma Violets?' asked Charity, at the same time.

Grace didn't say anything. She just stood there, rubbing her punching fist and looking blank.

'I wanted that gin,' sighed Brenda. 'That was nice gin.'

The Demon was still just lying there, not moving, its six eyes rolled back. The whole encounter had lasted less than ten seconds. Darryl and Janusz came hurtling into the food hall and stopped, breathlessly, taking in the scene. Brenda realised that they'd happened to end up near the entrance to the footbridge stairwell, where they'd agreed to meet anyway.

'Hey Charity,' cried Darryl, 'you'll never guess who I— shit on a biscuit, what happened here?'

'Everyone OK?' asked Janusz. 'It smells like my *Babci* round here.'

'What the Hell *is* that?' Darryl asked Brenda, nodding down at the Demon sprawled on the floor. 'Is it... dead?'

'Is what dead?' asked Charity. 'Mum? You *did* get it, right?'

'I think it's been knocked out,' Brenda told her son.

'OK,' replied Darryl, still aghast, 'but Mum, why does it look like Keira Knightley?'

CHAPTER TEN

Mister Peppermint

'We can't.'

'We can. In fact, I think we should.'

'But we *can't*. We can't interrogate a Demon.'

'We used to ask Murzzzz questions all the time.'

'Murzzzz was different. He was on our side. Mostly.'

'Well,' interjected Janusz, 'your father is the Demon expert…'

'Am I?' asked Richard.

'Of course,' replied Janusz, with his catalogue model smile. 'Don't you think that since we've managed to knock this Demon out, we should trap it and ask it some questions?'

Richard still looked bewildered. 'And you're absolutely sure we've knocked this Demon out?'

'It's lying on the floor right there, dear,' Brenda told him.

'Mm, I can feel it.' Charity was sitting on the floor, her hands outstretched, detaining the Demon with her psychic power. She seemed pretty at ease about the whole situation, although the fact she had demanded Grace sit with her and hand feed her crisps suggested it was using up a lot of energy.

'It's got Keira Knightley's face,' Darryl, still upset about the faces, noted for the fifth time. For the fifth time, everyone else just let it slide.

'It's pretty easy to keep a hold of, in this state,' Charity noted. 'You're quite sure it's not dead, Mum?'

Brenda nodded, watching it. 'Ben Whishaw's eye keeps twitching.'

'Why is nobody else bothered about the faces?' Darryl despaired. 'It's like David Cronenberg tried to make a RomCom.'

'I'm not even sure one can kill a Demon,' continued Brenda, 'at least, not in this dimension.'

'And I'm really not sure one could even knock one unconscious,' fretted Richard. 'How, exactly, did we manage that, again?'

'I told you – Grace punched it out cold.' There was a hint of pride in Brenda's voice. Grace gave them all a shy little smile.

'I've just…' Richard paused, and from his expression, Darryl could tell that he was trying to speak internally to Murzzzz – an impulse, a mental muscle memory reaching automatically for a part of him that was no longer there. 'I've never known that to happen before,' managed Richard, after a moment.

'Well, we've never tried hitting one with a vicar before, have we?' Brenda replied. 'Should've thought of it sooner, really.'

'I'm not a vicar,' said Grace, very quietly, slotting another crisp into Charity's mouth. Everyone ignored her.

'So Grace can see it?' Richard asked.

'No,' said Grace. 'Well. Sort of, maybe for a moment, but I can't—'

'Please don't say you can't remember what happened,' sighed Brenda.

Grace winced. 'Sorry. I still get so many blank spots, I really don't know what's happening with my brain. But, if I *could* see it when I punched it then I can't see it now.'

'Probably for the best,' muttered Darryl. 'It's got—'

'We know,' interrupted Charity. 'It stole the faces off the movie poster and it's weird. Demons are creepy. Deal with it.'

'Please don't use sweeping statements like that, princess,' said Richard. 'Not in front of Mur— not in front of your brother.'

'It's fine,' replied Darryl, archly. 'They *are* creepy.'

On the floor, the Demon began to stir. Six terrible doe eyes fluttered open. It wriggled, and tried to get up, but Charity held it fast.

'**What,**' it asked, in a voice that sounded like it was bubbling up through a pint of mucus, '**is the meaning of this?**'

'I can hear its voice,' noted Richard, 'anyone else hear its voice?'

Everyone nodded – even Grace and Janusz. Richard looked a little downhearted at that.

Darryl just sighed with relief. 'Oh, I'm glad *that's* its voice.'

'Why?' asked Charity. 'It sounds like a bucketful of slugs.'

'It's speaking through the Polar Bear's mouth,' explained Darryl.

'And?'

'And I was worried it might use the same voice for the bear as the movie does.' He nodded pointedly at the poster.

Charity glanced at it. 'Yeah, fair enough, I can cope with a Demon. Not sure I could say the same of a Demon that sounded like James Corden.'

'**I have no idea what you're talking about,**' burbled the Demon, '**but you're being incredibly rude.**'

Darryl took a moment to thank his unlucky stars that Demons seemingly had no access to IMDb, and steadied his nerve.

'What do we call you?'

The Demon leered with all three mouths. '**Your Stinking Mother.**'

'Hey,' Richard objected.

Brenda rolled her eyes. 'Childish lot, aren't you? Well, since you've decided to take the form of Mister Peppermint, we may as well name you after him.'

'**What?**' The Demon struggled again, but was still held fast in Charity's psychic grasp.

'Mister Peppermint.' Brenda waved a hand vaguely in the direction of the movie poster, which declared *Mister Peppermint* to be "delightful fun for the whole family". 'Can you not read?'

'**Not your language,**' replied the warped, Demonic Mister Peppermint, its voice dripping with disdain and slime. '**No point. Your time here is a blink of my eyes. You will release me.**'

'I will do,' Charity told it, 'after you've answered a few questions.'

'**How dare you?**' seethed Mister Peppermint. '**I have seen a thousand of your pathetic civilisations rise and fall, and will see a thousand more after you are gone and forgotten—**'

'In which case,' replied Charity, 'surely you can spare us just a few minutes of your infinite time to clear a few things up for us.'

'**I don't owe you answers. I don't owe you anything.**' Mister Peppermint continued to struggle, fruitlessly. '**It is the fate of the produce to languish in ignorance. Even the find-and-deliver unit operatives are too small and too stupid to deserve information…**'

'"Find-and-deliver"?' asked Darryl. 'Somebody else called us that, back at Coldbay.'

'**I will not be addressed by that *thing*,**' Mister Peppermint told the rest of the family. '**That disgusting hybrid mongrel you made is offensive to me on every level.**'

'Charming,' breathed Darryl.

'Is that why you Demons attacked us?' Janusz asked. 'Because Darryl is an outrage to you?'

'Or is it because we find-and-deliver and shut down your silly little Hell Holes?' added Charity.

Mister Peppermint scoffed. '**You operatives are so funny. You always think you're special, somehow. If only you knew.**'

'Yes,' replied Brenda testily. 'If only we knew – that's exactly why we're asking.'

'**You're cogs in a machine,**' Mister Peppermint told them. All three mouths smiled horribly. '**A machine that's about to be switched off and on again and there is nothing you can do about it.**'

'Oh, we can do something about it,' Charity told it. 'We shut down the last Hell Hole in Coldbay, and it was a lot bigger than this one.'

'**The destruction of the Coldbay door was a setback so minor we barely felt it,**' sneered Mister Peppermint. '**The purpose of luring you to Coldbay in the first place was to retrieve Murzzzz and bring him home. We achieved our goal. As far as my department is concerned, Coldbay was a success.**'

'The Manager wasn't from your department though,' noted Darryl. 'The Manager said it was in Head Office, and it didn't seem to consider Coldbay a success, considering how much it was complaining. Were you attacking us on Head Office's behalf? Do you report to the Manager?'

'I am *not*,' announced Mister Peppermint, its phlegmmy voice full of disdain, '**answering to this half-breed Spawn. There is no word in your language that adequately describes how disgusting and degrading to my kind its very existence is – the closest I can find is "blasphemy".**'

'That's funny,' replied Brenda, 'because our language has quite a lot of choice words for people with your sort of mindset. I imagine the other three languages Janusz speaks do, too.'

'Yes,' said Janusz, coldly.

Mister Peppermint laughed, horribly. '**Oh, don't tell me you've warmed to the mutt already? You all only just found out. Murzzzz didn't tell any of you because he assumed you'd find it disgusting too. But the pathetic self-delusion of the mother and the spouse is making you think you're fine with it.**' Mister Peppermint thrashed suddenly, violently, against Charity's psychic grip. Charity kept a hold of it, with difficulty.

'Guys,' said Charity, 'as fun as it is calling Darryl names, you know Mister Peppermint's just distracting you to buy it time to escape, right?' She concentrated, and Mister Peppermint struggled harder, as if the bonds around it had tightened. 'What did you do to all those people?' she demanded.

'**What people?**' Mister Peppermint snarled.

'The ones who were here! The ones who were alive only an hour ago! They're all lost and confused – there aren't even any bodies. What did you do?' She concentrated again and Mister Peppermint yelped a little.

'**Is that why you're being so uppity?**' Mister Peppermint replied. '**That wasn't my department. You people really have no idea what's going on.**'

'Actually, we did rather assume that was Head Office behind this rather than the Demons,' Brenda told it. 'From what we can tell, your department seems to be rather low down in the pecking order, certainly not capable of actually creating something as impressive as a Hell Hole. You just use them as your transport system in and out of the mortal world and – I assume – owe Head Office a fee for doing so. A fee like, oh, I don't know, doing a lot of its dirty work for it? Like attacking the people who shut the last Hell Hole before they could get a chance to shut this new one down?'

Mister Peppermint laughed. It sounded like jelly being flushed down the toilet. '**I can see why Murzzzz liked you, you're funny. You've got it completely back to front, you ridiculous monkeys. "Doing Head Office's dirty work", indeed. I'm not surprised that Manager didn't tell you the true pecking order around here, but even Murzzzz didn't tell you silly beings? That's precious. Mortals are amusing trifles at best – fun to play with. A nice little trip out for us, with barely any downsides, because when we come to your world to play, your torment increases, sharpens, becomes much better quality. Ultimately, you're produce. Batteries. A nothing of a dimension, filled with nothings. Electric meat, no more, to be farmed for your useful misery until the time comes again, as it has done now, to switch your dimension off and start over.**'

'We already know human misery is what powers the Hell Holes,' Charity told Mister Peppermint. 'We're fast learners, for unimportant electric meat. So, Head Office killed all these people to generate enough power to start opening a Hell Hole in a hurry. What we don't know is *why* the hurry.'

'Or where the bodies all went,' added Janusz, quietly. 'Or how come Reverend Grace could punch you.'

Grace looked up timidly from feeding Charity crisps. 'That might be more a question for when we finally get to Edendale.'

112

'We're not going to get to Edendale,' said Brenda.

Mister Peppermint started laughing that 'jelly in the toilet' laugh again.

'Not if they can help it, anyway,' added Brenda. 'Because *that's* the whole point of this, isn't it, Mister Peppermint? That's what the rush to make another Hell Hole was in aid of – that's why all these poor people had to die—'

'For crying out loud, you're dense,' interrupted Mister Peppermint. **'I'm amazed Murzzzz has any mind left at all after slumming it amongst you for a few decades. The freshest produce aren't even properly dead yet!'**

'Wait, they're not?' asked Richard.

'Head Office whipped a few hundred of them out of their bodies so fast, their bodies haven't had time to shut down,' Mister Peppermint told them, **'takes a couple of hours, last I heard.'**

'Where are they?' Darryl demanded. 'Where are they keeping the bodies? Charity, if the bodies are still alive, could you put the ghosts back, somehow?'

'Oh, yeah,' replied Charity in a tone that was probably only about forty per cent bluffing, 'it'd be just like re-stuffing a bunch of cushion covers. Easy pie.'

'Aww,' Mister Peppermint sneered, **'you know what? I think I'd actually like to see you try. You produce are at your most delicious when you're really striving for a false hope. You do have the slimmest chance of saving them, but you don't have long. Under an hour, I'd say. I'll even tell you where the bodies are – in the Waste Department.'**

'Ah,' said Brenda.

The mouths of Whishaw, Knightley and a once cute CGI bear grinned so widely that the corners of their mouths met each other to form one terrible mega-mouth. **'And,'** added

Mister Peppermint, '**your only way to get to Waste is through our interdimensional door.**'

'We still call it a Hell Hole,' said Darryl.

'**I am still not talking to you, chimera.**'

'Well you just did talk to me, actually,' grumbled Darryl, 'so there.'

Mister Peppermint studiously ignored him. '**You'd better release me and get on with it, if you're to save all these poor people, *and* close down the door, *and* get all the way to Edendale before it's Wine o'Clock.**' It cocked Keira Knightley's eyebrows at Brenda in a knowing fashion.

'Ugh,' groaned Brenda. 'Now I'm even getting lectured on my drinking by passing Demons?'

'**Oh, we've extracted some very fun information out of Murzzzz, since we brought him home,**' Mister Peppermint told them, cheerfully. '**None of it actually useful, so far, but then that's not really why we're torturing him, we just don't want him to get back to his nonsense after we've ended your world and started a new one.**'

'Wait, what?' asked Richard. 'What are you doing to Murzzzz? Is Murzzzz OK?'

'**Richard Rook, we are Demons, what were you expecting? We took him to our home dimension. Loads of your religions have plenty of things to say about what goes on back in our home.**'

'You mean Hell, don't you?'

'**If that's what you want to call it. None of you get it completely right, but we like to whisper little secrets about where we come from to your holy scribes, mostly to give them a tasty scare. Did Murzzzz not even tell you any of that?**'

'He said he didn't want to upset me,' replied Richard, shakily.

Mister Peppermint snorted a deep, wet snort. '**You silly little people and your silly little secrets. Never ends well, does it, Brenda?**'

'I don't think we're going to get anything else of use out of this one,' said Brenda, hurriedly.

Darryl allowed himself to stop concentrating on Mister Peppermint for a moment, and let his gaze travel to the spot in the food court that Brenda was studiously ignoring. There, he saw Constance's ghost, lingering by the falafel stand, looking distinctly unimpressed.

'Pop it back home, princess,' continued Brenda, 'and we can get cracking with saving a few hundred lives.'

Charity concentrated hard, again.

'**OK, well, best of luck getting to the door between multiple dimensions,**' grinned Mister Peppermint, its stolen facial features melting into one another. '**I'll pass on your regards to Murzzzz, although I think right now his only message back will be: "Aargh, the agony, the agony and the humiliation! Why was I cursed with eternal life so I can't even die to escape this torment?"**'

And with that, reality gave way a smidgeon and Mister Peppermint, or whatever its true name was, disappeared through the tissue-thin fabric of the living realm's space-time.

There was an awkward silence, through which two dead men sang about their drum that went 'pa-rum-pa-pum-pum'.

Charity exhaled hard, wriggling the life back into her hands. Clearly, trapping the Demon had been more difficult for her than she'd let on.

'Well,' announced Brenda, 'you heard the daft immortal racist, we don't have long to get to the Hell Hole on the other side if we want to reunite these poor sods with their living bodies, and I know how much you soft lot like helping ghosts out.'

'Murzzzz,' whispered Richard, shakily.

'Mister Peppermint was just trying to goad you,' Brenda told her husband, gently. 'It was trying to goad all of us – he called Darryl a mongrel and suggested I drink too much. Best taken with a pinch of salt.'

'The Hell Hole is a door between all dimensions,' said Richard. 'Including the door to where they're keeping Murzzzz.'

'Dear, you're not suggesting—'

'Brenda, they're hurting him!' Richard gazed pleadingly, desperately, around his family. 'They're hurting him. I know he made some bad decisions, but he's part of us. He's part of me.'

'Dad…' attempted Darryl.

'He's part of you, too, son. Like it or not. And they're hurting him. He wouldn't bear to see any one of you get hurt without stepping in to help.'

Over at the falafel stand, Constance silently threw her hands into the air in exasperation.

'Please,' begged Richard. He took Brenda's hands. 'Please. Can we at least try?'

Brenda sighed. And, from her sigh, Darryl knew that his dad was going to get his way. Darryl sighed that kind of sigh at Janusz all the time.

'I mean,' said Brenda, 'I suppose we're headed that way anyway. May as well see if we can pick Murzzzz up, while we're about it.'

CHAPTER ELEVEN

To Get To The Other Side

As soon as Brenda stepped onto the footbridge, she stopped and groaned.

'You said the footbridge was clear,' she said to her son.

'Yes,' replied Darryl. 'Clear of Demons, thanks mostly to Janusz.'

'You did help a little bit,' smiled Janusz.

'Obviously there's still ghosts here,' Darryl continued, 'there's ghosts everywhere.'

'But not for long, right?' said Charity cheerfully, through her third croissant. 'Not after we've fixed it. Can't believe we actually get to bring hundreds of ghosts back to life, this is some real Jesus level stuff... no offence intended, Reverend.'

'No, it's all right,' replied Grace, quietly, 'I'm sure it's what He would've wanted.'

Brenda started walking along the footbridge again, moving slowly, treading warily around the lost and mournful dead. The rest of the family followed her and Darryl's lead, sidestepping and shuffling about to avoid the patches of seeming nothingness that the two clairvoyants stepped around, so as not to accidentally go through the unpleasant experience of walking through a ghost.

'There's still too many ghosts, even accounting for the ones taken today,' said Brenda. She pointed at a few of them. 'Shell suit. Paisley dress. Nirvana T-shirt. So many old ones, for a services.'

'You think we can help the old ones, too?' asked Janusz. 'You said you wanted to help more ghosts in general, didn't you, Charity?'

'Yeah, sod it,' replied Charity, spitting pastry flakes, 'I'm just gonna Jesus *all* the ghosts out of this limbo place. Again – no offence, Reverend.'

'So, now you people want us to close a Hell Hole, reunite a few hundred souls with the bodies an all-powerful otherworldly being has just wrenched into another dimension, rescue Murzzzz from the demonic realm *and* help another load of old ghosts find peace?' Brenda asked. 'You lot do realise we only get two hours of free parking here, don't you?'

'That sounds like a "yes",' whispered Janusz to his husband.

'Just, if we get clamped, then on your own heads be it,' continued Brenda.

'Definitely a "yes",' murmured Darryl, pulling on Janusz's hand to steer him away from a ghost child that was, encouragingly, wearing a *Guardians of the Galaxy* T-shirt.

If it had been an X-Men T-shirt, Brenda might have worried that they were too late for the kid. She took a moment as she crossed the bridge to recognise that happy fluttering deep inside of her. It felt like hope. It had been a very, very long time since that feeling had flitted its delicate wings around her heart. And it simply wouldn't do. She took the fragile feeling, and stomped it with the reliable, familiar boot of pessimism. She also took a second to silently curse Charity for being the reason she even knew the difference between *Guardians of the Galaxy* and the X-Men.

She reached the other side of the footbridge. On the other side of the stairs lay a mystery. More Demons, probably. More ghosts, certainly. The new Hell Hole, which would only blur the boundaries of reality more, the closer they got to it and the more it grew. And they really did have less than an hour to get the new ghosts back into their bodies in time to survive their ordeals if Mr Peppermint was to be believed. And suddenly, she wasn't actually that worried about getting clamped. At the foot of the stairs, she glanced over her shoulder to do a quick headcount. Her no-longer-possessed husband, her part-Demon son, her son-in-law who she suspected of carrying Polish vodka somewhere about his person, her psychically powerful daughter, a hanger-on who definitely wasn't a priest, and Constance.

Bugger. Constance was still following her, then. Brenda told herself she'd deal with the whole Constance issue once this Hell Hole problem was over.

Brenda's been telling herself that since the last Hell Hole. Brenda's been telling herself that for much, much longer than the Hell Holes have been popping up. Brenda's been telling herself that since the night I died. Right now, Brenda doesn't believe Brenda any more than I do. Darryl spots me too, and draws breath to speak. Brenda notices.

'Total concentration please, Darryl,' murmured Brenda to her son, 'we don't know what's on the other side.'

'But—'

'Not now.'

You see? She's lying to herself. And the longer she does so, the more she betrays both of the people she calls her children. Tragic, really. If only I had the capacity to pity her.

Brenda descended the stairs to the food court on the other side of the motorway. The second food court was an odd mirror of the first one. The same octagonal space, with its sunken centre filled with bolted-down formica, the same brands on the frontage of shop enclaves and kiosks, but all arranged in a slightly different order, as if misremembered in a dream. Like the first food court, the silence was broken by old festive songs playing tinnily from the ceiling – in this case, it was currently a heart-warming song about two embittered drug addicts dying in New York. Also like on the other side of the motorway, there were no humans there save for the Rooks. The remains of the living were only abandoned food cartons and handbags. A half-drunk bottle of baby formula rested upsettingly on a counter next to an empty pram.

Brenda's 'gift' meant that she could see that the pram was not, in fact, empty. The baby was silently wailing for its father, who was standing only inches away from the pram – just as lost, just as distressed – unable to find his child. Ghost babies were the worst. The absolute worst, the most upsetting of all the deeply upsetting things, and Brenda had been forced to see them her whole life. She tried her best to avoid them. Their lost little faces were bad enough, but for the past thirty years, a baby crying alone always transported her back to that terrible night. The dead eyes of her friends. The baby, screaming and screaming in her dead mother's arms… and she knew – she *knew* deep down – when she scooped the baby up that she wasn't actually going to go to the police or through official routes with this child. Even as she'd told herself that she was simply taking little

Charity out of harm's way for the time being, she had known that she was just going to keep her. She had lied to herself, and she had known.

Brenda has never trusted Brenda. That's one of the things that used to separate her from me. I used to trust her with my life.

The baby's modern-looking pram and a *Hey Duggee* baby book suggested they weren't quite too late for this father and child, just yet but hope didn't dare flutter in her chest again. The baby weighed too heavily on her heart for hope to try to stretch its thin wings. Besides them, the food hall was just as busy with ghosts as the other side had been.

'Oh,' said Darryl. 'I was expecting this side to be scarier, but it's just... really sad, again. Oh no, a baby.'

'Oh no,' sighed Janusz, looking down at the pram. 'Is it OK?'

Darryl squeezed his husband's hand. 'Babe, never ask me if a ghost baby is "OK".'

'That's fair,' conceded Janusz, sadly.

'Come on.' Brenda started picking her way through the ghosts. 'Let's get this over and done with.'

There were no Demons here, at least so far. Brenda didn't take too much succour from that. The Demons clearly knew they were here, they were likely just biding their time, letting the family get closer to the Hell Hole, where the Demons would be stronger. The Hell Hole in question, the whole horrible reason why they were even in this miserable haunted hall of wipe-clean surfaces and despair, wasn't even above the building itself. It took Brenda a few attempts of looking out of the algae-and-soot darkened windows of the food court to spot it – a void hanging over the petrol forecourt on the other side of the car park. It was definitely bigger than it had been when she'd first spotted it from the car but at least it was still smaller than the one they'd encountered at Coldbay. But then, that Hell Hole had been a trap, to grab Murzzzz. But this new Hell Hole was also almost definitely a trap too, she thought to herself. Oh well, they were already more than halfway there and besides, she was adamant she was going to save that ghost baby, so there was no point in turning back now.

Old ghosts still milled around with the new, each drifting alone in their own little limbo. Only a handful of the ghosts seemed aware of the family. An old woman in a duffel coat stood and watched the family as they slowly picked their way through, a blank, confused look on her face, as if she'd half been reminded of something, but she wasn't sure quite what. Another woman, whose summer dress marked her out as too long gone to bring back, tried desperately to get Charity's attention. Brenda watched the woman's mouth silently repeating 'Excuse me?' at Charity, in annoyance. At one point the summery ghost tried clicking her fingers at Charity's face, and for that rudeness, Brenda decided not to engage with the dead woman.

'She's not staff,' Darryl told the summer ghost. 'Even if she *was* staff – ew. Don't click at people.'

'Wossat?' asked Charity, halfway through a biscuit.

'Just some rude dead woman.'

Charity shrugged. 'People always take their frustration out on pretty young girls.'

'You're thirty-one.'

'Yes,' Charity indicated to her bright, oversized kitty cat jumper. 'But I dress it much younger.'

As they passed the ghost in the summer dress, Brenda saw the woman's face crumple, and mouth an apology… dammit! She wasn't supposed to let the sadness in! This was how one got distracted from the work, and made mistakes, and—

And a man in a cleaner's tabard was suddenly blocking her way.

'Are you the support team?' Tabard Man moved his lips, but the voice came through Darryl. The family stopped in their tracks.

'*Zabko*, you're channelling ghosts again,' Janusz told his husband, excitedly.

Darryl was still upright and conscious, he just looked a little spaced out. The family were all still in the process of learning about Darryl's new-found abilities, but it seemed that his body was better at continuing to function when the dead decided, off their own back, to speak through him and did so politely and calmly, on a one-at-a-time basis. The free-for-all rabble of the seances had, so far, always turned him into a rag doll. Darryl gave Janusz a confused little glance before turning his eyes back towards Tabard Man, and speaking in a strong Manchester accent.

'I was told there would be a support team,' said Tabard Man, through Darryl. 'But instead I've just been fobbed off.'

'Do you feel like you need support?' asked Grace, gently.

'Um, yeah,' replied Tabard Man, 'there's that random with the knife, isn't there? We phoned it through. How am I supposed to stop him on my own? Bop him on the head with my squeegee?'

'There was a mass stabbing here, too?' Grace asked the family.

Janusz took out his phone, and immediately swore at the lack of signal.

Brenda craned her head to get a good look around the food court. Now that she knew what to look for, she could see two… no, three ghosts with stab wounds. She could just make out another ghost crouched only a few yards away, a young man, head in hands, blood running down from his throat to drip from his elbow onto an already bloodied knife by his feet. Tabard Man had probably been his last victim… or penultimate victim, depending on whether one wanted to include the knifeman himself as a victim of his own violence. From the fashions, the event had taken place around ten to fifteen years ago.

'Police can't have made it in time,' sighed Brenda.

'Police said they were on their way,' said Tabard Man, getting annoyed. 'And then…' he trailed off for a moment. Brenda could see in his eyes that he was struggling with the repressed memory of his own death. Tabard Man screwed up his face and swallowed the memory back down again. 'But this was after,' he continued. 'I was told *afterwards*, there'd be a support team. I deserve a support team! I've been left here by myself!'

Brenda couldn't stop looking at the young man with the knife. She'd come across a few hauntings like these – victims of a mass killing drifting around in the same spot as their dead murderer. The killers were often like this young man's ghost – too far gone, too cocooned in guilt and grief to do anything or communicate anything. They weren't in Hell – if there even was a 'Hell' for human souls to go to – but in a kind of hell, punishing themselves for what they'd done, as if that made anything any better. Brenda knew that there would be no point in asking the killer his motivations, even if her main question for him at that point wasn't the now pointless 'Why did you do it?', but rather 'Why do it *here*? Of all places?'

Helsbury was a bad place, that wasn't in question. The bloody great Hell Hole opening up over the petrol pumps was a bit of a red flag for that. Misery so often begot misery, and it could seep into a spot so badly that it set even non-psychic humans on edge. A place could become so bad that even dogs and cats didn't like it there, and dogs and cats were actually far less psychically inclined than humans, on account of being so much stupider. Brenda had seen a handful of places like this before – sinkholes of despair. Coldbay had been one. What was different about Helsbury was the clothes. The previous bad places Brenda had borne witness to had taken centuries of tragedy and frustration layered in the same physical area to get that bad. There had been ghosts in tracksuits, but also ghosts in flat caps and ghosts in bustles. Occasionally, ghosts in periwigs. Here, the fashion just stopped going backwards around the late sixties. There was no way for Brenda to tell what Helsbury *had* been, before being a motorway service station. From the look of it, there was a very good chance that it had been absolutely nothing at all.

'Do you know the history of this place?' Brenda asked Tabard Man, suddenly. 'From before the motorway?'

'Dear?' asked Richard.

Tabard Man looked put out at even being asked. 'What's that got to do with anything?'

'I thought we were in a hurry,' murmured Richard.

'Just a tick,' she whispered urgently to her husband. She turned back to the tabarded ghost. 'Was there a plague pit or something? There's often a plague pit at the bottom of all these.'

'Buggered if I know,' replied Tabard Man, 'I clean the bogs, love. Are you lot the support team or not?'

'Did you ever see weird things round here?' continued Brenda. 'Maybe on night shifts, on your own? Did you feel bad vibes, like something terrible was right at your shoulder?'

Tabard Man's expression became confused, and troubled. 'There was something bad. Screaming. And I called the police, the police said they were on their way. Where are they? Are they coming?'

'Besides that bad thing. Was there something else?' said Brenda, hurriedly.

Tabard Man's expression changed again. He looked now as if he were trying to remember an old, third-hand anecdote.

'Footbridge,' he said. 'Nobody likes cleaning it at night. They say in the nineties some teenager took an overdose, went up to look at the cars, and just… died. Customers would report humming. And then there's the smoking area. Nobody likes that smoking area. It's all wrong. Feels like something… Something was trying to get in. Someone *was* trying to get in. I called the police.'

'Ah!' crowed Janusz. 'Finally! Helsbury knife attack, 2009. Five dead including the attacker, something about him being a "lone wolf" and recently splitting with a girlfriend. So, three guesses what his race and background were. It was all over before the police got there. Hold on. There's a link to a thing about a Helsbury curse…' He stared down at his phone. Even Tabard Man watched him do so in awkward silence.

'Sorry,' muttered Janusz, 'it's taking a while to load.'

'Why do you have a Russian catalogue model with you?' asked Tabard Man after a moment.

'That's nice of you to say except for the bit where you call me Russian,' replied Janusz, still staring at his uncooperative phone. 'Oh! By the way, you said you were a janitor? This thing listed the names, if that's a help for you.'

'I know my name,' scoffed Tabard Man, defensively. 'I know…' he trailed off again, bewildered and embarrassed.

'Of course you do,' Janusz smiled, 'but forgive me, I'm Polish, so is it pronounced "Mick Car-le-SON" or "Mick CARL-son"?' Janusz knew how to pronounce English names. He also knew how to put people at ease.

Mick Carlson – a lost, nameless ghost no more – looked so relieved that he might cry. 'CARL-son,' he replied, shakily.

'Might go on a break,' he announced suddenly, and turned away from them, leaving Brenda's path clear again.

'Babe,' said Darryl, in his usual voice, 'I think you helped that guy. He looks more peaceful, now.'

Janusz looked proud. 'The lucid ones like to hear their names, don't they?'

'Well,' said Brenda, 'more importantly, he got out of our way, so we can get a wriggle on again without having to all walk through him and feel sick.'

She started carefully leading the family once more along the narrow path through the ghosts towards the exit.

'Maybe after we've helped the new ghosts we can work our way back,' said Janusz, 'help the nineties kid on the footbridge.'

'Nirvana boy,' chorused Darryl and Brenda, quietly.

'And *Zabko*, didn't you mention a trucker on the bridge? I bet we can help him.'

'Look at you,' said Charity, fondly, 'all cheerful. It's because he thought you were a model, wasn't it?'

'I just like helping people, Charity! So do you.'

They passed close by a woman in tailored bootcut trousers, a bolero jacket and an extremely early noughties hairdo, smoking at a table.

'I know, I know,' said Darryl in a woman's voice as the ghost's mouth moved. 'Not supposed to smoke in here any more. I just don't want to go out to that shelter, it creeps me out.'

'You could always quit?' suggested Grace, in a tone carefully chosen to sound as non-judgemental as possible. Brenda had heard that tone several times since meeting the little priest.

The smoking ghost scoffed. 'Round here? With no support, a creepy footbridge and deaths and curses and that *thing* in the car park? Nerves wouldn't stand for it, love.'

Brenda pressed on towards the exit, and left the ghost smoking silently in peace.

Annoyingly, the exit to the car park and the petrol forecourt beyond was also blocked by a ghost. This one was one of the oldest ones there, from his clothes. He was dressed head to toe in brown – brown checked suit with brown tie, brown hat, glasses with a brown browline, smoking a brown pipe. People really did used to smoke loads indoors, didn't they, thought Brenda idly to herself. Funny the things one didn't really notice about the way the world changed unless one was constantly presented with dead people still going through the motions of their everyday actions from a few decades ago.

The man in brown took his pipe from his mouth.

'Marvellous, isn't it?' Darryl spoke in crisp consonants of the Queen's English that even the poshest people didn't use any more. 'A gleaming palace, risen from the mire.' The ghost's expression suggested that he was nowhere near as certain about the marvellousness of it all as he was letting on. 'Little hiccups are to be expected, I suppose,' continued the man in brown, 'with a project of this grand a scale. I say, are you the clever fellows that were promised? They did say that there would be a support team.'

Brenda glanced at the others. This talk of a 'support team', again.

'Just a couple of hiccups, that's all,' added the man in brown, nervousness creeping into his tone. 'The, er, the unpleasantness, outside, in the verges by the car park, all the way to the filling station, sometimes.' He took a quick suck of his pipe. 'I wouldn't like to complain, only it upsets the women. And the children. Some of the chaps too, if I'm being brutally honest. And it, ah… It appears to be finding its way… in. Inside, that is. In here. It wasn't supposed to come in here. It wasn't supposed to be here at all. It was dealt with! All that bother with the locals. That wretched tree. All dealt with. We were building something marvellous. A gleaming palace. It got in, though. And it's rotted everything away, hasn't it? It's all… rotten.'

The man in brown gazed at Brenda, horror settling in his eyes, just for a moment.

'It's a trap. Not a palace, it's a trap, and it's full. No. Not quite full. Room for a few more – we can budge up. I was promised a support team, you see. the Manager promised me directly.'

'I knew it,' sighed Brenda. 'I *knew* the Manager was behind all this. I'd wring its neck if it had one.'

'It's definitely a trap?' asked Grace, sounding worried. 'Did… did we know this, before coming here?'

'Yes,' chorused the family.

'But we still have to try,' Charity told her. 'They've baited the trap with hundreds of people.'

'And Murzzzz,' added Richard.

'Yes, Dad, we haven't forgotten about Murzzzz.' Charity rolled her eyes.

'*Are* you the support team?' asked the man in brown.

'Do you know, I think maybe we are,' said Charity.

'Capital! Jolly good.' The man in brown's eyes didn't quite match the enthusiasm of his tone. He stood aside to let them pass without having to go through him. 'If you wouldn't mind taking a look at the unpleasantness outside? It would be really rather splendid if you could just make it all… stop. I would rather like it to stop. Just make it stop. Please.'

Brenda led the family out of the hall, and into the wet car park.

'Please,' entreated the man in brown, through Darryl's mouth. 'It has to stop.'

*

The door swung shut behind the family, and the voice stopped. When Brenda checked behind her, the man in brown was still there, watching blankly through the murky glass doors. His gaze drifted from them to the car park beyond – and whatever this 'unpleasantness' was that had been bothering him since the sixties. Details plucked at Brenda. The stuff about the locals, and a tree. Maybe this place *had* had misery layered on it for centuries after all, and the services had just acted as a catalyst, or had soaked up despair from an older misery sinkhole nearby. Brenda could already see that there was something wrong with the smoking shelter, but her eye was rather more caught by the bright strip lighting of the top of the petrol forecourt at the other end of the car park, and the swirling void above it. The Hell Hole had almost doubled in size since she'd first seen it from the road. Beyond it lurked beings from unknowable dimensions, and they definitely weren't there to fill up on unleaded.

CHAPTER TWELVE
Old Jack

'What's it like out here, then?' Charity asked, pulling a face at the weather. 'Besides damp.'

There were no clamouring ghosts or Demons in the car park at least, just abandoned vehicles, litter and a deep sense of unease, emanating from several directions. There was a troubling smudge inside the dirty perspex walls of the smoking shelter on the grass verge to the side of the car park. Some of the ghosts had been scared of that shelter, in life. So scared that it bothered them still, in death. The smudge wasn't moving, at least. It seemed contained to the shelter, for now. Brenda recalled what the man in brown had said about the 'unpleasantness' reaching all the way to the petrol station, and trying to get into the main building. If the 'unpleasantness' wanted to reach them, it would certainly be able to. She just had to hope that whatever was in the smoking shelter would remain as uninterested in them as it seemed right now.

'It's fine,' she said.

It would probably be fine. It wasn't as if any of her family were gasping to go and have a ciggie in a glorified bus stop –

they'd just give the smoking shelter a wide berth. It would be fine.

Darryl met her gaze and indicated silently to the smear in the smoking shelter, with an expression suggesting that he believed it might not be fine.

'It's fine,' she repeated. She started clicking and clacking her way across the car park, towards the distant petrol forecourt and the rapidly growing Hell Hole above it. The others followed.

'It'll stop being fine at some point soon though,' added Darryl. 'I hope we're all prepared for that, once we get to the Hell Hole.' He glanced anxiously at the smoking shelter again. 'Or maybe before.'

'I'm carbed up, I'm good,' Charity announced. 'And you've got your cute little Mogwai Demon thing going on…'

'Please stop calling the Demon thing "cute",' sighed Darryl.

'And if a Demon does get past you and attack us, the reverend can just punch it in the face,' added Charity, happily. 'We still haven't found out how you can do that, have we?'

Grace just frowned down at her hands.

'Murzzzz used to punch Demons in the face,' sighed Richard, wistfully.

'Oh,' exclaimed Darryl, suddenly. 'Charity. I meant to say earlier – you'll never guess who I saw.'

Charity's face lit up some more. 'Stan Lee?'

'No.'

'Because you promised you'd tell me if you ever see the ghost of Stan Lee.'

'I don't think the ghost of Stan Lee would be in a service station in Lancashire, Charity, do you?'

'I don't know – the man gets around.'

'In the movies. He doesn't make cameos in real life. Especially now he's dead.'

132

'Just tell me who you saw,' sighed Charity.

'Darryl,' interrupted Brenda, 'smoking shelter.'

'Yeah, I thought you'd seen it, Mum.'

'Of course I saw it,' replied Brenda, testily. 'But, it's started moving.'

'The smoking shelter's moving?' asked Janusz, frowning at the shelter on the verge. It remained stationary, for now at least. Large, immobile structures staying where they were supposed to be was not, in the Rooks' line of work, the given that most of us take for granted.

'There's a ghost in there,' noted Darryl. 'Or, at least, there was...'

The shadowy smear that had filled the smoking shelter was indeed on the move. It drifted straight through the walls of the smoking shelter as if they weren't there, and tumbled towards them at an increasingly fast pace. In only a couple of seconds it hit the approximate speed of a running human being, and kept on speeding up.

'Uh oh,' said Darryl.

The front of the dark smear was starting to find a human shape, like a doll being pulled out of a pool of treacle. It was a woman. Her features were too fuzzy to make out at first, but the cut of her dress suggested she'd last been alive during or shortly after the second world war. She drifted smoothly along the ground without moving her legs, her feet just hanging an inch or so above the tarmac. It happened quite often with ghosts, after a while they forgot that they used to walk. No matter how many times Brenda saw it happen, it was still upsetting. Also upsetting, as the ghost approached and emerged more clearly from her dark, viscous cloud, was the fact that she was wearing slippers and a pinafore. Something about the mundanity of it hit Brenda in the chest. When one saw ghosts in movies, they rarely looked as if they were doing a bit of haunting as a treat after finishing the ironing. Also, this was the first ghost they'd seen since getting here who was dressed as if she were at home. Then Brenda realised, just a moment too late to mention it to anybody else, that from her clothes, this ghost predated the service station. She would have been haunting the place before the motorway was even built. In her little pom-pom slippers.

The ghost was so fast now, it was practically upon them. She was very clear now, the swirling cloud she had emerged from flowed out in shadowy tendrils, like a dramatic cape, several feet long. It was utterly out of keeping with the ghost's drab, shabby housework clothes. Her hair was in curlers, for pity's sake. There was, thought Brenda to herself, more of this ghost than there ought to be. The ghost's very ordinary little face was set in determination. She was either going to attack them or try to talk to them.

'Are you from the Management?' the ghost asked; her meek, high-pitched Lancashire accent chirruping out from Darryl's mouth. 'I shan't be fobbed off again!'

Perfect. Another talky ghost. And yet another one who had been given hollow promises by the Manager. Well, at least the ghost wasn't attacking them. Brenda decided to walk and talk, with this one. This ghost could clearly keep up with her pace, and there was the issue of the Hell Hole, still.

'We're actually on our way to speak to the Manager now,' Brenda told her, resuming her click-clacking across the wet car park.

The rest of the family trailed close behind her, Janusz pulling a slightly spaced-out Darryl along by the wrist.

'What did that flaming ring of eyeballs tell you?' continued Brenda. 'That we were going to come and sort everything out for you as long as you detained us for as long as possible?'

The ghost drifted smoothly alongside her. 'I was promised someone would come, to sort out the dispute. They can't build here! They mustn't!'

'I think maybe they already did,' replied Charity.

'Princess,' chided Richard, quietly.

'They ought to go around,' continued the ghost, 'why can't they go around, please? I've been here all my life, old Adolf couldn't make me move out and neither will this. I've seen the brochure for the new flats and I'm sure having the loo on the indoors and all your whojamaflips running on electric is all very nice and modern, but I like doing things how I do 'em, and then there's Old Jack, they mustn't do that to Old Jack.'

At the mention of 'Old Jack', the ghost's incongruous shadowy cape swirled and writhed, as if it were a separate, faceless entity, reacting angrily to her words. The tendrils of it got in Brenda's way whichever direction she tried to take and forced her – again – to stop.

'And who might "Old Jack" be?' Brenda asked, bracing herself for the answer. It was going to be an older ghost, wasn't it – some older ghost that had attached itself to this meek woman in curlers and had railed against the intrusive concrete and glass of the service station before it was even built, cursing the place from the start.

'They want to cut him down. You mustn't let them! He's been here centuries, and all the starlings nesting in him…'

'A tree?' asked Charity. 'This Old Jack is just a tree?'

'Yellowhammers even, sometimes,' continued the ghost. 'And they're dead rare. Because Old Jack, he's special, isn't he? Everyone feels it, around him. They say all those birds who nest in him, they're the souls of the dead.' The ghost took on a dreamy look. Behind her, the tendrils of her cloudy cape floated high, branching off into smaller and smaller wisps like the boughs of a tree or the bronchi of a lung. 'There was a village here, once, long ago. Plague wiped 'em out. They say Old Jack grew on the graves, his roots all tangling through their bones.'

Of course. A plague pit. Brenda *knew* there'd be a plague pit at the bottom of this. There so often was, in haunted places. Plague pits were the supernatural world's answer to nuclear waste spills. They were areas of trauma, heaped on trauma, and then left in the ground to seep.

'He was never angry, though,' continued the ghost. 'Not him, nor his birds. Nature took the land back, and Old Jack grew, and it was peaceful. Even that horrible little berk Adolf didn't shake Old Jack. But now?' The tendrils behind the ghost thrashed angrily. 'They mustn't cut him down! Tell them! The Manager said, when I… after I'd been poorly… the Manager *said* you'd come and you'd tell them not to cut him down. They can just go round him, can't they?'

The tendrils thrashed, desperately. They extended far, far out of the ghost, now making her look deceptively huge. A mass grave for a village wiped out by plague could contain hundreds of the dead. Maybe thousands. All those souls, absorbed into a tree where they find peace for a few centuries, soaking in the sun, lovingly exhaling oxygen into the living world, only to be felled suddenly, violently, and turned into a hard, cold place for buildings and machines that looked to them like they belonged on an alien world. Of course those ghosts would be angry and bewildered. Of course they'd latch on to this woman who had clearly cared for and defended the tree while *she* was alive, and make her their mouthpiece. Maybe they'd latch on to and absorb more ghosts in the vicinity. Perhaps that explained why Brenda hadn't seen any ghosts on the motorway or in the car park. Maybe that's what the man in brown had meant about something trying to get into the services. Of course something

136

as big and as powerful and as filled with human souls would lash out against the sudden change that the motorway had brought. Of course it would add to the helpless cycle of human misery begetting human misery, wearing the barrier between worlds so thin that the Manager had only needed to cause one more mass tragedy in that spot to rip open a hole.

It had come to this, thought Brenda. She was empathising with a bloody haunted tree. It really was no good, at all.

'What's your name?' Brenda asked the ghost.

'Old Jack,' replied the ghost, on impulse, and then stopped herself, suddenly. 'No, that's not right, is it?' She laughed nervously, and thought. 'Lil?' It was more of a question than an answer, but it would suffice as a name for her.

'Lil. Look at this place.'

Lil shook her head, refusing to acknowledge the car park that was already there – that had been there for decades.

'It's OK.' Brenda gestured around the car park. Weeds pushed through cracks in the tarmac. Clumps of overgrown grass stood on the verge, little green islands in a sea of wet brown leaves. Beyond, the service station's building was, like its twin on the other side of the motorway, covered in a layer of moss and algae. 'I'd say nature's already starting to claim it back. Nature'll do that, if you leave anything for too long. It's entropy.'

'That's really not what entropy is,' whispered Janusz, very quietly.

'I think Old Jack might like nature to come back here,' said Grace, catching on, 'maybe even a new Old Jack can grow in his place. What do you think, Lil?'

Lil nodded. The tendrils behind her calmed themselves at the thought.

'But,' added Brenda, 'what entropy needs is time.'

'It's more about stars and heat,' whispered Janusz. 'Me and Darryl watched a documentary.'

'And, we don't think the Manager wants to give us any time,' Brenda continued. 'Not any of us – not people, not nature, not ghost trees. So, we need to speak to the Manager now, sort out a teensy little dispute we've got going on—'

The tendrils flailed again. 'Dispute, yes,' said Lil, urgently. 'The planning permission. They mustn't build here! There was a meeting about it, but then I got poorly.'

Brenda rubbed her eyes. They were back to this again. Why did she ever think she could have a sensible conversation with a ghost? Even the reasonably lucid ones would always circle back to the few petty issues that had been plaguing them since death. Whether it was a lost love, or a missing child or a missing dog or a missing sock. Whether it was *how* they died or *where* they died or who they died *with* or who they *didn't* die with. Whether it was money or property or family or sex – ghosts were stuck, just cycling through the same handful of obsessions. Most weren't even as self-aware as Lil, most were just smears of sorrow and there was no talking them round from it. Just as there was no talking Lil round from it. Just as there was no talking Constance round from it – no matter how much Constance followed Brenda about. They were just... there. They were there and they were miserable and they spread their misery like pollution, and Brenda had to see them all. Brenda had to bear witness to their sadness – all of them. From the silently wailing young men next to wilted bouquets on country roads to her friend, her beloved Constance, always around her with eyes burning with blame, Brenda had to see them all, so she knew – she *knew* – you couldn't talk sense to a ghost. So why was she trying? Of course this sad, stupid remnant of a dead woman was going to take everything back to planning permissions and unwanted constructions and demolitions, and— and oh! That was it!

Brenda took her hands from her eyes, met the ghost's gaze, and chose her next words with care.

'Yes,' she said. 'The planning permission issue here has evolved a bit, I'm afraid.'

'Oh Gordon Bennett, what is it this time?' cried Lil.

Brenda held her hands up, placatingly. 'It's the Manager, trying to open up a new transport hub, right here.'

It wasn't a lie. Not really. The Hell Hole was a sort of motorway service station, in its own terrible, multi-dimensional, Demon-riddled way. Part void between the living world and the great unknowables beyond, part service station and part airport. Really, if the universe had any sort of consistency to it, the Hell Hole should have a tiny little branch of Boots the Chemist tacked on to the side of it.

'Another one?' asked Lil, horrified.

'Without permission, either,' added Grace, getting into the spirit of Brenda's creative truth telling. 'Just trying to—'

'To bulldozer through without a by-your-leave,' Lil finished off for them both. 'Yes, I know the sort.'

'And that's why we need to speak to the Manager right away,' continued Brenda. 'Otherwise it'll go ahead, and we'll be too late – possibly too late to do anything at all.'

Lil nodded, earnestly. 'What can I do?'

'You can relax, Lil,' Brenda told her. 'Put your feet up, let us handle it.'

She wasn't saying it to be kind – she genuinely needed the ghost to calm down. The tendrils still blocked her way, and seemed in no mood to allow her to go around. This ghost was more layered than anything she'd seen before. Sometimes two or three ghosts could latch together to become one bigger, more powerful ghost, but this thing had to be made of many hundreds of ghosts, who with the exception of Lil, were so old that they had forgotten they used to be a whole village worth of different people. She wasn't sure they could fight this ghost – not even with Darryl's precious little Demon fangs. Not even with a Demon-punching priest. Not even with a carb-loaded Charity, and Charity could fight almost anything.

If this were a normal ghost clearance, Old Jack would be the root of the problem that they needed to purge before dealing with all of the knock-on effects that its rage had caused over the decades. Even with the Hell Hole to take into account, if the family could placate Old Jack then everything should become a little easier. Without Old Jack's fury at the core of this haunted spot to feed it, the Hell Hole could even become weakened. Anything that gave the family a little more of a chance to rescue those people who had just been ripped from their bodies…

Dammit, and now Brenda was worried about the wellbeing of a couple of hundred strangers. This was why she didn't like to do jobs sober, it really was all too much.

Lil looked unsure. The cloudy tendrils streaming out behind her became slightly smaller, slightly less agitated. 'You'll definitely stop it? Stop all of it?'

There was no way to tell Lil what she wanted to hear without lying. Brenda considered ways to talk around it – maybe tell Lil that after buying more time, she would have the family move as many of the remaining ghosts on as they could, maybe even set a couple of fires once the place was completely empty of human life, speed up the eventual destruction of the services and the return of the wilds. She remembered how closing down the Hell Hole over Coldbay had resulted in the

140

Manager's petulant destruction of the whole island. There was a perfectly good chance that this would happen again. In a fit of omnipotent immortal pique – it could just decide to fold Helsbury Services up into the void, like a sore loser kicking over the whole Monopoly board. None of those things were quite what Lil wanted to hear, though, since what Lil wanted was an impossibility: she wanted the service station that had already been built sixty years ago to not exist, and never have done. Brenda and her family were good at many uncanny, otherworldly things, but planning-permission-based time travel was not one of them. In the end, Brenda decided to go about the problem of the truth getting in the way of what she wanted to happen, using her tried-and-tested method – telling a bare-faced lie.

She looked Lil square in the eyes. 'Yes,' she told the ghost. 'We will stop it all.'

'Um...' attempted Grace, but Brenda was in no mood for moralising.

'Can you let Old Jack know?' she continued. 'He doesn't need to fight us. We're on his side.'

'Thank you,' sighed Lil. The shadowy cloak around her shrank right back into a gently swirling cloud. 'You don't know how long it's been, nobody listening, nobody talking to us straight...'

Grace gave Brenda a pointed look. Brenda rolled her eyes to look away, and found herself staring down the barrel of a completely different pointed look from Constance, halfway across the car park. She looked back at Lil.

'We *will* help Old Jack find peace,' she said. There, now. That one wasn't too much of a lie.

Lil smiled, calmly, and faded into the cloud, which wafted gently back to the smoking shelter.

'That must be where Old Jack grew,' said Darryl, in his own voice. 'Imagine cutting down an ancient tree for a car park. It's like the Joni Mitchell song.'

With Lil gone, Brenda started hurrying towards the Hell Hole again. 'You didn't have much to contribute there, did you, Darryl?'

'Yeah, well it was hard to get a word in.' Darryl and the others followed after Brenda. 'Lil's was the only voice that could form words, but there was loads of background noise going on with that ghost. You think Lil was confused and upset about the services? Imagine having a thousand people in your head who were uprooted for a car park and don't even understand what a car is.'

CHAPTER THIRTEEN

Edendale

The petrol forecourt was annoying to access on foot especially, as Brenda was sure to let everybody know, when those feet were wearing nice high-heeled shoes. Even Charity's trainers turned out to be inappropriate footwear for clambering up a steep wet bank, tangled with ivy and bracken, and then skidding muddily back down the other side.

She didn't have her mother and brother's clairvoyance, but Charity could make out the Hell Hole now. An upsetting absence of sky loomed over the bright canopy and the LED pricing board.

Charity's dad sucked through his teeth quietly at the petrol prices. 'That's dear,' he muttered. 'It's ten pee a litre cheaper at the supermarket. That's the motorway surcharge for you. Highway robbery. Literally.'

'Um,' said Janusz, 'also, I see a void…'

'Oh yeah,' replied Richard. 'And the void's pretty bad, too.'

'And those two people,' said Grace.

Brenda and Darryl both looked at the priest, surprised.

'You see them too?' Darryl asked. 'I assumed they were ghosts.'

And, oh yes, now that she looked, Charity could see them too. Her attention had been grabbed by the huge terrible nothingness hovering above, so she honestly hadn't bothered to pay much attention to the forecourt below the canopy. And she hadn't expected anybody to be there, least of all two people of above average attractiveness, wearing tailored grey suits and sitting peacefully out of the drizzle in folding chairs.

They didn't look a bit like Demons. They *did* look a bit like humans, but that was the thing – only a *bit* like humans. Not *completely* like humans. There was something… off about them, that bothered her.

The pair got up in unison, and smoothed down their suits, even though they really didn't look as if they needed to be smoothed. As Charity and her family approached, she was able to make out a little more detail about the two figures, or she would, were there not frustratingly little detail to be seen. The figures were flawless. Usually, Charity would mean that as a compliment, but not this time. Goodness knew, she was a fan of movie stars who spent hours a day burpeeing their way into corsets and spandex leggings. She had also had many a crush on comic book and cartoon characters – drawn to standards of big-eyed, lithe-limbed, pert-bottomed beauty that would be impossible for any real human to recreate. Even with cartoon heroes there'd be flaws though – a scar here, a mole there. Some sticky-uppy hair so you could quickly tell which cartoon character was which and so on. Flaws were a part of hotness. Crooked smiles, freckles – she could go on listing them. There was none of that with these two, and it unsettled her. There was something smooth about them that shouldn't be smooth.

She found that, no matter how much she looked at them, she couldn't determine their gender. Again, this usually wasn't an issue for Charity. She would happily spend a few hours adrift in her own imagination with sharp cheek-boned lovelies aboard the Good Ship Androgyny. But this time, it added to the sense of unease.

Their whole look reminded her of pictures she'd seen online created by computers. That was it, she realised. That was what seemed off – they looked almost CGI, like a computer algorithm had rendered them by layering the faces of thousands of hotties of various genders and races, to create one composite and absolutely average hot human adult. It was the same face on both of them. Same pretty nose, same pouty lips, same killer cheekbones, same uncanny valley CGI character eyes. The only thing that differentiated them was their hair. Both of them had objectively gorgeous hair, but one had long, wavy locks that spilled over their shoulders like a waterfall of soft, dark secrets, and the other had perfect curls on the top of their head, with close-cropped back and sides, showing off the kind of neck that would make Dracula drool uncontrollably and need half an hour of alone time in his coffin.

The average hotties folded their chairs in unison, and then the long-haired one rested both chairs gently against a petrol pump as they waited for the Rooks to approach.

'Oh,' breathed Richard, 'those things aren't human.'

'They're not ghosts or Demons either, though,' said Brenda.

'Murzzzz would know what they are,' Richard continued, ruefully.

'I don't like this,' whispered Grace.

'Somebody needs to find out what gender they are, so I can update my sexuality to Pansexual or whatever,' murmured Darryl. 'No offence, Janusz.'

Janusz shrugged. 'I'm Bi, you know this. I've got that T-shirt all about it, so why would I take offence?'

'You know, since we're married and all.'

'It's not disrespectful to still consider other people attractive,' Janusz sighed. 'This is the Krishnan Guru-Murthy conversation all over again.'

'I don't like this,' repeated Grace, with no more impact than the last time. 'Can we go back?'

'You fancy that newsreader?' Charity asked Darryl, with a snort. 'What is he? Fifty?'

'Shut up, Charity, you fancy cartoons.'

They came to the edge of the petrol station canopy, and stopped just underneath it. The two uncanny identical hotties walked over to greet them, their gait a synchronised confident catwalk strut. Charity half expected them to take their jackets off, hang them jauntily over one shoulder and do a coquettish half turn.

'You made it,' said the short-haired one, their voice in a pleasant temperate zone between tenor and alto.

'Listen,' said Brenda, 'we're in a hurry, so if you're going to make introductions, keep it brief, and if you intend to stand in the way of us and the people whose bodies were just snatched, I'd rather you told us so sooner rather than later. If you *don't* intend to get in our way, perhaps you could stand aside and we can have this little chat after we're finished?'

The short-haired one turned to the long-haired one, with a questioning look.

'She must want to retrieve that fresh produce,' said Long Hair.

'Stop calling them that,' Brenda told them.

'And Murzzzz,' Richard added. 'We're going to retrieve Murzzzz as well.'

The identical hotties laughed, together, the same blandly attractive laugh.

'Still worried about that resolved Red Sticker Issue,' said Long Hair, in the patronisingly fond tone one might use while watching a kitten trying to swat its own shadow.

Short Hair smiled, indulgently, and nodded at the little priest, who was trying to hide behind Charity.

'Hello again, Grace Barry,' said Short Hair.

Janusz narrowed his eyes. 'You were that voice at the seance. The one who knew her name.'

Short Hair just continued to smile.

'So,' said Brenda, 'we're on a tight deadline and I'm starting to think that you probably *are* trying to stop us saving those people.'

Long Hair sighed. 'That whole mess is down to the Manager – nothing to do with us.'

'We didn't even get cc'ed in for approval on the plans for Helsbury,' added Short Hair, 'we'd have said no to it. It was sloppy – smacks of desperation.'

'Well, that'll be why we weren't sent the plans,' Long Hair told Short Hair. 'The Manager knows it's in the wrong.'

'So… you're going to help us?' asked Charity.

They both laughed that upsettingly nondescript laugh again. It was like a recording of a laugh or a repeating WAV file.

'In a way.'

Brenda shook her head. 'They're a distraction, to make us run down the clock.'

'Oh yes,' Long Hair noted to Short Hair. 'Time's a real bother for their little dimension, isn't it?'

Short Hair smiled again. 'Here.'

And time just stopped.

There was no click of the fingers, no wave of a hand. It just stopped. There was no handy nearby clock that stopped ticking, no tumbling leaf that paused midway through its flutter to join the mulch on the ground – Charity simply felt time stop, the way one would notice when background white noise suddenly turns to silence. She wasn't frozen in time herself, she could still move and experience her own future-self rushing through her present into her past, it's just that she knew it wasn't happening beyond the bodies of the people that these uncanny valley supermodels had elected to speak to.

'Is that better?' asked Short Hair. 'Your countdown has stopped, so we're not interfering with your activities.'

'What are you?' Brenda asked. 'And why are you here, and what do you want?'

'I think you're probably bright enough to have worked out that we're not from your dimension,' Long Hair told her. 'So as for the "why" – as in "why are we at this specific dinosaur juice pump thingie?" – this is just where the Manager decided to open the latest door. Again, we didn't say yes to any of this, but you know what it's like with transport – anything that'll get one from A to B.'

'We're not picky,' added Short Hair.

'We were *planning* on going to Edendale for this,' continued Long Hair. 'Well. We were planning on *making* Edendale for this – I don't know if any of you had worked out yet that Edendale doesn't quite exist, yet.'

Charity frowned. No. That wasn't right. They were going to Edendale. Edendale was a place! It was on Tripadvisor! She was pretty sure she had read that there was a university and an annual poetry festival there.

'And then the Manager decided to rush its plans and drag you here, instead,' Long Hair told them. 'Infuriating. We were making a whole new county for it, next to Cumbria.'

'All rolling hills and lakes,' added Short Hair, wistfully. 'And Edendale was going to be this nice cathedral city with tea shops and an arts festival. You would have loved it.' Short Hair put an elegant hand on Long Hair's elbow. 'Shall we? We went to all that trouble.'

Long Hair shrugged. 'Fine.'

And they were no longer in the petrol forecourt. They were in Edendale. There were cobbled streets and tea shops and Edendale Annual Arts Festival bunting strung about amongst the early Christmas decorations, creating just the right level of jolly clutter. The glorious spire of Edendale Cathedral towered overhead and, in the distance, Charity could make out rolling hills and lakes. It was gorgeous but, as emphatically as she knew that she was existing outside of time right now, Charity knew that it was not real.

Short Hair opened the door nearest to them which, of course, led inside to the most aesthetically perfect tea shop that Charity had ever seen. And, suddenly, they were at a cute oak table with a seasonal floral display. And they were taking tea and cake.

'Isn't this so much better?' asked Long Hair. 'Honestly, that's what we get for outsourcing.'

'Outsourcing?' asked Janusz.

'Why haven't I seen any of you lot before?' asked Brenda.

'We generally don't get involved with this dimension,' Long Hair told her, 'not even for admin. We can't even just visit for fun, not like the… what do you call them again? Murzzzz's lot.'

'Demons,' said Richard.

'Yes, that's it,' said Long Hair. 'You see, your "Demons" can largely go around unnoticed, slither about, have a bit of fun…'

'Not that we're condoning that at all,' added Short Hair, in kind tones.

'Well,' said Long Hair, 'produce do yield a better quality of energy when they're distressed, and letting the Demons play in the mortal realm keeps them from getting bored and acting out.'

'It's cruel,' said Short Hair, emphatically.

'It also means they can help out with Red Sticker Issues,' Long Hair continued. 'Demons like to think they're these terrible, powerful things, you see, but they really aren't much stronger than you people. I don't need to tell you that, you had one latch to you, Richard, and it didn't harm you too much. It even managed to breed with you and your mate, here. We, on the other hand, could kill you, instantly, if you even tried to look at us.'

Charity frowned again, taking a big bite of the most perfectly delicious Battenberg she'd ever tasted. She was very definitely looking at the two hotties, and was quite certain that she wasn't dead.

'You're confused,' noted Long Hair. 'That's not your fault, I should have been clearer and explained it in a way your little minds can comprehend – I mean our true selves. These are just suits, so that you guys don't explode. Nobody wants you to explode. Right, Grace Barry?'

Grace still hadn't touched her cream horn. She was just staring down at it, looking incredibly worried. 'Huh?'

'Even when we do wear suits,' continued Short Hair, 'we run the risk of getting confused with some sort of all powerful creator-maintainer-destroyer deity, religions spring up around us – it becomes a whole thing. We prefer to just let your universe happen, at a respectful distance.'

'But you're involved now,' said Brenda.

'Yes, well spotted.' Long Hair took a sip of tea. 'So, you might have noticed, your world's ending. It's fine, it's happened before and it'll happen again. It's one of those things. We worked out a long time ago that humanity's just not an infinitely sustainable project, it gets to a point where it self-destructs and we have to essentially switch it off and on again. The Manager and Head Office were *supposed* to oversee this, but…' Long Hair took a dainty bite of a fondant fancy and shook their head.

'It's an absolute shambles,' said Short Hair.

'Total shambles,' agreed Long Hair. 'All these Red Sticker Issues.'

'That's what it called Murzzzz,' noted Richard.

'Yes, Murzzzz was a problem,' said Long Hair. 'Can't end the mortal world with interlopers from other dimensions still in it, can you? And then there was the issue of the Spawn.'

'Hey,' chided Janusz, 'the Spawn has a name, you know. He's my Darryl.'

'Please don't call me "Spawn",' said Darryl.

'So,' continued Long Hair, 'we intervened. Bit naughty of us, we know, but the Manager was supposed to use the Coldbay door to terminate the project. But first it had to extract Murzzzz and settle the Spawn problem. At the time it actually thought that bringing Charity to the Coldbay door would help matters.'

'Me?' asked Charity. 'What have I got to do with the Manager's silly plans? I ruined its plans, I'm the plan-ruiner.'

'Yes,' smiled Short Hair, 'we saw. Nevertheless. the Manager needed you all to be herded towards the Coldbay door. So herd you, we did.'

'You posed as Grace's diocese, didn't you,' said Brenda. 'You used a frightened woman, to get her to contact us and bring us to an attempt to end the world.'

The hotties laughed again, that looped sound file of a laugh.

'What a thing to say,' exclaimed Long Hair.

'Don't laugh!' Brenda tried slamming her cup down on the table. It made the same gentle 'tink' it would have done if she'd set it delicately on her saucer. 'She was terrified! Tormented for she-doesn't-know-how-long, and now she's been robbed of her memory – her whole past. Did you do that to her? Or did you sign off on the Manager doing it, so that you could keep your pretty hands clean? I know you're still meddling. You're the ones who manipulated us to decide to take Grace to Edendale – a very lovely city, I will admit, that does not exist. Were you going to give her memory back to her here? If you ever got round to finishing building it.'

'Brenda,' said Short Hair, soothingly, but Brenda was in no mood to be soothed.

'Were you going to give her her life back?' Brenda continued. 'Or was it another trap? Why make *her* the bait, of all people? Look at her – she's tiny, just a tiny, scared little priest.'

'Brenda,' said Short Hair, in the same placid tone. 'You know she's not a priest.'

That stopped Brenda. That stopped all of them. Yes. Charity had suspected it for some time. She could tell from the expressions of the others that they'd had the same doubts. It had just always seemed really rude to actually say that they thought Grace might not really be a priest. After all – she *was* small. Small and meek and nice and kind. One felt automatically inclined to protect her.

'I'm a priest – just, not a *vicar*,' said Grace, her voice low and shaky. 'Technically I'm a rector…'

'No,' smiled Short Hair.

'What?' asked Grace.

'No,' said Long Hair.

'But I'm—' attempted Grace.

'No,' repeated both hotties, in lovely, patient unison.

Grace just stared at them, trembling. It seemed as though the one person who hadn't suspected that Grace might not actually be who she claimed to be, was Grace.

'Grace Barry, do stop being silly,' Short Hair told her. 'The problems this has caused everyone. It isn't like you to be a troublemaker.'

'It isn't,' exclaimed Grace. She looked as if she were about to cry. 'I'm not! I'm not a troublemaker, I'm a trouble-solver, or at the very worst, a trouble-avoider.'

Long Hair ignored Grace's protestations and addressed Brenda instead. 'Grace Barry is not a rector or a vicar or a priest of any description, Grace Barry is a suit.'

'No! I'm… I'm…' Grace floundered.

'One of our more refined suits, in fact,' continued Long Hair, 'designed for slightly more intricate work in the living realm than the suits my colleague and I are wearing. So for the first part, we'd really quite like that suit back. We don't come to this realm often so we don't have many of them to spare.'

'Are you telling me Grace is a plant?' asked Brenda.

'No!' Grace was trembling. 'I had a home, I had a job, I had a collection of Fairtrade throws and blankets—'

'Which you don't remember buying,' interjected Short Hair. 'I…'

'Because you didn't buy them,' Short Hair continued. 'And you don't remember anything from before you contacted the Rooks, because contacting the Rooks was the first thing you did after putting the suit on and going to Coldbay. You don't remember interacting with any living humans on Coldbay before the Rooks arrived, because there weren't any. We ensured the whole island was completely harvested of produce before placing you at the church, and setting the trap for Murzzzz.'

Grace looked across at Richard, her expression full of confusion and sorrow.

'But, somewhere along the way, an error occurred,' said Short Hair. 'It must have happened before Murzzzz arrived at the island, but we didn't realise that until it was too late.'

'As we've stated,' added Long Hair, 'we're not used to having to work in this dimension, and on the rare occasions that we do, we prefer suits like this.' They gestured to their own beautifully rendered form. 'Keeps us in the right headspace. Keeps you people in the right headspace, too. The Grace Barry suit is designed for people to pity, to find likeable but a little pathetic and in need of protection. We now believe that what went wrong was, the colleague wearing the Grace Barry suit started to *like* Grace Barry. As a concept. Am I explaining that simply enough for you?'

Even Brenda looked surprised. 'You're saying Grace – my friend, a person we have had in our house—'

'I wouldn't call her your "friend",' interjected Long Hair.

'...is actually just some arrogant godlike being from a different dimension, who got lost in a role?' Brenda finished.

Charity looked at Grace. Grace was crying, now. She looked... likeable, pathetic, and in need of protection. Could she really just be 'Daniel Day-Lewis'-ing all of this? If so, Oscars all round, frankly.

Long Hair shrugged. 'It seems that way. We know these things can happen with the lesser beings you people call "Demons". Case in point: Murzzzz got totally carried away because he *liked* you people too much. We considered ourselves above that sort of mistake, but clearly we were wrong. Perhaps there's something about this base dimension that fundamentally corrupts. We'll have to look into that for when we start this universe of yours up from fresh again. Certainly, the colleague you've been calling

Grace Barry will be confined to administrative work for at least the next five cycles of your universe.'

'Oh no,' said Richard. There was a quietness about his tone that many people mistook for meekness in Richard, but Charity understood to be a very particular shade of anger. 'You people already took Murzzzz away, you're not doing the same to Grace.'

'She made the same mistakes as your Demon,' said Long Hair. 'Don't be flattered because it came from a place of fondness. It isn't fair on little creatures like you – it relies on secrets and lies and it is ultimately an illusion. Murzzzz was not one of you. Grace is not one of you. They are tourists at best, wearing humanity as a costume.'

'No, that's not it,' protested Grace. 'None of this makes sense, I *am* Grace Barry, I'm an Anglican priest, I only ever wanted to help—'

'And you *were* helping,' Short Hair told her, 'up to the point where you decided you liked Grace Barry and the Rooks so much that you went rogue, completely repressed your true self to fit your priest suit and ran away with these mortals instead of coming back through the Coldbay door like you were supposed to do. You were supposed to be helping to put a swift, merciful end to the inevitable decline of this mortal world by removing the outstanding Red Sticker Issue – Murzzzz's stubborn insistence he remain on Earth – so that the Manager could crack on with full project termination. And then, you had to go and mess it up, by doing exactly the same thing that stupid Demon did.'

Charity frowned. 'She… had a kid with a human?'

'Oh no,' said Long Hair. 'Eurgh! Imagine. It would be like you people trying to mate with a worm. Incredibly unpleasant all round and it would definitely kill the worm.'

Short Hair topped up Grace's cup of tea, with a gentle smile. 'I think you know what mistake you made, Grace Barry. And the Manager can't terminate the project with you in it any more than it could with Murzzzz running about inside a human body.'

Grace didn't look up from her tea cup. 'The new Red Sticker Issue is... me?'

Short Hair gestured around the tea shop. 'And isn't it so much nicer realising that in a lovely tea shop, rather than in some ghastly haunted petrol thingie, in the rain?'

'We will be requesting a different Manager for the project's next cycle,' added Long Hair, over their tea. 'This one is terrible. This is probably the sloppiest project termination I've ever seen.'

'On the plus side,' added Short Hair to Grace, 'that's probably a point you can make in your favour, once you're back.'

'I don't understand.'

'Just blame your mess-up on Head Office,' said Short Hair, 'they're going to be getting most of the flak for this anyway. Say that you were concerned about the way the produce were being... what's that reason you won't eat cheap chicken eggs, again?'

'Battery farming?' asked Grace.

Short Hair clicked their beautiful fingers. 'Battery farmed, that's it. Intensely piling human misery together to quickly open up these silly interdimensional doors the Manager is so fond of. You can say that – compassionate being that you are – getting confronted by the battery farming of all that unhappiness affected you in ways that had unintended consequences. Or there's the Manager's negligence when it comes to properly balancing the Death unit prior to termination. You can say you felt compelled to stay and attempt to refine its balance yourself before it was too late – especially with Murzzzz gone.'

'"Balancing Death"?' asked Grace. She gazed, bewildered and tear-streaked, at the family. 'I don't… I have no idea what any of this means, I'm so sorry, I…'

'Seriously?' snapped Long Hair. 'This "sweet and innocent little mortal" act is getting out of hand now, Grace Barry. Even Murzzzz knew it was important to get a decent Death unit before the end of the project, and he was a stinking lowly Demon. Why else do you think he intervened to change the initial plan for it and place Charity Xu with Brenda Rook and his Spawn instead?'

Charity paused, halfway through chewing her third slice of cake.

'What?' she asked, spitting a glob of buttercream that unfortunately came to a rest right in the middle of Short Hair's dainty china plate.

Short Hair didn't even mention the faux pas. Instead, Short Hair smiled indulgently at Charity, and Charity was struck with awe and gratitude that this beautiful creature had granted her such a smile. Yes, she could see how whole faiths might have been built around a single visitation from one of these angels, these gods.

'Charity,' smiled Short Hair. 'I think you already know, you're important. Very, very important.'

Well… yes. Yes, Charity knew she was important, she had all these psychic powers and all, but it was different hearing one of these otherworldly hotties actually saying so. There was something about her mum and dad's expressions that worried her. And she thought, she still hadn't been able to get her parents to tell her much about Constance and Harry. She hadn't been able to get anybody at all to actually tell her about their deaths, other than that Murzzzz blamed himself for them.

'All those stories you like,' smiled Short Hair, 'about orphaned "Chosen Ones"… Did you ever wonder why you have been saturated with those?'

Charity swallowed her cake. 'It's a narrative trope, isn't it? A tragic start in life becomes a part of the hero's journey.' She thought, a little. 'And, I suppose I liked reading those ones in particular because, you know… I *was* orphaned. And I *was* different.'

Short Hair's smile didn't falter 'And – bearing in mind we've established that your reality is an endlessly looping construct to harvest energy from human souls, and that we just created a whole city that exists outside of time just to have somewhere nice for a sit down and a chat – do you think it's at all possible that "the heroic orphaned Chosen One" exists as narrative trope because *you* needed to have that concept strongly seeded in your mind for what was to come?'

OK, no, that had never crossed her mind. Charity was aware that she had a teensy bit of a Hero Complex – but she had nowhere near the level of self-importance that could make her believe that the stories of Batman and Spider-Man and Harry Potter and a thousand other characters like them had been planted into the brains of their creators just so that Charity would eventually read them and absorb their heroic journeys. Was Long Hair *actually* suggesting that could be a thing? It was a joke, surely? Surely… *Did* those hotties tell jokes?

'But, those stories have been around for ages,' said Charity, 'long before I was born. And they come from all over the world.'

'Yes, and they always have,' smiled Short Hair. 'It's just that those stories *always* having been there is a reasonably new edit we've made, since we discovered that the plan had been changed, and you would need a lot of stories about heroic orphans. You're welcome.' That was the second time they'd mentioned a 'plan' that had been changed, somehow.

'And… this is to do with that "Death unit" thing?' Charity asked.

'It would probably be better if Murzzzz had told you all about it when he had the chance,' added Long Hair. 'However, since he's being tortured for his indiscretions…'

Richard interjected with a quiet, wordless, miserable whine.

'There is,' continued Long Hair, smoothly, 'someone else who can give you her side of the story. We really should allow you to hear her.'

The shop's door jingled, with the sort of tinkling bell-hanging-above-the-door sound effect that would indicate a shop's door was being opened in a comedy sketch even though shops hadn't had those kinds of bells in several decades. Charity turned her head to look at the door. It was still shut, but standing in front of it was a woman that Charity recognised from a handful of pictures, and, in part, from her own reflection in the mirror.

Hello, darling. It's me.

CHAPTER FOURTEEN

The Psychopomp

'Is that Constance?' Charity asked. 'Is that my birth mother?'

'Oh, yes,' said Darryl, in the sort of tone he would use if he had just remembered he'd left the hob on. 'I've seen her a few times, I meant to tell you.'

'Darryl!' cried Charity. 'What? Did you just forget you've seen my birth mother's ghost?'

'It's been a really busy day,' replied Darryl, apologetically.

'It isn't really Darryl's fault,' Short Hair told her. 'It's Brenda's.'

Charity turned to face Brenda. 'Mum?'

'Brenda's been ignoring Constance for longer than any of you know,' said Short Hair, blithely, 'and every time your brother tried to mention her, she has changed the subject.'

'Is this real cream in these eclairs, do you think?' asked Brenda. 'Or that chemical squirty stuff from a can?'

'It's all right,' Short Hair told Constance, 'come and sit with us, Constance. Everyone can see and hear you, while we're here.'

Constance walked over to the table, where a spare chair, cup and plate had suddenly always been there.

'Oh, good news for you by the way, Darryl,' added Short Hair as Constance approached, 'the Demon realm have decided you're far too human to be worthy of their dimension, so you get to stay in the mortal realm and ultimately perish with the others.'

'What?'

'Thought you'd like to know. It's nice for you – you get to die with your family and your husband.'

'What??' repeated Darryl.

'Shush,' Long Hair told him. 'You have a guest, now. Be more like Grace Barry, and shush.'

Grace was indeed in a constant state of shushage at this point. She gazed down at her uneaten cake. She had never looked so small and bewildered before – and she usually was pretty small and bewildered, just as standard.

Only Brenda actually paid any attention to Grace. The others were all looking at Constance.

Brenda.

Brenda kept her eyes fixed on Grace, and not on the dead woman sitting at the table.

Brenda. Look at me.

'Dear?' murmured Richard.

'Mum!' snapped Charity.

It was Charity's tone that finally made Brenda square her shoulders, and meet the gaze of Constance Xu.

I'm not angry, Brenda.

'Yes, you are. Of course you are.'

I'm just disappointed.

'Oh, come off it.'

The ghost turned her eyes to Charity, and managed a very sad approximation of a smile.

Charity. My Charity.

161

'Hello, um…' Charity faltered a little bit. 'You OK if I just call you "Constance"? It's just a bit weird and all… ooh, you really do look like me, don't you? I suppose that's genetics or something… Sorry, I'm babbling – I'm not sure what we're supposed to do here. Do we have a little moment where we hold our hands out at each other across the divide of death and you give me a little smile that says "We may not be able to be with each other any more, but I'm still watching you from the afterlife"…?'

I am still watching you from the afterlife, Charity. I'm watching all of you.

'OK,' replied Charity, 'that's—'

And I can be with you. Coldbay made me stronger, I've been following you ever since. Your house, your car, everywhere.

'Right,' murmured Charity. 'That's a little more intrusive than I was imagining. Not that it's not great to have a chat and all, just I thought maybe it would be more like Mufasa, you know? Appearing in a cloud occasionally to give pep talks and wise advice.'

'You know I can help you with that, right?' added Darryl. 'Other ghosts can speak through me, it's OK as long as you're careful and don't overwhelm me, I don't mind.'

Yeah, I don't really want to do that, though, Darryl. No offence. I've known you since you were a tot, I changed your poopy nappy one time when your parents were busy. It'd be weird.

'Oh. Yeah. Fair enough.'

Besides. Brenda should have spoken to you first, Charity. She never even told you about me or Harry. Where you came from.

'Actually,' said Richard, gently, 'as soon as Charity showed curiosity about her heritage, we told her all about the provinces where her birth grandparents came from and so on. We do Chinese New Year with her and stuff.'

162

'That's true,' Charity added, 'although I mainly asked about where my birth family came from out of necessity. Turns out when people ask about your background, they don't want to hear your whole dramatic backstory, they just mean like "So, were your birth folks from Japan or Vietnam or what?" And half the time with guys, turned out they were just being creeps about it anyway. Nerds can get pretty intense around girls who look like me. That's why I stopped going to conventions on my own. You ever tried to hide from a comic book guy while in full cosplay as Ryuk from *Death Note*?' She pointed both thumbs at herself. 'This gal has. It is not the best outfit for blending in with a crowd.'

I don't know what that is.

'It's one of her anime cartoons,' mumbled Richard, 'it's about Demon-thingies. Have to say, Murzzzz wasn't a fan of you dressing like a cartoon Demon. He felt it was sort of appropriation.'

Both Charity and Constance glared at Richard.

'Seriously?' asked Charity.

Richard looked sheepish, and picked at his cake.

They never told you about us, though. Our lives. What we did. How we died.

'I never asked.'

You shouldn't have had to! Charity, they just… picked you up, like an heirloom, like a prize for letting us die.

Brenda jabbed a finger. 'You *are* angry! I knew it!'

Brenda, I'm just sad. You were my best friend. After Charity and Harry I think I loved you most of all. I trusted you, and Richard, and the Demon inside him, and we were killed for it. And our daughter was treated as a commodity.

'Don't you dare. I'm sorry you were killed in that Demon attack, but the rest of us barely made it out of The Longest Night

163

alive ourselves, and as for treating Charity as a commodity, you know that's a vicious lie. There are many aspects of myself I could improve on, I know that, but I have always been a loving mother to both of my children, whether I gave birth to them or not. Charity is my princess.'

Not yours! Not yours to take!

'Well, what were we supposed to do with her then, eh? Leave her to the mercy of the Demons?'

You were supposed to read my will!

Brenda blinked. 'Ah.'

I had a sister. I think.

'Yes,' replied Brenda, 'in Wellington, a whole half a planet away!'

I don't see what difference that makes, she was a baby. I think I had nephews. She could have grown up around other children, her cousins.

'She did grow up around another child! Her brother! And look – thirty years on, still thick as thieves.'

Brenda indicated to Charity and Darryl who were, while still both looking steadily at Constance, having a very small, quiet fork battle over who would have the last Bakewell tart.

Brenda, I trusted you.

'I know you did, so it stood to reason I could be trusted to raise Charity properly.'

My sister would have raised her properly.

'No she wouldn't! Constance, she hated your psychic work, remember? You were always moaning to me about it, about the way she thought it was dangerous codswallop and kept trying to get you and Harry to pack it in and finish your medical degrees. And you'd better believe after you died she hated it even more. There's no way she'd have let Charity use her powers.' Brenda leaned towards the ghost, an intense look on her face. 'Our

164

princess has such a gift, Constance. She's so strong. Stronger than Harry and you combined. I couldn't bear it. I couldn't let an ability like that get crushed to death by a stupid normal life in stupid New Zealand. So. I made the call. For the good of... of humanity, the good of the universe. Just look at the work she's doing right now!'

What about the good of me? Of Harry? Of Charity?

'Charity's fine,' replied Brenda. 'Aren't you, Charity?'

'Oh,' said Charity, 'I get a word in about my own upbringing now, do I?'

Richard sighed. 'You always have, princess.'

Charity. Princess. It's OK. I'm here. I always have been. And, in this place the Angels made, we can speak freely...

'Woah,' interrupted Charity. The rest of the family stared at one another, and particularly at Grace. 'The what now? You think those sexy identical weirdos are Angels?'

It's what I've been calling them.

'We don't care for that term,' Long Hair interjected. 'It's reductive.'

We are here together, now, my Charity. You can ask me anything. Anything you don't trust the Rooks to give you the truth about.

'Hey,' complained Richard, quietly.

You can trust me, princess. I'm too dead to lie.

Charity nodded, and frowned. 'Did Murzzzz kill you?'

'Charity,' cried Richard, shocked and hurt.

'Would *you* tell me if he had?' asked Charity. 'Either of you?'

'Princess,' breathed Brenda.

Murzzzz didn't kill us directly. He swore to be our protector, and then came The Longest Night. Wave after wave of attacking Demons. He abandoned us, and was rewarded with you. I don't know Murzzzz's mind. But, if he had planned to artificially manufacture a Death unit that would put him and his favourite humans in charge of controlling the end of the world, I'd say he went about it perfectly.

'Well,' interjected Richard, 'I *do* know Murzzzz's mind. Sort of. And he would never do that sort of thing. At least, not on purpose.'

'People keep talking about this "Death unit",' said Janusz, politely. 'Is this another English turn of phrase? I have trouble with those.'

'No turn of phrase,' replied Long Hair. 'Death is one of its names. Others are The Grim Reaper, Charon, Azrael, Anubis, Valkyrie, Xolotl. Charity.'

'What?' asked nearly all the members of the family, at the same time.

'Charity is a fair name for it,' continued Long Hair, cheerfully. 'While the produce have always seen it as fearsome, they can also consider it a kindness. A guide, through the unfathomable. We just call it The Deliverer, I suppose you could call The Deliverer in partnership with a Finder "Death".'

'What?' asked Charity, again.

'This wasn't actually the unit that all the departments signed off on,' added Long Hair. 'Murzzzz did have a little fiddle with the plan. Perhaps he felt that, for the end, the unit should include a sort of bodyguard, as well. Or maybe he was just enjoying his visit rather too much, and wanted to insert himself into the equation. Anyway, Death units or whatever you want to call them have always existed – sorting out the produce, sending them to the right departments. The produce always prefers to have other mortals deal with it, it's less scary for them and frankly it's easier for us. It helps all round to have a particularly strong Death unit for the end of your world, since you've got a few billion all going at the same time. Could be one mortal, could be a group, we don't really care as long as it does the job.'

'The last time we switched your universe off and on again, the team was a group of four,' added Short Hair, conversationally. 'They had horses.'

'I think that covers just about everything,' said Long Hair. 'Don't you?'

Short Hair nodded in agreement. 'Constance, Charity, the Death unit thing, project termination and Grace Barry. Yes, that's all the bases, I think you've all been suitably brought up to speed. Isn't our way just better? Maybe we shouldn't outsource the next project to Head Office after all.'

Long Hair rolled their lovely eyes and said, 'No.'

'We're more efficient,' reasoned Short Hair.

'Yes, but it's *boring*.' Long Hair set their fork down on their empty plate with a decisive clink – the type that usually precedes a tap of the table and the words 'right then'. Long hair tapped the table. 'Right, then. We should be off. Grace Barry?'

Grace looked up, miserably.

'You're with us, obviously. Let's get you back home, out of that suit and we can find out what went wrong.'

'Wha…' managed Grace, in a tiny voice. 'I don't—'

'You're the one causing this whole hold-up, Grace Barry,' snapped Long Hair. 'You don't really want to go back to that horrible place in the rain, do you? You know you're the reason the Demons are going after the Rooks, now that the Murzzzz issue has been settled.'

'Well,' added Short Hair, 'also they do think it's fun. So, it's not *all* your fault.'

'Yes,' sighed Long Hair, 'but it mostly is. The Demons want this world over and done with so it can start again, like us. Like everyone.'

'So,' said Grace, still in the same meek little voice, 'if I stay, the world can't end?'

'If you stay,' glowered Long Hair, 'the Demons will keep coming, not just for you, for all of this family you've decided you "like". Just as they kept coming when Murzzzz was with them. The Rooks may even experience a second "Longest Night", to streamline the unit, and get rid of any dead weight, like the first one ended up doing with Constance and Harry Xu.'

Brenda got to her feet with a sudden violence that would, in a normal café, have made her chair topple over dramatically. Because this was a special celestial tea room that existed purely for their benefit, outside of time and space, her chair merely slid backwards, modestly and silently. 'Don't you dare say that about my friends!'

'But they *were* dead weight,' replied Long Hair. 'All that actually mattered was that Charity be placed with a Finder. After she was born, Murzzzz knew that Constance and Harry were expendable.' Long Hair stood up, and there was an unusual spark of malice in their eyes. 'Just as Richard Rook is expendable now that Murzzzz has left him – look at him, he's useless.'

'Don't,' replied Brenda. It wasn't a plea. It was a coldly furious command.

'Just as Janusz Wosniak has always been useless.'

'Hey!' Darryl was on his feet now, too.

'Don't,' repeated Brenda.

Short Hair also stood, and held out their lovely hands, placatingly. '*We* won't. We don't hurt or kill mortals, there's no point. But the Demons enjoy it, and we can't guarantee they'll leave you alone until the Red Sticker Issue of Grace Barry is resolved.'

Brenda didn't budge. 'You are not taking any more of my friends. None of you. Not Demons, not the Manager, not even if you're all androgynous and sexy in tailoring. Now, if you'll excuse us, I'll thank you to return us to the petrol station and make time start moving again, because we still have a few hundred people to save. Grace? Come on. You're with me. You too, Constance.'

What?

'Brenda Rook, you're being difficult,' replied Long Hair.

'Oh gracious, had you only just worked that out about me?' replied Brenda. 'Yes. I'm difficult. And, as you *just* pointed out like an *idiot*, I am also a small but necessary cog in your "destroy the world" machine. You need us to work as a unit to be Death, or the new version of the four horsemen or whatever, right? To get your precious produce where they need to be? A nice bumper harvest of the energy of seven billion frightened souls to use as fuel in your own wretched realities, or whatever it is you do with them? Huge mistake, telling me I'm part of your plan – huge. Because now, I have a bargaining chip, and I love having bargaining chips because they make me extra difficult.'

'But Brenda,' Short Hair smiled warmly. 'You're not the only Finder in your family. Death can work in balance with just Charity and the Spawn.'

'You think *I* would comply, if you hurt my mum?' cried Darryl, incensed. 'After you threatened my husband and my dad?'

'And called you "the Spawn",' added Janusz, helpfully.

'And called me "the Spawn", yes. Thanks for that, babe.'

Charity didn't say anything at all, for a moment. She was aware that this wasn't like her, but she had a lot to take in. She was special. She *knew* she was special, but... Death? Fricking Anubis levels of special? Parents getting killed so that she'd be put in a special unit from babyhood levels of special? That was... that was fine, *in cartoons*. But she wasn't a cartoon. She wasn't a cartoon, and looking at Constance hurt. The sadness of Constance consumed her. This wasn't a heroically tragic backstory, it was just a tragedy. No. Not a tragedy. With a tragedy, it's a sad accident, nobody is to blame. There was blame in Constance and Harry's deaths. And now what? Now these Angel-Hottie-Whatevers were arguing with her family about who else was expendable, as long as she continued to be Death.

She didn't want to be Death. She wanted to be a cool superhero! She wanted to be the kind that helped! She wanted to rescue those 500-odd people from the Hell Hole. That's what she wanted to do. She too got to her feet.

'I'm going back,' she told the two hotties. 'You can't stop me. Because I'm Death.'

'You do know,' Short Hair told her in kind tones, 'it's just an honourific given to a powerful but mortal Deliverer, you haven't magically become an immortal psychopomp.'

'Don't call me a psychopomp,' railed Charity, '*you're* a psychopomp!'

'Princess,' attempted Richard, '"psychopomp" just means—'

But Charity carried on. 'And you're not taking anyone away from us in this little cake shop of yours. Which – although congrats on the ambience and ten out of ten on aesthetics, this place is *really Instagrammable* – has only served to make Death angry. So stop congratulating yourselves because you're no better than that Manager.'

Long Hair rolled their eyes again. 'Well, that's what we get for trying to be nice. Fine. See if we care. If you want the Manager to settle this, so be it – that's its job, after all. And the Demons can have a little end-of-project party extracting Grace Barry, if she won't leave peacefully.'

'Also, just for the record,' added Short Hair, 'Edendale actually isn't Instagrammable. Light works differently here, so it's impossible to take photos. Not that it matters, now.'

Charity glanced out of the tea shop window and saw beyond the lead latticework that Edendale was disappearing. The rolling verdant hills on the horizon had already gone, and now the colourful bunting advertising a non-existent festival and the impressive gothic spires of a fake cathedral were drifting away like candyfloss in water.

Janusz and Richard also stood up.

'Thank you for the cake,' said Janusz. 'Screw you for the rest of it – but the cake was delicious.'

'Last chance to come nicely,' Short Hair told Grace.

Charity grabbed Grace's hand. Silently, Grace rose to stand with the rest of the family. Brenda took her hand on the other side.

Constance looked around awkwardly, the only one still sitting.

What did you mean, 'me too', Brenda?

'Well, you can't stay here, can you? You were going to follow us, anyway. May as well do so with our blessing.'

But, back there, I won't be able to speak to—

And, they were all beneath the lurid canopy of the petrol forecourt yet again. A miserable drizzle slicked the tarmac beyond. The hotties in the suits were gone. Only the neatly folded chairs remained. A cold, damp wind blew, and above, the Hell Hole swirled into countless different dimensions.

Time was running again.

And therefore, they were, again, running out of time.

CHAPTER FIFTEEN

Waste

'Well, that was unpleasant,' announced Brenda. 'Time to save a few hundred idiots, I suppose.' She turned to Charity. 'Princess, you're up, did you want Grace to get you some more crisps?'

'We're just going to carry on as if nothing happened, are we, Mum?' replied Charity.

'Nobody's suggesting that, princess,' said Richard, 'we can talk about all of this on the car journey home. We're just sort of on a deadline right now.'

Charity held her hands up in the direction of the Hell Hole for a moment, then lowered them again, distracted.

'Is Constance really still with us?'

Darryl glanced over his shoulder. Yes, Constance was still there, looking rather at a loose end.

'Yep,' he told his sister.

Charity nodded, still distracted. 'And her will really did say I was supposed to go to Wellington?'

'Wellington would have repressed you, princess,' replied Brenda. 'It would have locked away everything that's special about you – at best. At worst, you'd have grown up with all those abilities, around a family who didn't share them or understand them. You don't know how miserable that is. I do.'

'Bloody Hell, Mother,' breathed Charity. 'And this anti-psychic aunt who I have obviously never met, by the way – she was cool with a random clairvoyant friend of her dead sister going against the will and yoinking a baby so it could be raised as a ghost hunter?'

'Can we *please* discuss this in the car home?' asked Richard.

'Yeah,' added Janusz, 'I hate to be That Guy, but we made it all the way here, we've got people to rescue and the end of the world to stop. Can we not wreck it all by having a big argument right now?'

'Right, so this kind of sounds like you're still keeping something from me,' said Charity.

'Princess, please,' cried Richard. 'Think about it – wasting our time while the Hell Hole grows more powerful is just playing into those Angels' hands.'

'I thought they didn't like being called that because it was reductive,' interjected Grace, quietly.

'Well,' replied Charity, 'you would know, wouldn't you?'

'I…' attempted Grace, and then fell back into miserable, hunched silence once more.

'Guys,' said Janusz. 'Please! We've all found out things in the past few days that aren't so nice, but we just have to make the best of it for now! Look at me and my Darryl. We just found out he's part Demon but it's OK because we look for the positives – like how his Demon form looks like a cute little kitty cat, and—'

'Oh my *God*, Janusz,' cried Darryl, exasperated, 'will you *stop*? Will you stop saying the Demon is cute? It's not cute! It's gross! And stop pretending you're immediately fine with it! It is not fine! None of this is fine! OK!?'

'Wow,' replied Janusz, and that one 'wow' contained a multitude of disappointments and hurt.

Darryl cringed inwardly, remembering various agreements he'd just broken, about shouting, and telling each other off in front of other people. Remembering quiet conversations in bed about Janusz's past, and why men's voices raised in anger still prompted the fight-or-flight reflex in him, and how it made him feel sick when he refused to fight, and had no way to flee.

'Sorry,' said Darryl, immediately, but the damage had already been done.

'See?' said Brenda to Charity, 'and now Janusz is upset.'

'That's not my fault, it's Darryl's for being a bad husband!'

'I'm not a bad husband, I'm just… really stressed right now. I'm sorry, Janusz.'

'Just, please.' Janusz pinched the bridge of his nose. 'Please! Stop arguing and save the world. As your admin guy, I am begging you to get this job done on time.'

'Fine.' Charity turned from the others. 'For Janusz.'

'Just, you're always doing this,' added Janusz, under his breath. 'Always we have a job constipation for the ghost hunting bookings. We can't afford a job constipation for saving the world.'

Charity walked back out from under the petrol forecourt canopy. Darryl broke into a jog to join her. Death – if his sister was indeed Death – still needed a Finder, a pair of clairvoyant eyes to point her in the right direction. He and his sister had always worked like this. It was just weird now that strange immortal creatures were talking about it like it was some unwritten, eternal rule of the universe. Giving grand names to their ghost hunting work and comparing them to Valkyries and ancient deities.

'You OK?' he asked his sister.

'Not really,' she replied. 'It's just a bit much for one afternoon. I mean… from what they just said, I'm pretty sure Batman was created specifically for my benefit.'

'You think Batman was made especially for you alone?' Darryl managed a faint, mocking smile. 'And you're quite sure you're not a straight white man?'

'Oh, shush.'

They got far enough away from the canopy for Darryl to be able to see the Hell Hole properly.

'You see the people?' asked Charity.

Darryl just saw a void. 'No. Can… can you pull them out, anyway?'

'Not if I don't know where they are. There's nothing for me to grab hold of.' She sighed, shakily. 'Even if we could find them, I don't know…' Was that self-doubt in his sister's tone? Darryl wasn't sure he'd ever heard that in her before. It really didn't suit her. 'If they're right – if I'm Death, actual Death, the Grim Reaper…'

'They said it was just a title, you know.'

'Still, though. Aren't I supposed to just be sending people *to* the realms beyond ours? It might explain why I'm not very good at pulling them back into our world.'

'Charity, you're great at it.' Darryl continued to squint into the void, desperately looking for some sign of the prematurely snatched bodies, but seeing only the void. 'I've seen you bring back people who were taken before their time, more than once.'

He didn't say out loud what they both already knew – that by 'more than once', he meant 'twice'. And that on both of those occasions it had taken her hours and hours of concentrated effort just to get one person out at a time. It wasn't her strongest skillset. All of this remained moot, because he still couldn't find the people.

'Where have they hidden them?' he asked, with increasing desperation. 'Mum!' His mother clacked over. 'Can you see them? I can't see them.'

Brenda peered at the Hell Hole. 'No,' she admitted. 'And it's getting bigger.'

As they spoke, a couple of slug-like Demons squirmed out of the vortex and landed silently on the brightly lit canopy.

'Bugger,' grumbled Brenda. 'Grace! Angel-in-a-Grace-Suit! Not-A-Priest, whatever you are, get over here, we're going to need you and your magic fists.'

Slowly and sadly, Grace began to shuffle over.

'Chop chop please, Your Grace. Yes you've had some bad news – join the club. Since your Angel fists can punch Demons out cold, we shouldn't let that go to waste.'

'Waste!' shouted Darryl. 'That thing with Keira Knightley's face said that the bodies that weren't quite dead yet were being stored in Waste.'

'Waste,' repeated Charity. 'That's the dimension where ghosts automatically go when I move them on, isn't it?'

'Yeah.' Darryl was still thinking about that Whishaw-Knightley-Bear thing. He really hated being reminded of that thing's face. It wasn't a pleasant memory.

'Great,' replied Charity. 'So, we know what we're looking for. Now, how do we find it?'

Darryl continued to peer up at the void. Several more Demons emerged from it.

'I have no idea.'

Brenda turned to her children. 'Find a way – fast. I'll help our Fake Vicar fight these Demons.' Grace had barely made it over to them when Brenda grabbed her by the arm and started dragging her towards the approaching Demons. 'Come on, you, you're one of us now, make yourself useful.'

'Can you not just access the Waste dimension?' Darryl asked.

Charity shook her head. 'I didn't even know that's where I was sending the dead until recently – it was automatic, I just concentrate on making them leave the realm of the living, and… off they pop.'

'So, if you had a ghost to pop…'

'I don't even like doing that to them, any more,' said Charity. 'Now I know that's what happens to them, it feels mean.'

'But, if you did, could you access the Waste dimension for long enough to grab hold of the people stuck there?'

'Maybe? But as I said—'

'Charity, if this place has a surfeit of anything, it's ghosts. For a few hundred of them, it's still not too late to bring them back. But for loads of others, it's definitely too late. There's no bringing them back to life, and they're miserable here – they're trapped.'

'But they'd probably be miserable and trapped in Waste, too,' argued Charity. 'At least here, they've got posters and Blackpool tower keyrings to look at.'

'Yes, I get it. It's a Trolley Problem, all right.' Darryl paused. 'The Trolley Problem is when—'

'Yes, Darryl, I know what the Trolley Problem is, I watched *The Good Place*, too.'

'Stop mansplaining the Trolley Problem, Darryl,' called Janusz, which at least meant Janusz was still speaking to him.

The first of the Demons had successfully slithered down from the forecourt canopy. Brenda pushed Grace in front of her as a Not-Actually-A-Human Shield and launched her at the Demon. Grace yelped, flinched and swung with both fists, making contact with the Demon's side. There were now over a dozen more Demons headed their way.

'I… don't think I want to do it,' said Charity. 'Like, is *this* my destiny? Sending those poor sods to Waste? They're all just dead and sad, like Constance. Her eyes…'

And suddenly, Constance was right there, next to Darryl, and yes, her eyes were so like Charity's, only devoid of joy and hope. Only sadness remained. Sadness and – in spite of Constance's protestations that she never felt it any more, there was still some buttoned down fury there. Constance, silent once more in this realm, was indicating wildly.

Send me.
    It's OK.
    Send me to Waste.
    Charity is in danger. The Demons.
    It's OK. I've spoken to her now. She's seen me. My baby. I just wanted to be there for my baby. I can still protect her, I can still help her. She can send me. Send me. I can help her find the Waste.

Darryl had absolutely no idea what Constance was trying to say.

'I mean – who am I supposed to send?' Charity continued.

Me! Send me, princess!

'They're all just people,' said Charity. 'The lady who just wanted a cigarette, the posh bloke under the impression that the services were brilliant and that poor woman who kept wanging on about Old Jack…'

'Old Jack,' muttered Darryl, thoughtfully.

Brenda pushed Grace at another Demon. 'Have you done it, yet?'

'No,' called Darryl.

'It's a Trolley Problem,' shouted Charity. 'Darryl wants me to send some poor bugger to Waste.'

I'll go, Charity. You can send me to Waste. It's OK.

'I'll go, Charity,' shouted Grace. 'You can send me to Waste. It's OK.'

Oh shut up, Grace, you're not even human.

'Oh shut up, Grace,' replied Brenda. 'How's that even supposed to work?'

'I'm not mortal.' Grace blinked, clearly admitting this truth to herself for the first time. 'I'd probably survive it.'

'But if you leave this dimension the world will end, genius.'

'Oh, yeah.'

'Plus,' continued Brenda, 'we need you here for punching Demons. Speaking of which…' She shoved Grace at yet another Demon. 'No idiots sacrificing themselves, understand? You too, Constance, I recognise that face.

Oh.

'Well, if we're not letting any of our lot willingly sacrifice themselves, it makes it even worse to think about doing it to some random dead person who *doesn't* consent,' said Charity, 'doesn't it?'

'Charity, I cannot believe you're having an ethical crisis at a time like this,' said Darryl, helplessly watching more and more Demons pour forth. 'It's not like you.'

'I know! I hate it! I want to go back to just *assuming* I'm special. *Knowing* it is too much pressure.'

Darryl grabbed her arm, remembering something from earlier. 'Old Jack,' he said. 'That thing was huge – biggest ghost I've ever seen, thousands of spirits in one.'

'Even if I wanted to pop Old Jack, I probably wouldn't be able to, as it is,' argued Charity. 'There's too much of it, and it's too rooted here.'

'Exactly,' replied Darryl. 'What if you just... nudged Old Jack? With Lil's permission? Do you think you'd be able to move it towards Waste enough to open up the way, without any of Old Jack actually being sent through?'

Charity thought about this. 'It's possible.'

'Usually, "possible" is all you need.'

'Yeah.' Charity set her face. 'Yeah! Yeah, I can do that. Janusz! Dad! Get out the smelly candles, we're going to summon the ghost of a haunted tree and save the frigging world.'

CHAPTER SIXTEEN

No Naked Flames

The Rook family were not good at a lot of things. Quizzes, cleaning the bathroom, remembering what night to put the bins out, three-legged races – as Darryl recalled from primary school sports days. What they were very good at was creating a passably occult-looking set-up out of odds and ends, while fending off attacks from the undead. They did it a lot in the ghost hunting business, and had it down to a fine art, like an emergency service speedily and professionally cordoning off a dangerous area as smoke billows and civilians scream. Except that instead of traffic cones and striped tape it was chalked sigils, salt and smelly candles.

The effect, for ghosts, was similar to the effect on the living public. It told them that this was a place where it was all kicking off, and the people marking the area out were in charge of the situation. If there were a supernatural version of hi-vis gilets, the family would have all popped them on by now.

To an outsider, it might have looked a lot like they were preparing for another seance, but this was messier and more hurried. They had no table, and wouldn't be able to spare the time to sit around it and hold hands together even if they did. Instead, Janusz and Richard placed candles here and there while dodging Grace's blindly flying fists as Brenda physically pushed the not-a-priest at approaching Demons.

'I don't really want to light the candles,' called Richard. 'This is a petrol station – naked flames are just asking for trouble, I don't even use my phone in these places.'

'That's what I packed the LED ones for.' Janusz showed Richard the candle he was holding. He flicked a switch on its base and a small, fake flame lit up.

'Janusz, you bobby dazzler, you.' Richard held out his hands and Janusz tossed him a fake candle.

Darryl also held out a hand towards Janusz as an offer to help place the fake candles, but was ignored. Right. So he was still in the craphouse with his husband, then. Probably fair.

Richard and Janusz didn't put out quite as many candles as they usually would because – fake or not – they were still causing a trip hazard for Brenda and Grace. There really were a lot of Demons now. Grace was surprisingly good at getting rid of them, windmilling her little arms around in a panic as Brenda steered her. It was like watching a two-person combine harvester at work. That said, Darryl really wasn't sure how long she'd be able to keep it up, at the rate things were going.

Richard looked around at the tarmac. The chalk markings were already starting to run in the drizzle, and one of the electronic candles was making a troublesome fizzing noise.

'How's that?' he asked. 'That do?'

Probably. It wasn't the best of set-ups, but it was only window dressing. This was far from Lil's usual haunting spot, but as the man with the pipe had said, her ghost was known to get as far as the petrol station at times. Darryl had no idea quite how far the ghostly roots of Old Jack spread. Probably hundreds of yards. Maybe a mile, or more. He just hoped that it would become aware of the candles and chalk, at least enough to pique Lil's interest.

'Lil?' he called. 'Lil, we've found the door to the Manager's office, but we wondered if you could help…'

Lil was there, suddenly, right in front of his face.

'What do you need, chuck?'

Bless her. Helpful as ever. Darryl felt bad. What if this didn't work? He decided to give it to her as straight as he could.

'There's some people who are… stuck. Because of the Manager. Because of this place.'

Lil shook her head. 'I *told* them this'd end in tears, but did they listen?'

'We need to find the place where they're trapped, and for that, we need someone who's…' he trailed off. 'Who's… already a ghost.'

Lil looked at him. For a moment, there was a tiny spark of realisation, of horror, like someone waking from a dream to discover their house was on fire, and then horrified lucidity was pushed right back down again.

'Like Old Jack,' she said. 'Or like the ghosts Old Jack sucked up from the ground.'

'Yes,' replied Darryl, brightly. 'So, we just need Old Jack to take a quick look for us, through… there.'

He pointed up at the void in the sky. Lil's gaze followed his finger. Her expression darkened.

'So, that's what they built. Without permission. Without consulting any of us.'

'Yes. But we're…'

Lil's expression kept getting angrier and angrier, until it wasn't Lil's face any more. It was a mess of lines with dark knots

183

and holes. It was not any kind of face at all, but the illusion of a face that you can only see by squinting sideways at the trunk of an ancient oak tree. Somehow, Lil was still little Lil, with her curlers and her pinny, and shadowy tendrils all around her, but also she was not Lil, and she was not little. She was simultaneously five feet tall and ninety feet tall. The tendrils were at the same time writhing shadows and thick wooden boughs, swaying angrily in some gale that had raged hundreds of years ago.

'We don't like it,' said Lil, and when she spoke it was with hundreds of voices.

'Woah.' Charity blinked at Darryl. 'You all right, there?'

Darryl realised that the words were coming from him – they were speaking through his mouth. If all those voices seemed weird coming from Lil, it would have been even more disconcerting for the rest of the family, perceiving them coming out of him. Darryl couldn't do anything, couldn't speak with his own voice. Old Jack wanted to talk, and the rage of it all filled his throat. He'd never known anything like it. It was one voice and it was thousands of voices. It was a mass grave, howling together, one thought and many.

'We don't like it! It doesn't belong here!'

Darryl could taste blood. He could no longer feel the ground beneath his feet. He could no longer feel anything beyond Old Jack's rage.

'Darryl?' Charity looked alarmed.

'*Zabko?*' shouted Janusz, his eyes wide.

This wasn't right, this was too much – too much. It was becoming like a seance, with all those voices of the dead pushing his own consciousness further and further back. And Old Jack wasn't stopping: it was too big, there were too many. Beyond, he could see his mother, surrounded by Demons now. The Hell

Hole still swirled into nothingness, Demons still crawled and buzzed out of it. The arrival of the Demons only made Old Jack angrier. Trespassers! On Old Jack's land! Building things without permission! All wrong!

'All wrong, all wrong!'

He couldn't breathe, now, and the part of Darryl that was Darryl was still being pushed into a smaller space at the back of his mind. He didn't lose consciousness though, Old Jack was too angry to allow it. As a panicked last resort, Darryl tried to fight against the invading tree ghost by taking Demon form, but Old Jack pushed that back, as well.

'Stop it,' shouted Janusz in an admirable attempt at a businesslike tone. 'Stop it!'

'We will stop it,' replied Old Jack. 'We will stop them!'

'Right you are, then,' said Charity. She grabbed Darryl by the shoulders, and pushed.

It wasn't a physical push. It was different. It was a push only against the rage in Darryl's throat and mouth and mind, only against the part of Old Jack that had entered his body to use Darryl as a sort of mortal megaphone. Old Jack stuck in Darryl's windpipe for a second – the strength of it was still extraordinary. Charity screamed, and Darryl's throat cleared, allowing him to cough up globs of dark blood and, upsettingly, sawdust. For the briefest moment, Lil was discernible again, amongst the shadows. She pulled a determined face, nodded at Darryl and was gone again, lost in the bark and branches.

And Old Jack was so tall that it reached all the way up to the Hell Hole.

And Old Jack was filled with the dead, so the Hell Hole automatically shifted to take the dead to where the dead are supposed to go – to Waste.

And Old Jack was so big, and so many, and so old, and so angry, that the Hell Hole choked.

Darryl spat out one more mouthful of woody blood. 'There! Charity? Do you see?'

Darryl had never seen the dimension that the immortal beings kept referring to as 'Waste' before. Whenever they'd sent a ghost there before, they had simply slipped out of the realm of the living – no muss, no fuss. Actually *seeing* it was different. To call it a 'desert' would be a misnomer, because a desert has an up and a down, land and air, a north, south, east and west. From what he could make out, Waste had none of these, and yet it did still remind him of a desert. A desert where there was no distinction between the sand and the sky.

He wasn't able to get a really good look at Waste for several reasons. One was that it was the other side of a Hell Hole hovering in the sky. Another was that the Hell Hole was being held open and blocked by the thousands of shadowy branches and roots of Old Jack. Another, happier reason was that right at the edge of the Hell Hole, around five hundred bodies dangled, lifeless but not yet too late.

They hung together, awkwardly, as if hooked by the shoulders. Their heads lolled heavily against their chests, long hair dangling over faces like veils. Assuming they managed to get everyone out safely, a lot of these people would have terrible cricks in their necks.

'There!' He pointed his sister towards the sight. 'Do you see it, Charity?' Eurgh, Darryl's throat was really hoarse, he felt like he'd swallowed a pint of splinters.

'Smudges,' replied Charity.

'It's them,' croaked Darryl. 'I recognise that kid's *Guardians of the Galaxy* T-shirt.'

'Aww, a little Marvel fan. I think I can grab hold of them.'

She grimaced, and thrust her hands towards the Hell Hole. Around a dozen of the hanging bodies began drifting towards them, like flotsam caught on a tide.

'You got a big load of them, there,' Darryl told his sister, scraping a bit of tree bark off the roof of his mouth.

'Yeah, well, I'm in a hurry, aren't I?' Charity was already sweating profusely. 'Ah man, this is giving me a headache. Is it working? It feels like trying to get a load of bits of eggshell out of batter. Only, the batter's got a big angry tree in the way.'

As Darryl watched, the dozen bodies floated to the edge of the void and the branches of Old Jack parted to let them past. At the edge of the void, the living world's laws of physics kicked in, the first and most immediately dangerous of these being gravity. Body after body flopped like horrible meaty slinkies from the void to the canopy of the petrol station, which was thankfully only a couple of feet below.

The sound of it, from below the canopy, was obscene.

'Eurgh,' said Richard, understating things as usual.

'It's OK, it's working,' shouted Darryl, instantly regretting raising his voice, with his throat feeling the way it did. 'Everyone keep it up – you OK there, Mum?'

Brenda didn't reply, which was fair because she was very busy guiding Grace from Demon to Demon. With the Hell Hole stuck at Waste, no more Demons were able to come through it at least, but there were still around forty Demons in the forecourt, which against one middle-aged clairvoyant and one frightened Angel-being disguised as a priest, wasn't really fair. Brenda and Grace were still holding them off, but only just, and they were getting tired. Darryl really didn't want to go into Demon form again today, especially since it was the source of an ongoing falling-out between himself and his husband. But, it seemed today wasn't Darryl's day. He felt the full-body chill

187

of the Demon inside him manifesting. Who was he kidding – Janusz aside, no day was Darryl's day.

Brenda desperately tried to just concentrate on the task in hand. Unfortunately, when the task in hand was 'fighting a few dozen attacking Demons Hell-bent on enabling the end of the world, in a petrol station full of trip hazards, armed only with an immortal amnesiac having an existential crisis', that wasn't easy. The heavy, meaty sounds of bodies hitting the canopy above were off putting to say the least, and were getting louder and more frequent as Charity picked up momentum. Turned out that it quite literally raining men was nowhere near as joyful as the song made it out to be. Cutting through the torrential thuds of human precipitation came a new sound – a now familiar tiger-cub roar. Out of the corner of her eye she saw Darryl, all teeth and claws, come bounding over to the attacking Demons.

'Well, look who's decided to join us,' she muttered, turning Grace towards a Demon that was trying to slither up behind them.

Grace swung wildly out with both fists, and managed to catch the Demon with a left hook on the second try. Her breaths were fast and shallow, and Brenda imagined that it wasn't simply due to physical exertion – if physical exertion even so much as affected Grace's kind.

All Brenda could do for Grace at that moment was to pat her on the shoulder.

'Panic about it when we're done here, eh?'

'How can you be OK with all of this?' Grace's voice was high and shaky. 'How can you just… carry on? I'm a… whatever those things in suits were! I was put here to end your world! I… I just…'

A Demon lunged at Grace from the left. Brenda turned the not-a-priest to face it, hurriedly.

'I've been able to see ghosts and Demons since I was a baby,' said Brenda, quite calmly, 'my husband was possessed for decades, my son is part-Demon, my best friend's ghost is stalking me and I just found out my daughter is Death. I'm pretty good at compartmentalising. I have to be.'

Grace punched the attacking Demon right back into its own dimension.

'I think for now I can cope with being friends with an Angel, or whatever it is you are,' added Brenda. 'I'll just get drunk about it later.'

That was a thought, realised Brenda, shoving Grace at yet another Demon – she was still stone cold sober. Had been all day. She simply hadn't had a chance to drink yet. It was an odd sensation, doing all of this sober. It wasn't great, but maybe it wasn't as bad as all that either. Obviously, she wasn't intending on retaining this accidental sobriety for any longer than she needed to, but still, it wasn't the worst thing about today.

Grace punched a Demon so hard that it didn't just sink back into its own dimension, it managed to pull a second Demon back with it.

'We're friends?'

'I think so.'

'That's nice.'

'It's not *that* nice. I got my last friend killed.'

By the petrol pumps, Richard and Janusz watched the scene. Charity was just about holding out, although her nose was streaming blood and she was shaking with sustained effort. She'd need more carbs, very soon. Janusz searched through his bag. He usually kept some honey roasted peanuts to hand for just this sort of occasion.

'Typical Charity,' he said, rooting through tissues, hand sanitiser and old receipts, 'tell her she's *Śmierć* and instead of reaping she brings hundreds back to life. Ach ha!' He retrieved the nuts from the depths of his bag, and shot a glance at Richard. 'You OK?'

Richard shrugged, watching the scene. 'Just feeling a bit useless, is all.'

'You're not useless,' replied Janusz. 'You're just part of the support team now, with me! Am *I* useless?'

'No,' replied Richard. 'You brought fake candles and peanuts.'

'Exactly,' said Janusz, cheerfully. 'And you are good at spotting fire hazards, which in a petrol station is very useful.'

Beyond, Darryl, grappling with two shadowy smears that Richard assumed were Demons, stumbled over one of the electronic candles and crushed it accidentally beneath his claws. The wrecked little electronic light sparked, dangerously.

'Case in point,' noted Janusz.

'Oh no,' shouted Richard, 'where's the bucket of sand? There should be a bucket of sand!'

Janusz didn't really have time to help Richard look for a bucket of sand. Charity was visibly struggling, now. He ran to his sister in law, opening the peanuts as he went, ready to shove handfuls straight into her mouth. Saving the world was a team effort, after all, and sometimes that involved being the one with the snacks.

Richard didn't like being this panicky. Usually, when he got stressed, Murzzzz would take over, meaning that he rarely had to worry about the thing stressing him out any more – although the flipside was, he did have to worry about clearing up all the mess left behind by his inner Demon going on a rampage, instead. He was used to that, though. He wasn't used to having to do all of it – having to face all of this danger and feel all of these feelings, without someone inside him to pass the reins to when he didn't feel like he could carry on. He berated himself silently. His family were having to do so much, he was just looking for a bucket of sand, and for the love of Jeff, where *was* it? There was *always* supposed to be a bucket of sand, it was basic health and safety! At a loss for what else to do, he scooped the crushed electric candle up by one of its smashed plastic shards and scurried away with it from the petrol pumps. Still not sure what to do with it, he wrapped it in a tissue from his pocket and threw it into a bin. But then he worried that that could be a hazard too. Maybe he should keep it until he was able to take it to a recycling centre or something, since it had LED lights and batteries. As he pondered this, something shadowy grabbed him by the shoulders and yanked him off his feet. He was dragged painfully across the tarmac along his side, the rough friction of the ground scraping his coat, jumper, shirt and T-shirt up towards his armpit. Honestly, four layers and still he managed to badly graze his torso. The nearby Hell Hole was increasing the Demon's power so it was just about visible to Richard as it dragged him, but it was still extremely nebulous. And Richard couldn't fight against it – it was far too strong. Richard couldn't fight anything, without Murzzzz. He probably couldn't even battle some ghostly patch of sadness that used to be a kid. Not that he'd hit a kid – dead or not. Why had he thought about hitting a ghost kid? For pity's sake, Richard! Such were his spiralling self-pitying thoughts as he was dragged horribly across the forecourt, the skin scraping off his ribs. He did also think 'Ow, my ribs,' but that was a given.

*

Charity's mouth was full of blood. She was aware that it was streaming from her nose as well. She had to keep spitting mouthfuls of it out so that she could take a breath. All of this wasn't good for her kitty cat jumper. Post-mission laundry was a nightmare as it was, but honestly – had the family expected to have got caught up in another otherworldly ambush today, they probably wouldn't have worn all this knitwear.

She was also exhausted. Pulling people back into the realm of the living was much harder than pushing ghosts out of the living world – she had done the latter countless times, indeed, it now seemed that she was literally born to do it – but she had only achieved the former task twice before. Once, she'd managed to free an old woman from a haunted painting, and recently she'd been able to extract Janusz from an extremely cursed stained glass window. Both of these jobs had taken hours, and huge amounts of energy and concentration. While it was a little easier to pull living bodies out of a Hell Hole than out of a two-dimensional depiction of a Judean pasture, trying to do five hundred within a few minutes wasn't just pushing her powers to the limit, it was quickly pushing them far beyond every limit she thought she had. If her limit were a fundraising thermometer, she'd currently be sticking several fresh sheets of A3 to the top of it, all the way up to the ceiling, and wondering if she needed to invest in a new red marker pen. Her everything was shaking. Her knees were two blancmanges on a condemned rollercoaster. She was almost there, but it felt like her body was going to give way at any second. The idea of having to give up after pulling out all but the last fifty people or so felt even less fair than the idea of not being able to pull anybody out at all. The thought of saving everyone but that last ten per cent, of sending home carfuls of people with a child or a spouse missing, enraged her. She felt her legs give way beneath her, and the Hell Hole disappeared from her view as she collapsed completely to the wet ground. No. No! Unacceptable! Come on, stupid body! If she was going to be Death or whatever then she needed to be considerably more badass than this. She was supposed to loom over London in lithographs swishing a scythe about and looking bony and menacing, wasn't she? Not collapsing outside a petrol station with her task bar only ninety per cent full because she was a bit tired. Admittedly, if she was Death like the Hotties had said, then she shouldn't be bringing people back to life at all, but that was beside the point, right now. She tried to get back to her feet. Her limbs were like Play-Doh.

Strong hands grabbed her and hauled her upright. There was a flash of Catalogue Model smile, and a handful of slightly sweaty honey roasted peanuts were shoved into her mouth. Janusz!

Leaning heavily on her brother-in-law's shoulder, Charity chewed and swallowed the peanuts. They tasted manky, and had a lot of her blood on them. But it was fine – fuel was fuel. She allowed Janusz to prop her up entirely, and held out her hands towards the remaining people in the Hell Hole. She psychically grabbed as many people as she could, opened her mouth for more nuts, and pulled. Bodies tumbled out of the Hell Hole again, falling a few feet for a now mercifully soft landing on the mound of inert humanity on the canopy. Charity hoped that the ones at the bottom of the pile weren't getting too squished. She tried to grab as many as she could again, and suddenly found it much, much easier. Only five bodies fell out, at a speed that surprised her. The last one, a child of around ten, rolled gently down the hill of bodies and came to a stop, face up, on the bottom. There was something about the sight that repulsed and fascinated Charity in equal measure. She held her hands towards Waste again, and found there was nothing to grab.

That was it. She had done it. She'd brought them back from the realm beyond, the Waste from whence no human soul was supposed to return.

Now what?

'Now what?' shouted Janusz, to be heard over the continuing Demon battle by the petrol pumps. 'They still look all dead.'

Charity nodded. 'Yeah.'

She didn't know what to do. If she really were Death, she'd know what to do, surely.

She tried shouting 'Wakey wakey' at them. It didn't work.

'Mum?' she called, but her mother was still stuck in the fray, wielding Grace as a small, frightened weapon against the remaining half dozen Demons.

'Dad?' she attempted, but her father was screaming and being dragged by one leg while a Demon-form Darryl clawed at the wispy, cloudy head of his attacker.

Charity looked up at the Hell Hole again. The shadowy shape of a huge tree still loomed in front of it, holding the rift open with branches that squirmed and shifted like tentacles. Darryl was still fighting in Demonic form, so he couldn't channel whatever it was Old Jack had to say, but that didn't matter. Charity could feel Old Jack's rage. It went beyond words, beyond worlds, beyond everything and it was determined to find whoever was responsible for all of this. With Waste emptied now, and no Manager to be found, Old Jack thrashed and thrummed with frustration.

Charity knew something she could do. She could find the Manager. She'd done it before. She just needed a dead person who really wanted to speak to it.

'Lil,' she called, and for a moment, Old Jack's rage turned into something else. Something in the heart of the giant ghost tree's wordless fury felt like a person – a tiny little angry woman.

'Thank you for waiting,' Charity told the ghost. 'I can transfer you to the Manager now.'

CHAPTER SEVENTEEN

Nope

Charity concentrated on Lil, in the centre of Old Jack. She concentrated on Lil's interminable wait over the decades. The woman deserved some answers – deserved to have her say, even if it was just for once. And, even as the branches of Old Jack clutched at the Hell Hole, choking it, the dimension beyond the Hole shifted yet again. What was behind it now was no longer the eternal nothingness of Waste, nor was it the dark, slimy mysteries of the Demon realm. What was behind it now felt pristine, shiny, pretty and yet oddly uncomfortable. It felt like a strange combination of control and chaos, but the ordered element of it was only on the surface hiding a truth that was a tumult of everything. Like that idiom about the duck – calm above water, but paddling desperately beneath. Yeah, thought Charity. This dimension was metaphysically a duck.

And there, burning bright, right in the centre of it, was a familiar nightmare of interlocking rings of fire, covered in countless eyes. The Manager. One did not need to be in any way clairvoyant to see the Manager because there was so much of the Manager it could not help but be seen, in all its impossible, fiery glory. If *you* suddenly had an immortal being of flame and eyeballs hovering over you, spinning away like infinite burning hula hoops in far more dimensions than your own universe is used to incorporating, you'd probably notice it, too. The Manager appeared to be resting upon some sort of beanbag. It was like no beanbag Charity had ever seen before. It was at the same time not quite a beanbag and yet also the ultimate cosmic beanbag. There was something about it that exuded exactly the right levels of uncomfortableness and impracticality.

'Plato's chair,' breathed Janusz, next to her.

'Who?' asked Charity.

Charity, being more one for reading Manga than the philosophical pontifications of long-dead Ancient Greek wrestlers, wasn't familiar with Plato's concept of there existing in the ether the impossible, universal blueprint of the perfect chair. If she had done, then perhaps she'd have been as upset as Janusz was that it turned out the cosmos' idea of a perfect chair was a beanbag.

The Manager had very obviously not been expecting them. All of its uncountable eyes swivelled to look at them. It managed to look surprised and more than a little bit upset, which was quite a feat, considering it didn't have a face.

The Manager spoke, and the word it spoke was 'Nope'.

Charity felt the Manager's dimension – the Duck Dimension, or Head Office or whatever its real name was – getting pulled away from her. The Manager was fighting her, trying to wrestle its own dimension out of her grasp. At another time, she would have no chance of fighting against the Manager's will, especially in this exhausted state. At another time though, there might not have been a massive ancient ghost tree made out of a whole medieval village's worth of angry spirits grasping at the

Hell Hole, trying to get to the Manager. Even with Old Jack gripping the Hell Hole, its ghostly branches reaching towards the Manager, Charity still felt the Duck Dimension paddle so hard against her that it slipped away from her hold on it. The Hell Hole shifted again to become a portal to the murky depths of the Demons' dimension once more.

In the Demon realm, the beings that dwelled there took advantage of the freshly opened portal. They stampeded suddenly, many of them joyfully, like thrill seekers running straight to their favourite rollercoaster as soon as the theme park opened. Not all the Demons were full of glee, however. Some were thoroughly sick of this cycle now, and just wanted to hasten the bumper harvest that came with ending this mortal universe and the nice fresh start of beginning the next one. A couple of Demons were not even thinking of that, but were consumed by their grudge against the Rooks. And, one Demon hid amongst the surging crowd, flitting in the shadows, making himself seem smaller than he was. This was his chance! His only chance!

Somewhere else in the Demon realm, sirens wailed at an intensity that would cause a mortal to pull their own brain out through their ears just to make the sound stop.

'He's escaped,' someone called. 'He's broken his cage! He's out!'

'Charity!' Darryl was in human form again, sweating and panting. He pointed at the Hell Hole. 'You've lost Head Office – that's the Demon realm.'

'Yes,' shouted Charity, 'I know!' She could see yet more blurry Demons pouring out of the Hole, even as she fought to pull it back to Head Office.

No. This will not do.

Darryl watched as Constance flickered over to Old Jack.

Old Jack. So big. So old. So many. There's so much of Old Jack, and its roots want to suck more of the dead up into it, plucking the lost and lonely dead up from the bewildering roar of the huge, rushing road. It wants even more to join it. One more soul to push against the Manager. It offers… not 'peace', exactly. Old Jack offers a part in a collective. An end to the loneliness of wandering as a ghost. Its ancient boughs whisper sweet promises about the new purpose I would find within the tree. Old Jack is family, they say. Old Jack is home.

That is their truth. Their family, their home, not mine. My family is scattered, my home is lost. But, my daughter needs Old Jack to be just that little stronger. She needs just that bit more of a shove against the Manager.

Fine.

I got to speak to my princess, at least. You could say that's kind of dealing with my unfinished business. And I sort of gave Brenda a piece of my mind, even though I don't think she really listened. That's… well, that's more closure than a lot of other ghosts have had, every cloud and all that. The point is, Charity needs my help. They all do. Everybody else here is already helping, in their own ways. And, I did say I wasn't going to be a dick. So, here I go, not being a dick.

Darryl continued to watch helplessly as Constance added her ghostly force to Old Jack's, pushing against the Manager. The tendrils of Old Jack wrapped around her like a terrible hug, and absorbed Constance into it.

Darryl wasn't sure what to do. He couldn't stop Constance. It had happened so quickly. Should he tell Charity and Brenda what had just happened? They'd want to know, but they were both so embroiled in the fight against the Hell Hole and the Demons, it really wouldn't do to distract them with the news that Constance had just disappeared into an ancient ghost tree. He decided not to mention it for now, and just add the trouble it would eventually get him in to the trouble he was already in with Janusz. He swallowed the words down, and they hurt his stomach. He wondered if this was how Brenda felt all the time, and hated that he was following in his mother's footsteps.

The incorporation of Constance made Old Jack even bigger, and with a great heave of joint effort by the ghost tree and Charity together, the dimension behind the Hell Hole shifted from the dark viscosity of the Demon realm to the uncomfortable clean lines of Head Office yet again.

The Manager vibrated with bright rage. 'No, I said! Stop this! Stop it!'

'Keep it up,' shouted Darryl. He glanced around the forecourt. He, his mother and Grace had pushed almost all of the Demons back, but the Manager sending the Hell Hole back to open up the Demon realm, if only for a few moments, had allowed several more to join the fight, including a couple of really big, powerful-looking ones. He was going to have to go Demonic again. It was getting easier for him to control the change, he noticed. This was not a good thing. He still wasn't at all comfortable with this just being a thing he could do, now. That was something else he was going to have to worry about once the world had been saved and they were out of Hell's own service station.

Looking around he could see that there were two flying Demons buzzing towards his helpless father, and both of the worryingly huge Demons had vanished, which Darryl took as an ominous sign. He allowed the chill to take him, shifting his form again, and – oh no – it was getting as easy as putting on or taking off a pair of jogging bottoms and he really didn't like that at all. And he was worn out from fighting. The first time he'd used this form to fight Demons, it had only been for a few minutes. Today, he'd had to turn Demon three times within an hour.

He took a few bounds towards Richard, teeth bared, before something huge and incredibly strong walloped him side-on and sent him rolling and skidding across the tarmac. Oh. So *that's* where one of the huge Demons had got to.

'**Oh,**' said the Demon, in a familiar, wet voice, '**I have had it up to *here* with this nonsense.**'

A terrible face, made out of six large, bright eyes, three mouths and a lot of cheekbone loomed over him. 'Mister Peppermint' was still using the features of two doe-eyed RomCom stars and a CGI Polar Bear, then. Fresh back out of the Demon realm, Mr Peppermint was bigger than it had seemed earlier. It was probably the biggest Demon Darryl had ever seen. Bigger than Murzzzz. It loomed over him, a good twelve feet tall, maybe more and a writhing mess of Christmassy coloured limbs and shining teeth. Darryl remained adamant that his own Demon form was not 'cute', but compared to this thing, he was a squishy little baby koala of a Demon.

'**You weren't supposed to actually raid the bodies out of Waste, you disgusting half-breed Spawn.**'

Darryl growled. OK, Darryl still really wasn't happy about one of his parents being a Demon, but *he* was the one who got to call it 'disgusting'. Not this massive interloper who didn't even know him. That was just rude.

'**Taking the bodies out of Waste is the opposite of what the Death unit's supposed to do! This is the most shambolic** reset I've ever seen,' continued the Demon. It looked up into the Hell Hole and addressed the Manager. '**And the worst find-and-deliver operatives ever chosen, I'd say. All of this is going to go into my review, you know.**'

'I understand your frustration,' boomed the Manager, from the Hell Hole, 'but perhaps if you and the Executives hadn't interfered—'

'**The Executives are nothing to do with me,**' replied Mister Peppermint.

'Then why lead us to them, by telling us we still had time to rescue all those people?' growled Darryl through awkwardly pointy Demon fangs. 'And how to find them?'

'**Because,**' shouted Mister Peppermint back at him. '**I thought it would be funny, watching you try, only to find out you were the Death unit so your efforts to save mortal lives were meaningless.**'

'Couldn't help yourself, could you?' the Manager said. 'Couldn't help tormenting the mortals, even while I'm trying to reset.'

'**Well yeah, of course. Isn't that what mortals are for?**'

'That's not what the produce are for,' argued the Manager.

'**Don't you talk back to me. This is your fault. This has been the worst Mortal Universe yet,**' railed Mister Peppermint. '**Barely any fun at all. Two stars at best. Now, are you going to fix it, or do we have to intervene properly?**'

The Demon began striding towards the stricken Charity, who was still wrestling with the Hell Hole, with Janusz propping her up.

'I do have the situation under control,' replied the Manager, its voice tinged with panic. 'You don't need to do anything. There's a Death unit and a Hell Hole, everything's in place – bar the last Red Sticker Issue, which wasn't even my fault – so it would be a perfectly smooth and efficient apocalypse if you could all just stop poking at it.'

'**Stop fobbing us off,**' railed Mister Peppermint. '**Your Hell Hole is rushed and your operatives are faulty. Why you haven't simply terminated this Death unit and installed a new one yet is beyond me.**'

Darryl leaped at the Demon, grabbing one of its Polar Bear legs and sinking his fangs into it. It didn't even slow the massive Demon down.

'**I remember the good old universes, when we used to end the world ourselves,**' continued the Demon, still heading towards Charity and Janusz. '**Entrails everywhere. Happy days. But no, that was "inefficient". Well, I ask you, how "efficient" is this, eh?**'

'Stop!' cried the Manager.

'**I'm putting my claws down. Just install a different Death unit and I'll terminate this one myself. I do assume you've got backups?**'

'Charity! Princess!' Brenda shouted a warning. From the corner of his eye, Darryl could see Brenda still trying to fight with Grace, but they were too far away, and surrounded by smaller Demons. 'Janusz! Run!'

But there could be no running away from a Demon of this size. Darryl tried using his claws on Mister Peppermint's leg as well as his fangs but he was still simply dragged along by the Demon.

'You don't have the authority to change our Death unit. You're infringing on Head Office's jurisdiction here,' continued the Manager, using the tone of voice a hapless fast food server would use if a gobby customer had decided to leap over the service counter and help themself to ice cream straight from the machine.

'**Oh, who's going to stop me?**' sneered Mister Peppermint.

Darryl scrabbled desperately at the ground with his back claws as he continued to plunge teeth and front claws into Mister Peppermint's leg but he wasn't strong enough. Even as a Demon, he wasn't actually good enough at anything to be of any real help. Mister Peppermint was practically on top of his sister and his husband, and Darryl couldn't stop it. Nobody was going to stop it…

There was a roar, from somewhere near the pumps. A familiar roar. A horribly familiar roar.

A *wonderfully* familiar roar.

There had been two big Demons on the forecourt. And there had been something recognisable about the second Demon, but Darryl had been too distracted by Mister Peppermint's attempt to take the end of the world into its own claws to think too much about the odd familiarity.

Mister Peppermint stopped at the sound of the roar, and turned, just in time to see Murzzzz leap straight onto its face, claws slashing, teeth flashing, and with a familiar mortal-world physicality to him.

The torture had been one thing. Obviously, it had hurt – it had been torture, that had been the point. But, there had been something understandable about the torture. It was punishment. Murzzzz had transgressed: he'd delayed the mortal world's termination, and, more taboo still, he'd Spawned with a mortal. He'd accepted the punishment, because he had no regrets about Spawning Darryl, or about being a Red Sticker Issue to frustrate the Manager.

What Murzzzz could not abide was the newfound loneliness, after he was ripped from Richard. It felt cold, in a way he'd never experienced before. It was like suddenly becoming lost and disorientated – surroundings once familiar turned into bewildering, empty shapes. The pain was worse than having his eyes repeatedly gouged out, only for them to grow back almost instantly – and he meant that literally, because they did actually do that to him, for a while.

The others kept saying they'd brought Murzzzz home, but they were wrong. The Demon realm wasn't home to him any more. The Rooks were his home. Richard was his home. He felt like he'd been torn in half. It wasn't a desire to get away from the torture that had given him the strength to break his cage, or the drive to hurry through the door to the mortal world in the shadows of the jostling crowd of Demons. He wasn't running away from anything. He was running *to*. He needed to get home, to Richard, to be Richard again, to have his whole self back. Also, he was aware that he owed the other Rooks an apology, not to mention Constance Xu, and he couldn't very much do that with his tongue being pulled out in a whole different dimension now, could he?

He had run straight to Richard, flitting through the shadows. And, oh, Richard had welcomed him without a second thought, like long-separated partners rushing into a wordless, tearful hug at an airport arrivals lounge. And the hug remained. The hug became them both – two beings in one body – they were home again. He could breathe again! They both could. They were *them* again. No longer half, no longer cold, no longer alone. Home.

But, there was urgent work to be done. He had a place in this family, after all. He was their protector. And right now, they really needed protection.

'**Leave them alone,**' screamed Murzzzz.

'Murzzzz?' gasped Brenda.

'Murzzzz??' cried Charity. 'Wait, what's Murzzzz doing back here?'

'See what you did?' wailed the Manager, as Mister Peppermint flailed against the powerful Demon clawing at its face. 'You went and let Murzzzz escape! This is why I said not to intervene on this – it's delicate, and your department clearly has its own security issues.'

Darryl pulled his fangs and claws out from where they'd been uselessly accosting Mister Peppermint's leg, dropped to the ground and allowed himself to become human form once more.

'Dad?' he shouted.

Murzzzz glanced down at Darryl very briefly as he attacked, a delighted expression on his face. '**Son?**' he called.

'Not you!' yelled Darryl. 'Where's Dad-dad? Where's Richard?'

'**He's fine,**' shouted Murzzzz. '**We're us again, Darryl. The joy in us both!**'

'We were told you were captured! We were told you were being tortured!'

'**I was! I escaped. Came here on this one's shadow...**' Murzzzz barely stopped attacking Mister Peppermint to address it. '**Did you know you have the faces of two humans and a cuddly bear?**'

The Manager thrummed. 'Murzzzz, you were *told* about this. You were *warned* to stay in your own dimension.'

'How is torturing someone "warning" them?' called Janusz.

'You all know Murzzzz isn't supposed to be here,' continued the Manager. 'Charity could send him back?'

'Oh, no doubt,' shouted Charity, 'but I'm not going to – not least because he's stopping John Carpenter Presents Keira Knightley from "terminating" me for being faulty.'

'You wouldn't *be* faulty if you just did what you were chosen to do,' replied the Manager. 'You're supposed to bring balance and peace to the end. You're supposed to be a gentler, kinder alternative to... well, to entrails everywhere, like this Demon said. You're supposed to help me to help you: resolve the Red Sticker Issues and send Murzzzz and Grace Barry back to their homes so we can just end this mess and guide the produce towards Waste. And instead, you're just... being very annoying and making me look like a bad Manager in front of the other departments.'

'Ha ha,' replied Charity, in a mocking, sing-song voice.

Mister Peppermint crumpled to the ground with a horrible wail, still trying to protect its three faces against Murzzzz's furious attack.

'It was hard work creating a new door,' continued the Manager. 'I had to cull a load of produce prematurely, and now I find it lying in a pile in your universe! It's not supposed to be there!'

'You are not taking those poor people's lives today,' shouted Grace, punching a Demon back to its realm. 'You are not ending this world, not today, not if I have anything to do with it.'

'Grace Barry,' boomed the Manager, 'the situation has been explained to you, has it not? You were supposed to guide this unit, instead you have allowed them to guide you to... to chaos! You're faulty! All of you! The Death unit, Murzzzz, Grace Barry – all of you. Get it together right now, or... or, you're fired. I totally have a backup unit. It wouldn't be a problem to replace you at all.'

'**I don't work for you,**' snarled Murzzzz. '**You can't fire me.**'

'And from what I could tell from the Edendale meeting,' added Janusz, 'I think Grace actually outranks you, so you certainly can't "fire" her. Aren't you basically just a cosmic subcontractor?'

'I…' began the Manager, before pausing, briefly. A momentary hesitation that spoke a thousand words. It changed the subject, suddenly. 'Why,' it said, in a voice that vibrated its terrible glowing rings of flame and eyeballs, 'is there a *tree* in my *door*?'

'We are Old Jack,' said Old Jack in its thousand and one voices, that made Darryl's throat feel like it was full of splinters as it emanated from him. 'And we have been waiting very patiently. No more.'

And out scattered the ghosts, like a torrent of autumn leaves in a gale, out of Old Jack and through the Hell Hole, to the Manager's dimension.

'Stop,' cried the Manager, fruitlessly. 'Charity! You already sent all of the Coldbay produce to Head Office, we're still trying to process them all. This produce is supposed to go to Waste! Waste!'

'You told them to wait,' Charity told the Manager. 'You told all those spirits, in Coldbay and the ones here, to wait for you.'

'Yes, so I could use them to create doors! I didn't actually mean—'

'A good Manager follows through on their promises.'

'Not promises made to *produce*!'

'Is that all we are, to you?' The voices coming out of Darryl had dwindled to just one voice – the quietly angry little voice of Lil. As the ghosts poured out of Old Jack, the tree's trunk and shadowy boughs shrunk down to take the form of a small woman in a pinny and curlers. 'Just stuff? To be ignored and used?'

The Manager paused, again. 'You really think I'm the bad guy here, don't you?'

'You left us waiting and waiting. To create this… hole thingie in the sky without our permission.'

Another shape split from the dwindling trunk of Old Jack. It was Constance. Darryl allowed himself the slightest exhalation of relief that – whether it was due to a particularly strong sense of identity after death, her tenacity, or just an urge to linger around Charity – Constance still remained after all. It meant he didn't have to worry about how he was going to break it to his family how he'd let her leave the living realm. Also, it was nice that Constance hadn't been turned into part of a big spooky tree, he supposed.

Every soul that is going to the Manager's dimension is doing so out of choice, to try to have a little agency, to try to find answers that they'd been left waiting for in this world where they've been drifting in limbo with no purpose other than to wait for something that would never come. Lil still has purpose here – to oversee the undoing of the services, and the return of nature to this place. My purpose still lies in this world, as well. Charity is still here, and the rest of the Rooks, and Murzzzz. Even the Manager is here, right now. This world still contains the focus of all my love, and of all my rage.

Wait. Rage?

Yes! Rage! I'm angry. I'm actually angry, I thought the sadness wouldn't allow room for anger and yet yes, here it is! The thrill! The rush of fury!

The Longest Night. Was that Murzzzz's doing? Was it the Manager's fault? Was it a combination of both? Killing me? Killing my Harry? Taking our baby girl like she was a tool or a utility and handing her to someone else? Treating all of us like disposable things?

'Constance Xu,' boomed the Manager, 'before I'm blamed for your death as well as everything else, I had no part in what happened to you and your husband, I signed off on a completely different proposal, I was actually on your side. So, take it up with the Demons please and thank you.'

Darryl watched as Constance turned, and glared at Murzzzz.

'I am not a bad person,' continued the Manager.

'You're literally trying to end the world,' called Charity. 'Look at all the people you hurt doing it. And it's the second time in a week, at that!'

'We were waiting and waiting,' railed Lil. 'And then you call us "Produce"! Who put you in charge, anyway? You don't care!'

The Manager glowed bright. 'I do care! I do! Nobody had any of these issues with my management when I was just maintaining your reality. The Demons enjoyed all the extra leisure time they had to visit your dimension and play, the Executives enjoyed taking a back seat, without having to worry about ethics. And I was ethical! Produce was Produce – they didn't talk back, and the Death units did their jobs properly. Do you think Anubis kept whining and bringing people back from the dead? No they did not! It was efficient. No more suffering than was necessary. The reset is just an extension of that. A compassionate and efficient end. A bumper crop of produce, to keep the other departments sweet. A better end for the produce than the Demons ending it, or just… leaving it all to rot. *I* didn't set this date for termination arbitrarily, I was led by you people. When you all got to a point of no return where you'd completely wrecked your world, I tried to end it fairly, swiftly, without too much suffering. You think the other departments care if I let you lot choke your little planet to death as you boil yourselves alive? The Executives don't mind as long as produce keeps coming, and honestly the Demons prefer a protracted, miserable end of mortal reality because then there's more suffering for them to play with. And I'm starting to believe you lot are no better! If everything had ended with Coldbay, like it was meant to, the suffering here wouldn't have had to have happened. I could have just let the potential door over Helsbury go, same as all the other potential doors I've got on the simmer. Lil, Constance, you could be at peace by now, out in the gentle nothingness of Waste. But, no. Murzzzz and Grace Barry had to go rogue and lead the Death unit astray along with them, and now we have this wretched mess. And who ends up looking bad? Muggins, here. Even though I'm the one now stuck with thousands of unprocessed Produce cluttering up the Lavender Floor Break Room of *my office*. You know what? That Polar Bear Demon was right. You people are faulty. This isn't even the correct Death unit I signed off on. Charity, Darryl, you're fired. I have other options.'

'Fired?' cried Brenda. 'You can't just fire Death.'

'Yeah,' added Charity, 'you can't fire me, because I quit.'

'You quit?' sighed the Manager. 'You. You, who wanted to be The Chosen One your whole life, and then as soon as you discover that you actually *are*, you react by immediately doing the exact opposite of what you were chosen to do. And now you've decided – minutes later – that you want to quit.'

'Yeah,' replied Charity. 'Now that I've actually experienced it, I feel like being The Chosen One is overrated. It's overdone. I feel like I better fit the scrappy rebel superhero trope.'

'You are not a superhero!'

'Yeah, well. I'm not Death, either. I've decided.'

'No you haven't! *I* decided that!'

'Yes,' cried Brenda in proud delight, 'that's my girl!'

'Don't you start, Mum,' Charity replied, 'I'm still really pissed off at you.'

'Honestly,' continued the Manager, 'I probably should have done this a while ago. But I didn't. Because I'm nice. So there

211

you go. Demons, the Rooks are no longer the Death unit, so you can stop complaining about them to me. Just leave them be or destroy them. Don't care. Executives, you can extract Grace Barry from the Rooks yourselves. Rooks, you can go back to just being the workaday ghost hunters you thought you were this morning. The end of the world is officially no longer your problem. So wind your collective necks in. And now *if* you will excuse me, *I* have a break room full of mortal souls to deal with.'

And then, the Manager was simply no longer there. The Hell Hole swirled into a vast, empty chamber of perfectly clean, bright, uncomfortable lines, with an empty beanbag – the ultimate ideal of beanbaggy impracticality – in the centre.

'Is... that it?' asked Grace. 'Did we just have to really annoy the Manager until the end of the world just... stopped?'

The Manager was suddenly there again, thrumming with irritation. The family collectively sighed in disappointment.

'No!' snapped the Manager. 'No, that's not it! You mortals have still irrevocably broken your world. I'm still resetting and there will still be a Death unit. It's just not you any more. I'm giving it to the runner up... or at least the runner up to the unit *I* signed off on. Because you know what the alternative to resetting the universe is?'

'People get to carry on with their lives?' asked Charity.

'Rot,' replied the Manager. 'Murzzzz knows what rot looks like – true rot. Do you? Do you even know what I'm saving you people from?'

'**Leave them be,**' shouted Murzzzz. '**You've put them through enough.**'

'I would,' replied the Manager. 'But honestly, Murzzzz, I am fuming right now. They need to see. They need to see that I'm right.'

And, it was gone again. This time, the gleaming impractical lines of Head Office were gone, with it. Instead, something new began to stream from the Hell Hole. The colourful neon lights in the pumps flickered out. Algae and rust crept from the corners of the pumps. The tarmac beneath their feet began to crack. The canopy, still covered in hundreds of unconscious human beings, began to groan and crumple.

The Hell Hole was pouring out time. It was pouring out entropy. It was pouring out neglect. It was pouring out rot.

CHAPTER EIGHTEEN

Rot

'Everyone else seeing this?' Darryl asked.

The others nodded.

'It's really happening,' added Janusz. 'The Manager is throwing another tantrum. It's going to destroy this place. But we've got all those people to save, this time. What do we do?'

The rot flooding out of the hole seemed to only be affecting the structure of the petrol forecourt rather than them so hopefully it wouldn't be affecting the people dumped onto the canopy, Darryl thought. But he had no idea how long that would last, and besides, there was also the issue of how much the canopy was groaning and drooping with sudden rust and wear. The thought of those poor people being rescued from the nothingness of Waste, only to succumb to decay was horrific enough but just as horrific was the threat of them collapsing several metres onto a dozen pumps – now starting to fall apart but surely still full of fuel – along with tonnes of splintered metal, plastic, and, crucially, an electricity source. It would only take one spark to turn this wave of destruction into a real 'entrails everywhere' affair.

'We have to get them out of here,' Darryl shouted. But how? These weren't ghosts, these were flesh and blood people and really, not his family's forte at all.

'Murzzzz?' asked Brenda. 'How many can you move at a time?'

Murzzzz was already bounding towards the canopy. '**Twenty at a time, perhaps?**' replied the Demon. '**Darryl, can you help?**'

Darryl could help. Not as many as Murzzzz, but maybe he could save five or six? Maybe, if he just took the kids, he could rescue a few more? Urgh, he hated this. He hated that they might not have time to save everyone and would have to choose. He hated that the choice would come down to himself and a Demon. He also hated how easy it was to slide into Demon form and he hated that Murzzzz was already calling on him to be his little half-Demon sidekick, as if that was just the way it was always supposed to be. In fact, he hated that Murzzzz was just *here* again, within Darryl's father, without so much as a by-your-leave, without consulting anyone… He'd think about it later and he would sulk about it later – and yes, there would be sulking. For now, he'd just have to swallow all of these feelings, change yet again, and…

'Murzzzz?' Grace stepped forwards. She looked exhausted from the fight. Her coat was torn and her hair was in disarray. Grace had been having, contemplated Darryl, quite a day of it. They'd all been having quite a day of it, but honestly if Darryl had had Grace's levels of day today, he'd have needed a quiet sit down about it by now. And yet, there was a fresh determination to the little not-a-priest. There was something about her voice that carried, that jangled the mind. There was something about the look in her eyes that hurt. 'If you could stand aside,' she asked, and the authority to her tone made even the Demon part of Darryl feel that ignoring her request would be agony.

Murzzzz stopped, just short of leaping up to the groaning canopy, and turned to look at Grace. The Demon's expression was strangely meek – like a little kid who'd been told to stop running by a favourite teacher.

'I found you,' Grace told the bodies… No. She wasn't talking to the bodies. She was talking to the bodies' lost souls, right on the other side of the motorway. Her voice wasn't loud, it was level and calm, but Darryl could feel the size of it. It was a soft announcement that carried over a huge distance. It was a tide, lapping gently at a distant shore after starting out far at sea, pulled by the moon. 'You need to wake up,' she said, 'and you need to get away.'

And inevitably like the moon's silent tug flooding a wet beach hundreds of thousands of miles away, the canopy and all the people on it did as they were told. They simply went away.

'Er,' said Darryl, looking at the empty space where an awful lot of comatose people and rusting metal had just been.

'Did you,' breathed Brenda with more than a hint of admiration, 'just do that with willpower alone?'

'I don't know how I did it,' replied Grace, her tone returning to its usual setting of vague anxiousness. 'But I don't like it.'

Darryl still gawped at the forecourt. The petrol pumps were continuing to rust and crumble before his eyes. The stubby bottoms of the pillars that had, up until now, held the canopy aloft ended in jagged plinths of rusty metal after only about a foot, now covered in algae and choked with weeds.

Like so many mortal empires that came before, 'My name is Shell Oil, king of kings. Look on my works, ye mighty, and despair.'

'We really should get out of here too, you know,' said Janusz. 'Really. Right now.'

The roof of the little shop attached to the forecourt caved in with a crash, broken beneath the weight of decades of neglect that had been concentrated into a few seconds. The electric lights inside sparked dangerously.

Janusz turned to the others, urgently. 'Really, *really* right now!'

Olivia woke up, which was weird, because she didn't remember going to sleep. The last thing she could remember was calling for a customer named Yasmina to come and collect her soy macchiato.

And this was not even the weirdest thing about her situation. Instead of being in the food hall at her kiosk, she was outside, in the thin November drizzle. She was in a huge pile of strange people, with a middle-aged lady groaning faintly underneath her and an unhurt but terrified child in her lap, wearing a *Guardians of the Galaxy* T-shirt. She was not usually on top of a middle-aged lady, and the only time she ever had a child on her lap was when she saw her nephews. This was not one of her nephews. She was also several metres up in the air, on top of a very old, very messed-up flat roof. It made a horrible, grating sound, and whatever had been holding the roof up buckled underneath them. The pile of people screamed – Olivia included. She tried to push herself off the woman and hold on tightly to the kid as she fell. Helplessly, they all crashed to the ground. It was an unpleasant jolt, but mercifully not a freefall – as if whatever was holding them up had collapsed at the knees. Their landing was into really rather a lot of mud which spattered everywhere, like a mortar hitting a trench in an overzealous World War One movie. Something on the side of the roof came off it at the impact and slid away as Olivia watched, mesmerised. It skidded to a slow, sad stop, coated in mud. A huge plastic shell shape – yellow, rimmed with red.

Wait, was this the petrol station? What was she doing in the petrol station? And what were all these other people doing in the petrol station? And what was the petrol station doing in a wet field? She wiped the mud off her face and tried to look around. There was hazy grey and a dark, damp green in almost every direction, punctuated by the off-white blobs of some very startled looking sheep in a field nearby. As she craned her head around, she could just about make out a thin river of flowing white and red lights in the distance – the motorway. As she ran her gaze along the motorway, she could pick out something squat, angular and a slightly different grey-green to the rest of the environment. Was that the services? But it had to be a good mile away – maybe more.

''Scuse me?' said the middle-aged woman, still sort-of underneath Olivia. 'Do you know what's going on?'

Olivia shook her head. No, she did not. There were only two things she knew for sure right now. One: she was going to tell Narin how she felt. Two: she was getting a new job.

'Oh,' said the woman, sounding put out that Olivia didn't know why she was suddenly part of a frightened mound of people in the middle of bloody nowhere.

On the horizon, worryingly near to the squat dark building that was probably Helsbury Services, something quite big exploded. People screamed. Olivia didn't. She hugged the panicking child and told herself that yep, she was *definitely* getting a new job.

The screams died down, and the child spotted a frightened man who had his eyes – eyes that were red and wet with gratitude as he scooped his son out of Olivia's arms. Amongst the families and friends emotionally finding one another, an awkward silence descended amongst people like Olivia who didn't have family or friends here to find. She just sat for a while, bewildered, wondering what to do now.

'Well,' said the similarly lost-looking woman after a while, 'do you at least have my coffee? I ordered a soy macchiato ages ago.'

The family ran. Brenda kicked off her high heels to make it across the warping, cracking tarmac without tripping. She didn't have time to pick them up and carry them. A perfectly good pair of Marksies stilettos, lost forever. She knew that if she complained about it, her family would – yet again – advise flats for work, but honestly, what was the point of living if one had to do it in sensible loafers?

Even Constance wafted along with them at speed, as they tried to make ground between themselves and the imminent explosion that was the collapsing remains of the petrol station. The only one who didn't move was Lil. Brenda glanced back as she scrambled over the weed-choked ridge that separated the petrol forecourt from the car park and saw the little ghost, resplendent in her pinny and curlers, with an expression of total bliss on her face as she watched the forecourt crumble to nothing. She was getting her way, at long last. The buildings she'd fought against for so long were being removed, the metal and glass and plastic that had been jammed into her home against her will were finally being extracted. It was like shrapnel being pulled from a wound. Brenda hoped that the sight of it would finally bring Lil peace.

Eurgh. Since when had she started worrying herself about ghosts finding peace? Honestly, she blamed Darryl for this nonsense.

The tarmac was falling into ruin so fast that it seemed alive. It buckled under like untreated subsidence, slanting this way and that. Brenda watched as sinkhole caved away into nothing, right in front of Darryl, causing Janusz to yelp and yank his husband out of harm's way. Darryl put his arm around Janusz, gratefully. At this point they all knew Darryl could easily just go Demon again and leap over it but, if it made the husbands happy for Janusz to play the big dashing hero, then where was the harm in it, right? It was, as little as Brenda wanted to admit to it out loud, a sweet gesture. Brenda remained grateful that Darryl of all people had landed himself a Janusz. It was the sort of idle, fond thought more suited to a family dinner over wine, or even a family brunch… over wine – and not so much for a race for their life across a warping car park away from a forecourt of twenty petrol pumps that was about to—

And that's when the petrol forecourt exploded.

They say that cool guys don't look back at explosions. Well, nobody in their party was particularly cool and all of them looked over their shoulders at the pluming fire and smoke, and had a good swear about it in English and Polish. Even Murzzzz said something in Demon language that was so terrible it made all the weeds in a three-metre radius curl up and go crispy.

'Keep running,' shouted Darryl, even though yes, that was obvious and they were already running as fast as they could.

'OK,' panted Charity, 'but in my head, we're all walking away from this in slow motion.'

They approached the door to the services' main building. The man in brown was still there, pipe dangling from horror-slackened lips as he stared out of the murky glass, aghast.

'I'm sorry,' Darryl told the man in brown as they entered and hurried past. 'It's over.'

The man in brown looked around himself, his expression set in sorrow and loss. The rot was still spreading. It corroded the door behind them as black mould climbed the walls. Perhaps the rot had always been here, Brenda wondered. Perhaps the monster had not been Old Jack out in the smoking shelter, spreading roots and tendrils, but the services itself. Squatting on the land, refuelling transient cars and their drivers, home to nobody – in fact, by its very nature, a place that was not home, but rather a waiting area for the exhausted, the stressed, and those who wanted to get away from there as quickly as possible. Temporary yet permanent. A nowhere space. A mortal manifestation of Limbo. Or, maybe she was just being overly dramatic about a building for people to stop for a wee and buy some Lilt. Again, she blamed Darryl.

There was one matter Darryl was definitely right about, though: whatever Helsbury had been, it was over, now. The rot wasn't stopping at the door. It was spreading through the whole building. The man in brown had been here from the start, when they'd had such high hopes. He'd remained here as the place had declined, albeit at a far slower pace than it was doing now. Had he been aware of the slow rot? Had he persisted in seeing a gleaming glass temple all this while, or had he noticed the paint fade and the damp set in but tried to ignore what was happening? Well. There was no ignoring it now. Brenda was suddenly, acutely aware of the fact that the man in brown wanted to leave. His cathedral was broken and he saw no point in remaining in its ruin.

'Charity, love?' asked Brenda.

Charity gave her a faintly dirty look. Right, so Charity still wasn't happy with her about the whole 'Constance' thing. That was probably fair. But, it wasn't this man's fault. She grabbed Charity and positioned her in front of the man.

'This one wants to pop off. If you wouldn't mind…?'

She suddenly had a worrying thought. She didn't know if Charity could even still expel spirits. Her daughter had been Death, all along, and Brenda hadn't figured it out. And now, Charity had been fired… or had quit, depending on who you asked. What if the Manager had stripped her of all her psychic powers, just like that? What if she now had to deal with her daughter's grief at her lost abilities, as well as trying to do something about the imminent end of the world with no Deliverer? What if—

Charity held her hands out to the man and popped him away as easily as if he were a soap bubble.

'Done,' she announced.

Oh, OK, fair enough. Well, at least that was one less thing to worry about, wasn't it?

'Guys.' Janusz grabbed Brenda and Charity by the shoulders. 'Come on. The Manager's destroying this whole place, like Coldbay, and our getaway vehicle's still on the other side of the road.'

The food hall was making some very upsetting noises, as its structure began to disintegrate. The ceiling groaned and sagged and corroded pipes began to spurt water of dubious cleanliness. The piped festive music grew more tinny than usual, before turning into an unpleasant electronic static, right as Paul McCartney was in the middle of telling the world what a simply wonderful Christmas time he was having. The family hurried along, through the food hall, filled with mould and moss with the occasional McCartney vowel breaking through the audible fuzz. It was filled with ghosts who had been lingering for years, with their flares and their wet-look perms. Brenda still had a persistent sense of the dead wanting to leave now that the services were decaying away. For a multitude of reasons, they had been waiting at Helsbury Services, but there would soon be no more Helsbury Services for them to wait at.

'They all want to go,' muttered Darryl, before Brenda could even mention it. He glanced at Janusz. 'Do we have time?'

Janusz sighed. 'To help the lost? Always.'

'Aww,' cooed Darryl.

'Still annoyed with you,' Janusz reminded him.

Her children moved as fast as they could from ghost to ghost through the food court, with Darryl manoeuvring Charity around as she held out her arms blindly to pop the dead away to Waste. It was just like in the good old days, she thought, when the kids were younger and didn't answer back, and there was none of this 'half-Demon and freshly sacked Grim Reaper' nonsense to contend with. In spite of the kids doing their best, it still took a few minutes to make it to the stairs up to the walkway, while all around them windows and walls cracked, letting in noxious fumes from the continuing inferno. The smoking ghost, that poor cleaner, the panicky lad with the knife, all the others that had been stuck here for years, they were gone, now. At peace, or whatever approximation of peace was to be found in Waste.

'Come on!' Janusz grabbed Darryl's hand at the stairwell.

Murzzzz, anxious to escape the rot, was first to bound up the stairs, landing halfway up after one leap. The step collapsed into a sad heap of damp splinters as he landed on it.

'**Uh,**' he managed through his surprise, '**watch your step. Stairs are rotten.**'

'Yeah,' added Darryl, ascending the stairs rather more carefully, 'nobody jump on them with great big Demon feet.'

Murzzzz pulled the most sheepish expression it was possible for a powerful and ancient Demon, who has seen countless civilisations rise and fall, to pull on being mildly rebuked for breaking a stair. He continued the scramble up to the footbridge pressed down flat on his belly, his limbs scuttling out at his side like an alligator's, distributing his weight as evenly as possible.

'There were a few more long-haul ghosts up here too,' added Darryl as the family climbed. 'Guy watching the motorway, lady in paisley, kid in a Nirvana T-shirt.'

'You never know, Nirvana Boy could have been one of the fresh ones that we just saved,' said Charity. 'They're like The Beatles, aren't they – lead singer long dead, band long gone, but the T-shirts endure.'

'This is true,' Janusz added. 'You have a Nirvana T-shirt.'

'Yeah, but only for sleeping in… Oh, crap.'

Brenda gingerly joined the others on the footbridge. Oh crap, indeed. The whole bridge was bowing dangerously in the middle. Murzzzz, still flat, tried shifting back into Richard, which didn't help matters at all.

'Er, no,' managed Richard, in a panic and unable to get out of the alligator stance, 'can you do this bit, please?' And he changed back into the Demon.

There was the ghost of the youth in a Nirvana T-shirt, as well as the anxious-looking woman in paisley and the man in a shell suit gazing out at the motorway, hands still on the cracking glass. The motorway below was no longer the twin flowing streams of fast traffic. The cars and lorries were crawling through the smoke from the petrol station fire. Brenda hadn't even thought about that – hadn't contemplated that human civilisation was still trying to pass by this haunted place on a dangerously busy road. She realised that the Manager's little hissy fit could cause even more death below.

'What do we do?' Brenda asked. She turned to Grace. 'Could you do your trick, again? Like with the canopy?'

'It wasn't a "trick"! It's… I don't know what it was. Some sort of Celestial Will. I wanted them to move to a safe spot, so they did.'

'And could you want to put that fire out? Could you want to stop this rot? Overrule the Manager entirely, even?'

'I don't know,' fretted Grace. 'I don't know what I can do. I barely know what I am, besides a… a priest suit that some otherworldly stranger inside of me is wearing, and—'

'OK fine, *don't* put the fire out, then.' Brenda nodded at a set of flashing blue lights approaching. 'Nee-naws are coming, anyway.'

'Oh good,' breathed the not-a-priest.

'So, stand down on the Celestial Willpower,' continued Brenda, 'we don't need it this time, at least.' She very carefully and slowly started walking along the sagging bridge and thought about what a coincidence it was that fire engines had started arriving the very moment she'd asked if Grace could do something about the fire. 'You could maybe Willpower this bridge into being a little less structurally unsound?' she asked. 'Charity, princess, there's a woman in front of you and a fellow up against the window on your right. The fire's upsetting them and they want to leave.'

Charity popped the woman in paisley directly in front of her, then brushed a hand along the window until it sank into the ghostly form of the distressed shell suit wearer at the window. She concentrated and pushed, and the man popped away, right as the whole pane of glass smashed against her hand. She screamed a little, drawing her hand back in shock. Brenda watched helplessly as great shards of glass fell from the bridge towards the trapped traffic below.

'Murzzzz,' screamed Darryl. 'Help them…'

But Murzzzz was already gone – leaping straight through the broken window, snatching glass out of the air in his huge claws. Brenda hoped that the smoke was thick enough for none of the drivers to have seen that.

There was a thunk, and the sound of complaining, rusting metal. Brenda could see distinct dents in the floor of the bridge where Murzzzz had grabbed hold of the underside of it from outside.

'**Go**,' cried the Demon. '**Whole thing's coming apart!**'

The rest of the family ran. The bridge buckled and swayed, dangerously. A huge crack opened up in the middle of the floor, between the dents. Looking back, Brenda could just about make out through it that Murzzzz was now all that was holding the bridge together. From the way the thing was moving, they surely only had a matter of seconds before the whole bridge just fell apart. Nirvana Boy was still standing in their path, looking sad and frightened. She was sorry for him, truly she was, but if they didn't get off here right now, not only would the family be killed, but surely several motorists below would be crushed by the bridge as well. Lives were at risk, so they just couldn't spare the time to help him out.

Darryl grabbed his sister as they ran, and shoved her towards Nirvana Boy. 'There! Help him out!'

'Nirvana Boy?' Charity asked. Without even waiting for an answer, she held out her hand into the youth. 'Off you go, love.' The boy vanished in an instant.

OK, well maybe they *could* spare the time to help him out, after all. Brenda and Grace overtook the kids, and Janusz desperately held out his hand again to hurry Darryl along.

'If you see Kurt,' called Charity into the empty space behind them, 'tell him "Violet" was an epic tune.'

'That was Courtney Love,' Darryl told her, dragging her onwards.

Brenda reached the stairwell, with Grace and looked back. The bridge lurched suddenly, ripping itself away from the stairwell, leaving a gap of about a foot between them and the others. Charity leaped and just about made it, tumbling painfully to her hands and knees right at the edge. Behind them, Murzzzz wailed with effort at keeping the bridge from falling to the motorway. Darryl and Janusz leaped together, and at that moment, the bridge jerked at a wild angle, knocking both men off their trajectory.

'No!' Brenda instinctively held a helping hand out towards them, but they were too far away, they weren't going to make it. Darryl screamed, and his body blurred as he took on Demon form, before reaching out with one long limb to grab the broken wall of the stairwell and the other to grab Janusz's wrist. Sharp claws on one Demonic hand anchored like knives into the concrete, and, automatically, the knife-like claws on the other hand sank into Janusz's flesh. Darryl's husband cried out in pain. Darryl's eyes widened in panic, and became human again... human, and so physically weaker – certainly not strong enough to keep himself latched to a wall with one hand while holding a full-grown man dangling in mid-air by the other. Brenda grabbed her son around the waist, and Grace grabbed Brenda to steady her. Charity reached down and grabbed Janusz's other hand.

'Heave,' shouted Charity, and they did.

Janusz and Darryl were hauled up to safety, blood pooling out of the claw wounds on Janusz's arm still clasped beneath Darryl's now human hand.

'Baby, I'm sorry,' breathed Darryl, trying to wipe away the blood.

'You saved me.'

'I hurt you! I... that *thing* hurt you.'

''Tis but a scratch,' smiled Janusz through the pain.

At that moment, the bridge completely gave way. With a tremendous cry of effort, Murzzzz landed on the roof of a slow-moving lorry below, the broken halves of the bridge raised above his head, then leaped up high, swung the bridge and threw it. The two halves of bridge span magnificent arcs through the air before crashing to their final resting places in a nearby field, harming nobody and nothing except for whichever farmer owned that field and now had the logistical nightmare of getting a very broken, very rusted footbridge off their land.

'It's not *just* a scratch,' protested Darryl back on the stairwell.

'He was quoting *Monty Python*,' Charity told him.

'Shut up, Charity, you don't know the difference between Nirvana and Hole.'

'You can't expect me to just know the difference between old bands, Darryl. I'm a busy former Grim Reaper.'

Murzzzz landed on the stairwell with them. That too was beginning to crumble.

'Blimey, this is all very *Tomb Raider*, isn't it?' added Charity. 'Come on!'

They continued the race against the spreading rot at their heels, hurtling down the stairs that crumbled every time Murzzzz accidentally put his full Demon weight on them. They burst into the food hall on the other side. Thankfully there were now far fewer distressed spirits than had filled the place before, since the few hundred new ghosts had been rammed back into their bodies and flung into a field. The food hall still smelled tantalisingly of the lovely booze that Brenda had had to use up fighting off the first wave of Demons. She was struck again by the horrible realisation that she was still stone cold sober. It really wasn't fair.

The handful of older ghosts that remained were watching the decay spreading fast through the building and radiating that same feeling that Brenda had felt in the others – a realisation that they had been waiting too long, in this transient place. Waiting for help and guidance that had never come. And now, this octagonal limbo was disintegrating away. Their wait was over. Like everybody who ever stops at a service station, they had to continue on their way. Brenda knew that Darryl could pick up on the feeling too. She expected him to usher Charity to them, as he had been doing, but her son was still clasping his husband's bleeding wrist and apologising as he ran – too distracted by his own misery to help with anybody else's. Brenda took hold of the faintly protesting Charity and guided her into the casino corner. The few remaining unhappy spirits of dead gamblers disappeared easily into Waste, as the fruit machines corroded before their eyes. The flashing neon lights fizzled out, along with the electronic bleeps and bells promising all the good times and fortunes that a roadside fruit machine could possibly provide. *The Simpsons* themed machine by the door went out just as Charity sent away the final casino ghost. The colourful buttons, which up until now had been merrily depicting the cartoon family enjoying hijinks with their little cartoon friends, went dark, and the endlessly looping burst of the show's jaunty theme tune slurred into something eerily slow and deep, before falling mercifully silent. There was something peaceful about the darkened corner now, in spite of the crawling rot drawing a long, dangerous crack along the ceiling. The brief sensation of peace was shattered by Constance manifesting in front of Brenda suddenly and gesticulating wildly for them to get out of there.

'Yes, yes,' said Brenda, turning with Charity to run and join the others, 'we were just going. Honestly.'

There were a few more ghosts to help on the way out. Some were near the poster for the *Mister Peppermint* movie – now missing the pictures of its two stars and winsome CGI bear. There were a couple next to the WHSmith display racks selling neck pillows and – for reasons Brenda *still* couldn't understand

– wetsuits. And one by the wrecked and raided coffee stand. The rot crept over the coffee concession as Brenda watched, turning the one remaining muffin into a shrivelled green husk, and collapsing the merry red Christmassy paper cups into mulch. The family hurried to the door, which fell off its hinges as soon as Charity pushed it.

The smoke wasn't quite so bad on this side of the motorway, but it still choked the throat and stung the eyes. The car park's tarmac on this side was warped and sprouting weeds just like the other one. As they hurried away from the service station, one of its walls collapsed, taking a chunk of roof along with it. Murzzzz looked back at the collapse, shifted in focus, and became visible as Richard again. Brenda always likened the shifts between Murzzzz and Richard to one of those optical illusions where you could make yourself see an old woman or a young woman depending on how you thought about it. Both were always there, even if you could only see one at a time. Of course, up until very recently, both had *not* been there, and frankly both Richard and Murzzzz still owed everybody an explanation as to why he was back inside her husband without consulting the family.

Richard indicated vaguely to the collapsed wall. 'That's a subsidence issue, that is. It's a miracle they hadn't had any major structural problems before this, frankly. Right.' He fished in his zip-up jacket pocket and pulled out the car key. 'Car. Let's get out of here.'

As they approached where Richard had parked the car, Brenda allowed herself to wonder – what if this wasn't like Coldbay after all? What if the Manager didn't intend to simply swallow up the haunted hotspot of misery it had created to open the Hell Hole? What if the rot spread beyond Helsbury? What if it kept chasing them? What if it covered the whole world? What if this was it? What if—

'No!'

Richard broke into a sprint. All of the cars in the car park were rusted and broken, and Richard's new car was no exception. The tyres were flat, and the exhaust was hanging off. He no longer had to worry about the bright red colour being a bit too garish or making the car look like a Royal Mail van, since the rot had faded the remaining paint that hadn't simply corroded away.

'My car,' he wailed. 'That was new! I only *just* wrangled the insurance for the last car, they're never going to believe it happened again!'

Murzzzz briefly shifted into view. '**Ooh, you bought yourself a Citroen?**'

Richard shifted back. 'Yeah, although I never really thought I could pull it off.'

Murzzzz came back. '**No, no, I can see you driving a French car. *Very* "ooh la la".**'

'Not now,' snapped Brenda. She stood and watched, as smoke still billowed, and the rot continued to collapse the services building. Masonry crashed to the ground. In the car park, vehicles fell off their corroded axes. When would this stop? How would this stop? She suddenly felt horribly cold. She tried to rub her arms but her coat fell apart, rotted away. It was spreading to them. It was spreading to all of them. Maybe this was the end, after all.

CHAPTER NINETEEN

Death

Thirty years ago

'I'd say it's got about another three decades,' said the Celestial Executive.

'Yes,' replied the Manager, testily. 'Although some might say that's towards the more pessimistic end of the scale. The consensus suggests it's more like sixty years or so.'

By 'the consensus', the Manager meant 'what the Manager thought'. And frankly, the Manager believed that that was a much more informed opinion than that of a Celestial who had literally just wafted in to Head Office – all eye-achingly beautiful and powerful and whatnot – and started telling the Manager how to do the job that the Manager had been doing for the entire cycle of this mortal universe's existence. To its chagrin, the Manager also knew enough about the job to be wearily aware that, if the Celestials said the mortal realm only had three decades left, they expected the Manager to ensure it would end in three decades' time, and no later.

'I mean,' added the Manager, with dwindling hope, 'they didn't blow themselves up, this time.'

'More's the pity,' sighed the Demon delegate. Demons loved it when the humans blew themselves up.

'They still could,' replied the Celestial. 'Bombs are all still there.'

The Demon beamed.

'But that stand-off's all over now,' the Manager told them.

'Is it, though?' asked the Celestial.

'Yes, they knocked down a wall in Germany – it was a whole thing.'

'Listen,' said the Celestial, 'I don't know what a "Jemminy" is so whatever. Point is, bombs are still there, that ozone hole is getting bigger, and then there's the carbon dioxide thing.'

'Yeah,' sighed the Manager. 'The carbon dioxide will probably be what does it.'

'So, termination plans are in place?' the Celestial asked.

'Yes, of course,' huffed the Manager. It was the Manager's job after all, for crying out loud. Creator, Maintainer, Destroyer – that's what the subcontract said.

'We still have a few of our people down there,' added the Demon.

Well, of course the Demons still had 'a few of their people down there'. They always did. One of the hardest aspects of the Manager's job was that the Demons didn't just see the mortal realm as a power source, they saw it as a playground. They were constantly scampering over there for little pleasure trips, having fun tormenting the mortals and drinking up the misery they caused like a holiday daiquiri. And the Manager couldn't say boo to them because the Demon Department was one of his clients. He already knew the arguments they'd come up with. This was one of the reasons they got the Manager to organise the mortal universe this time instead of doing it themselves. Yes, it was technically to cause fewer bust-ups with the Celestials, but also it gave the Demons much more leisure time to play, and go on their little jaunts. The Demon Department would also swear blind that it was only ever quick little trips and no harm done, even though the Manager knew full well that several Demons had been knocking around the mortal universe for thousands of years. One had even Spawned. Hence his current Death unit plans.

'For the Death unit there's a couple of options,' said the Manager. 'Patel has the potential to be a very good all-rounder, but I'd prefer to combine Xu and Rook.'

The Demon and the Celestial looked at the Manager, curiously.

'Rook?' asked the Celestial.

'As in, Murzzzz's wife?' asked the Demon.

'Actually, I'm talking about the children. The Xu girl has excellent prospects and the Rook child.'

'You want part of your Death unit to be Demon Spawn?' the Celestial asked, incredulously.

'I thought it would be fitting,' the Manager told them. 'And, he *is* mostly human. And he would be raised by human parents, of course.'

'So,' replied the Demon, 'when you say "combine Xu and Rook"…'

'Brenda Rook and Constance Xu are working together at present,' the Manager told them. 'Perhaps if a large party of Demons were to go to the mortal realm and… get a little rowdy? You need to extract Murzzzz before the end anyway, so we may as well kill two birds with one stone, as it were…' The Manager rumbled a laugh at its own joke. The Celestial and the Demon just stared blankly. 'Because "Rooks" are a type of bird, you see.'

The Demon didn't even smile. It was a good pun, thought the Manager. For pity's sake, these people were impossible.

'So,' confirmed the Demon, 'you want us to kill Brenda and Richard Rook.'

'Yes. Constance and Harry Xu will adopt the Spawn rather than let him go to humans who don't understand his powers, so in thirty to forty years' time we will have a solid sister and brother Death unit in Charity and Darryl Xu.'

'It's worth a try, I suppose,' said the Demon. 'We do need to pull Murzzzz out of this ridiculous extended sabbatical he's been having, and my guys do enjoy getting rowdy and killy.'

'And if it doesn't work out?' asked the Celestial.

'There's always Patel as a failsafe,' said the Manager. 'We'll leave him to get on with things for now, but I can activate him as the backup any time.'

'Fine,' said the Celestial. 'We'll allow you to sign off on the Xu–Rook idea.'

Oh, the Manager was being *allowed* to sign off on its own plans, was it? How *magnanimous* of the Celestials.

'We always have suits to help out down there if it looks like you're struggling,' continued the Celestial. 'Oh, just one more note – not forty years, that is too long. If you could start the proceedings in twenty-five years or so?'

'So,' replied the Manager, '2016-ish?'

'Yeah. Ish. Because it takes a few years for everything to snowball to a point where you can actually terminate, you see. May as well get it in early, especially since this is your first apocalypse.'

'Possibly your only apocalypse,' added the Demon, 'depending on how it goes.'

'You're doing great,' added the Celestial, in a tone that dazzled, but didn't quite reassure. 'I'm sure the end of the world will all go swimmingly.'

*

But it hadn't gone swimmingly. The Manager blamed Murzzzz. Murzzzz could have gone back peacefully. He could have adhered to the plan. But, no. He'd been so 'attached' to his human host and the woman he'd spawned with that he'd sacrificed the Xus in order to save the adult Rooks, and the Manager's preferred Death unit had ended up all back to front. Well, no more. The Manager was miffed. The Manager wasn't the smiting type, at all, but still. It was miffed. Failed doors needed to be expunged anyway, but the Manager had to admit, it found it cathartic to expunge this one with rot. Especially with the Rooks and Murzzzz and that ridiculous rogue Grace Barry to witness it, because they would realise that, if they carried on resisting the mortal world's termination, this was what awaited them. Rot. A decline which, while certainly not 'gradual' in the grand scheme of things, would draw out the suffering of the end. The Manager's original plan had been benevolent and merciful. These people didn't know what was good for them. These people were impossible! Well, they could watch the rot. They could watch their transport fall apart and their clothes fall off their bodies. Maybe the Manager would make their hair and teeth fall out, to teach them a lesson, maybe they could lose a couple of fingers, maybe—

'Enough.'

The voice was calm and gentle, and spoken from some distance away, and yet it carried, directly through the half-collapsed Hell Hole and straight into the Manager's mind.

Grace Barry stood in the car park at the opposite side of the motorway, surrounded by rusted cars. Her coat was decomposing and falling off her shoulders in shreds.

'You've made your point,' said Grace Barry. 'We're all very impressed. Now, pack it in.'

And, since it was the will of a Celestial Executive – even a rogue one like Grace Barry – for the Manager to 'pack it in', then the Manager had to 'pack it in'.

Fine. Fine! With a huff that huffed across the mortal universe, the Manager stopped the rot from pouring out of the door. The Manager had important work to do now, anyway. It closed the door over Helsbury. It would certainly see the Rooks again, especially since they still had a Celestial and a Demon as hangers-on, but they were no longer the Manager's issue to try to manage. It would simply go with its backup plan. Its secret weapon, the young man who had been quietly honing his skills as both a Finder and a Deliverer for decades now, thousands of miles away from the Rook family. They had no idea. They had no idea what terrible new Grim Reaper they had imposed upon the mortal world.

In a small, sunny first-floor apartment on the outskirts of Winnipeg, it was a little after nine in the morning, and Krish Patel was having his breakfast. Cornflakes with almond milk, Fairtrade OJ in his second favourite cup and a vegan croissant with a nice bit of homemade conserve as a treat. It had been a tiring job last night – getting the ghost to leave that nice old lady's house – and he needed carbs today to build his strength back up. It had been worth it, of course. It was a lonely job, ghost hunting, but he always took such satisfaction from the relief he brought to others. Clients who'd spent weeks, even months, being tormented by the paranormal until they contacted him – often as a last resort. But also, the ghosts themselves often seemed relieved. There was a desperation to them that Krish could feel. It had definitely been getting worse, too, for a while now. Since, ooh, 2016 he reckoned. On the rare occasion that he swapped notes with other ghost hunters, they said they'd felt it recently too – well, everyone except Aurora Tavistock, but she was apparently too busy to get back to him, as she was doing the rounds on breakfast TV telling people she was in touch with the spirit of Lady Di. Krish was pretty sure that Aurora Tavistock was a fraud.

He scrolled the news on his phone. Climate crisis, economic crisis, climate crisis, war, pandemic, ramped-up tension between superpowers, climate crisis...

His phone froze. 'Dangit!' Krish tried jabbing at it with his thumb. Nothing.

Well. Nothing for a second or two, at least. Then it went on fire.

'Argh!' He dropped the burning phone onto the table and then, realising that dropping a burning electrical item onto a wooden table wasn't the best idea under any circumstance, let alone when your apartment and all the furniture therein were rentals, shoved his croissant into his mouth and tried to use the plate to scooch the unfortunate phone into an empty saucepan.

His morning had taken a really weird turn. So, obviously, things immediately got weirder. The fire engulfing his phone in the saucepan spoke to him.

'Krish Patel?' it boomed, vibrating the whole pan.

'Mmf?' replied Krish, his mouth still full of croissant.

'Try not to be afraid,' said the talking saucepan full of fire, in spite of the obvious.

'Mmf!' was all that Krish could say in reply.

'Here's the thing, Krish,' said the saucepan, 'I've got a little bit of bad news, but also quite a lot of good news. Let's start off with something nice. Have you ever thought about visiting Britain? I hear it's lovely this time of year.'

*

This particular part of Britain at this time of year, was not lovely at all. At this time of year, this particular part of Britain was a cold, damp rectangle of warped, weed-choked tarmac covered in wrecked cars, with a collapsing ruin of a sixties service station at one end of it. It was, at least, no longer the focus point of an attempt to end the world, and it now only had one ghost and one Demon in it, instead of hundreds of the former and scores of the latter. This wasn't a huge aspect in its favour, but at least it was better than it had been an hour or so beforehand.

Darryl shivered, and pulled rotten bits of his coat off him. Janusz's wrist was still bleeding.

'We need to get you to A&E, love.'

Janusz sighed, looking at the wound. 'Usually I'd say I'm fine, I think in this case, you have a point. We'll say a dog did it.'

'I am so, so sorry, again.'

'You were catching me. Saving my life.'

Darryl shook his head, miserably. 'It's that *thing*. That *Spawn*. I… don't want to use it any more. I won't. I went thirty-five years without turning Demon, I'll just go back to that.'

'Don't talk about yourself like that, son,' said Richard, gently. 'The Demon side is a part of you. You can control it, use it for the good of—'

'It's got nothing to do with you, Dad! I know you're like in love with bloody Murzzzz or whatever, but not all of us are willing to put the Demon inside of us ahead of our own family!'

Richard looked like he'd been slapped. 'What a thing to say. Apologise to Murzzzz, this instant, please and thank you!'

'Absolutely not!' Darryl fumed. 'Who told him he could come back into our family anyway?'

'I did! It's his family too!'

'No it isn't. He is not my father. You are.'

'He *is* partially your father as well—'

'No! No, I'm not having that. It's always been you and Mum and he's always been… just there on the side. But if he's now going to make some kind of claim to me, then he can just sod off entirely.' Darryl looked around at the rest of the family, despairingly. 'Right, guys? I'm not being unreasonable, right?' Insecurity plucked at him so much that he barely waited for a response. 'Oh, why am I even asking you? I'm the one who's actually *in* this crappy position. Like you guys would understand.'

'Er, excuse you?' said Charity, offended.

'*Zabko*,' breathed Janusz in the quiet warning tone he used when Darryl was about thirty seconds away from feeling the need to apologise.

'*I* wouldn't understand??' asked Charity. 'I just found out my birth mother or biological mother or… I don't know what the preferred term is these days, Janusz could you look it up for me please?' Janusz couldn't look it up for her because he was still keeping pressure on his bloodied wrist. Darryl was aware that they should probably find new transport to the hospital instead of having a row, but Charity was in full flow now. 'Anyway, I just found out she's been with me all this time. And, Bee Tee Double-U, you two buggers didn't even tell me!' She indicated to Darryl and Brenda. 'And you're all "Boo hoo hoo, my name's Darryl. I have three parents and one of them's paranormal. Woe is me." Did none of you stop and ask whether maybe I might have quite *liked* having three parents with me? Having a ghost Mum to watch over me? Could have been cute, could have had, like, nineties sitcom vibes or something. But *no.*'

'I'm sorry,' mumbled Darryl, fitting his apology in just less than thirty seconds after Janusz's warning. Honestly, you could set your watch by it.

'No,' Charity continued. 'Mother had to go and make all of my decisions for me, didn't she? Just like you always do! Just like keeping me away from my aunt in New Zealand, I could have thrived in New Zealand! Christmas in summer, hobbits everywhere. Being all "Australian But Less So"... But no, you went against Constance's wishes...' She indicated to her left.

'Other side,' muttered Darryl.

Charity indicated to her right, where Constance was standing in still, quiet sadness. 'Which, Mother, the more I think about it, sounds less like legitimate adoption and more like just straight up kidnapping. And then you wouldn't tell me about her, wouldn't tell me she was with me – watching over me. You wouldn't tell me how she died, because what? You didn't want me to hate Murzzzz for it?'

Darryl perked up a little now that Charity's rant was swinging round to everything being Murzzzz's fault.

'Well,' said Charity, glaring at Richard, now. 'I'm afraid I think that boat has sailed.'

Richard looked utterly horrified. 'You too?'

'Did he get Harry and Constance killed?'

'He didn't kill them,' argued Brenda.

'But did he *get* them killed?'

'Now... isn't the time, princess.'

'It's *never* "the time", Mother! It hasn't been "the time" for thirty years! How did you get around my birth parents' will? Did you have a certain otherworldly being use his powers to tinker with official legal documents and change the names on it?'

She glared at Richard. Murzzzz shifted into focus, briefly, looking guilty. '**It was for the best...**'

Oh, my God.

'Oh, my God,' breathed Charity and Darryl, in unison.

'Princess, we can go through this later,' maintained Brenda. 'We're all exhausted, I had to take my shoes off so my feet are freezing, Janusz needs the hospital—'

'I do quite need the hospital,' interjected Janusz, quietly.

'I just…' Charity sighed. 'I think I'm going to need some space, to think about all of this.'

'Of course,' Brenda breezed. 'We'll Uber it to the nearest train station given the state of the car. We can all go home, chippy tea, watch the final of that metalworking show—'

'I don't want to watch metalworking with you, Mother! That Greg guy's going to win it anyway.'

'OK fine, you can have some alone time – watch your cartoons in your room all night if you think that'll help. Grace? Happy with chippy tea…? Oh, where's she wandered off to this time?'

Darryl noticed at the same time as the rest of the family that Grace wasn't with them.

'Don't tell me she's been raptured?' asked Brenda, with just a hint of worry seeping into her tone. 'Or… a Celestial version of whatever it was the Demons did to Murzzzz with the last Hell Hole?'

'*Thank* you for acknowledging what a horrible time Murzzzz has been put through, dear,' interjected Richard. 'And all after putting himself in peril to protect this family—'

'Oh, pack it in, Dad,' breathed Darryl, looking around desperately for Grace. She'd been right there! She'd willed the Hell Hole shut and stopped the rot spreading. She'd definitely been there when it had shut. They'd been so distracted by Janusz's injury and their horrible car park argument that none of them had noticed when she'd just… gone. Was her work on this world done? Had she gone in peace – just quietly returned to the dimension she'd come from – or had she been snatched away by those curiously attractive androgynous Celestials? Was she OK? Why hadn't she said goodbye? He *liked* Grace. Why were they being stuck with bloody Murzzzz but not allowed to keep Grace? It wasn't fair. And they were still facing the end of the world, what were they going to do without Gra—

'Oh, wait,' said Janusz, 'there she is.'

Oh.

Darryl followed his husband's eyeline and saw a rather battered minibus coming towards them from the 'coaches only' part of the car park. It had a logo on the bonnet that incorporated a dove made out of hands and a chunky, modernist cross – which strongly suggested to Darryl that it belonged to the sort of church that held harvest festivals and pet blessings for the kiddiwinks and preferred an acoustic guitar and a tambourine over a pipe organ when it came to hymn accompaniment. It was keeping steadily to the ten miles per hour speed limit of the car park in spite of the fact that they were the only people in it. Grace's tiny little determined face was visible behind the wheel.

There was an awkward pause when it became clear that, at this speed, it was going to take her a while to get to them.

'I didn't just mean watching anime in my room,' said Charity. 'Although… I do have a couple I need to catch up on before I get spoilered. I meant more than that, Mum. I… don't think you quite understand yet. This isn't "chippy tea and *Attack on Titan*" upset. This is "I don't think I can live with you and Dad any more" upset.'

'What?'

'Especially if Murzzzz is going to be hanging around again,' added Charity.

Richard sighed. 'And Murzzzz is the bad guy, again.'

'Yes!' Darryl cried, exasperated. 'He is! And, you know what… I'm with Charity. Either he goes, or I go.' He patted his sister on the arm. 'The three of us can pool our money, get a little two-bed flat, Janusz has been talking about moving out to a place of our own for a while now, haven't you, babe?'

'Please don't bring me into this argument while I'm losing blood.'

'Er, I'm still angry with you as well, Darryl,' added Charity.

'Yeah, but not *as* angry, right? Also I do come with a free Janusz.'

'Yay,' said Janusz, weakly.

At long last, the minibus came to a sensible stop in front of them. Grace rolled down the window with an air of triumph. 'I found us a minibus! Janusz, I really think I should take you to a minor injuries unit or something.'

'You found it?' asked Janusz, trying and failing to open the door to the back of the minibus. 'The only working vehicle in the whole car park?'

'Well… yeah.'

Darryl pushed forwards and opened the door for Janusz. 'The logo says St Catherine's, Coldbay.'

Grace looked confused. 'Yes. Good old St Catherine's.'

Darryl guided Janusz into the minibus before the rest of the family got in. St Catherine's church – the church where Grace had been placed by the Celestials in Coldbay, to wait for the family, to guide them to the apocalypse. The place where she had become so enamoured with her disguise as the priest of a lonely, damp church on a sad little island that she had forgotten the otherworldly mysteries of who she really was. Grace had had such plans for St Catherine's. Such small, kind, lovely plans – nothing like the great and terrible world ending plans she'd been supposed to follow through on. Plans that likely involved learning how to accompany modern hymns on the acoustic guitar, holding pet blessings and the sort of harvest festivals where people would bring in a slightly out-of-date tin of sweetcorn, and she'd put it in a hamper with a ribbon around it. The sort of plans that would probably involve fundraising for a minibus so that she could take pensioners out on day trips.

'Good old St Catherine's,' added Brenda, 'that got thrown at us before the whole island vanished into the void a few days ago. And which, as I remember it, didn't actually have a minibus.'

'Dear,' sighed Richard, 'don't take it out on Grace.'

'No, it's OK,' said Grace. 'You're right. I think I must have just *really* wanted there to be a minibus, and so there was one. It's even got an air freshener that smells like a jelly bean and is also shaped like a jelly bean.' She pointed at it. 'I always used to think "Those look like fun – pity I don't have a vehicle to hang one in". And now I do! Kind of weird, finding out I can just make stuff by wanting it to exist. Now that I know that I'm a... you know, one of those thingies.'

'An incredibly powerful Celestial being,' said Charity, strapping herself in. 'And you're using your new found power to make novelty car accessories. I'm actually genuinely proud of you, right now.'

'Really? I know I'm probably not utilising the power to its fullest, but I don't really understand it yet, it's all so new. Well, I don't need to tell you about that, Darryl.'

'Hmmph,' said Darryl.

'Darryl, she has a point,' Brenda told her son as Grace drove the minibus towards the car park's exit at the same excruciatingly slow speed. 'All your life you've been whining that you didn't feel like you were quite enough, just because you could never keep up with me or your sister. And now you have all these new powers, thanks to Murzzzz, and you've decided to throw a tantrum about it all being too much, instead.'

'So, you're siding with Murzzzz, too. Well, that just makes my decision easier, Mum.'

'I am not siding with anyone.'

'What decision?' Grace asked. 'What's happening?'

'My children have decided to respond to saving the world for the second time this week by throwing a joint strop,' Brenda told her.

'It's not a strop,' said Charity and Darryl at the same time.

'They think they're upset with me and their father,' added Brenda.

They were still a considerable distance away from the car park exit. They'd have been faster if they'd jogged.

'Darryl and Charity, what are your thoughts on that?' asked the not-a-priest.

Darryl narrowed his eyes. 'Are you trying to give us sneak family counselling?'

Grace kept her gaze on the car park exit ahead, and didn't reply.

'I just can't do anything right for you kids,' railed Brenda. 'I haven't even had a drink all apocalypse this time, and I've *really* needed one.'

'So what?' Charity asked, glumly. 'I've needed a wee this whole time, sometimes you just have to hold it.'

'It's a bit different, Charity. You've all been nagging me for ages about the booze and look at me – stone cold sober and you ingrates haven't even noticed.'

'We did notice,' Janusz told her. 'Well done, Brenda.'

'*Thank* you, Janusz.'

'It's not enough, Mum,' Charity told her. 'I should be able to trust you. It's not just that you lied, ran roughshod over everyone else… you can't even understand my anger. Neither of you… well. All three of you, if we're including Murzzzz, and Dad seems adamant that we *are* going to include Murzzzz again. You just… don't get it. Darryl didn't tell me Constance was with us either, but at least he gets it – at least he's apologised. And I'm still mad at him but, God, at least it's a *start*. And, I know I tease him about the Demon thing, but I do get why he's angry about it.'

Darryl met eyes with his sister and nodded at her, gratefully.

'But you guys? Mum, Dad, Murzzzz… you won't bloody listen. You never have. It's always been "We'll discuss it later, princess, after we've finished this job." But the job never ends, does it? There's a constant supply of the dead, and I think you guys rely on that. Not just in terms of keeping the ugly sides of this family from us, but from yourselves, too. Stay busy with the work, stay in denial, kick the can along the road… Well, I think we might have come to the end of that road.'

Grace finally pulled out of the service station's parking area and onto the slip road for the still smoky motorway.

'I mean, also us "kids" are all in our thirties and Darryl and Janusz are a married couple, so we really should move out anyway,' added Charity.

Grace blinked over her shoulder at her passengers. 'You're moving out? That's what this is about?'

'So they say, at least,' snorted Brenda, rubbing the feeling back into her wet, frozen feet.

'Watch the road please, Grace,' panicked Richard over her, grasping his seatbelt.

'I think we could all do with some space to think,' Charity said. 'Mum and Dad more than anyone.'

Darryl noted that his father still hadn't said a word about his ultimatum that it was Darryl or Murzzzz. And Richard didn't have to. Darryl knew the answer. More upsetting was that his mother hadn't pushed Richard on it. Richard hadn't exactly asked Brenda's permission for the Demon to return. Yes, it was to Richard's body, but it was also to their family, to her marriage. He took that to mean his mother had chosen Murzzzz's side, too. He understood the logic – he hated it, but he did understand. He understood that devotion to one's spouse. He put a hand on Janusz's knee and pulled up directions to the nearest injuries unit on his phone. Darryl would never let the Demon inside himself out, ever again. The scars on his husband's wrists would act as a reminder. It was too much. Too much. Even in the face of the end of the world, he would not hurt his Janusz – his brave, soft man who had been betrayed by so many other men in his life. Oh yes, he could understand his mother's devotion to Richard. But he would never, ever, as long as he lived, understand the way Richard loved and protected Murzzzz. He would never understand the way his father had mourned the loss of the Demon, or the joy in him now at being reunited, even in the face of his children's rage and despair. Darryl knew that, even now, his father was more interested in being a horrible backseat driver than in actually listening to what Charity was saying. He knew that, when he and Darryl's mother had finally accepted that their 'kids' weren't just bluffing to get attention, Richard would be frustratingly supportive about the whole thing. He would offer to help with the move, help them pay the deposit on the new place, and pop round with frozen homemade dinners, claiming to have accidentally cooked for six and saying he didn't want the food to go to waste. His father would do all of these things with a gentle, kind smile. But he would steadfastly refuse to take in their reasons for leaving.

And, what did all of this mean for the business?

'And what does all of this mean for the business, might I ask?' interjected Brenda. 'There are still ghosts and Demons out there…'

'And in here,' muttered Darryl, glancing at Constance, who was sitting in the back, still clearly visible to him, with an unusually peaceful expression on her face. Wherever he and his sister were moving to, it would definitely be haunted. Maybe that was for the best. Maybe he could help the ghost of Constance Xu reconnect properly with Charity.

'And the mortgage still needs paying – as will the rent on a two-bed flat, if you ridiculous children are to be believed,' continued Brenda. 'Also we do still rather need to save the world, you know.'

This was true. What *did* it mean for the business? Could he still work with his parents, if they'd chosen Murzzzz over him? Could Charity work with them if she felt she couldn't trust them? Did their parents even truly ever work *with* them? Or did they use their children as psychic tools, to be lied to and not listened to, to be taken out of school, kept out of other work, to be taken and raised against the dying wishes of the Xus? It was a lot to think about, and Darryl had already had an exhausting day of it.

They drove out of the smoke, and Grace was able to speed up. The remains of Helsbury station fast became a sad grey cloud against a backdrop of yet more sad grey cloud.

'Let's just get Janusz to hospital for now.' Darryl passed his phone to Grace, to show her directions.

'And after that?' asked Janusz.

'Well, you can't exactly pack your little bindles and move out tonight, can you?' Brenda asked. 'As I said, we'll go home, chippy tea. Charity can watch her cartoons And you kids can see how you feel in the morning.'

Darryl sighed. 'Sure. We'll see how we feel in the morning.'

*

249

Think about home. Think about what it is, to you. Think about who it is, to you. Think about a kitchen, in the early morning light. The clouds that have led to a series of dark grey, damp, closed-in days have finally cleared, and a crisp, bright, early winter sun floods through the windows now. The kitchen smells of today's coffee and last night's chips. Think about a priest who is not a priest – who doesn't even yet know the full extent of what she is, let alone what she isn't. She sips her coffee from 'her' mug – a mug featuring a kitten, warning the world not to talk to her until she has drunk said coffee. She wouldn't mind talking to the others, coffee or not, but nobody else seems to be in the mood. She thinks about home, about whether hers could ever be here. She wonders whether this home might be breaking, so soon after she'd come to stay. Its fractures seem too deep to fix, right now. She wonders whether this is her fault. Perhaps the stress lines were always there, but her arrival added too much pressure, and broke a deep, jagged line right down the middle.

Think about two husbands. One wears a bandage on his arm. The other wears an expression of guilt, and distress, and determination. They sit at the kitchen table in the bright winter sunlight, drinking coffees, not talking to the not-a-priest, but looking at flats to rent online.

Think about a woman, a Princess, the deliverer of the dead and the only Grim Reaper to resign, currently wearing a Batman onesie. She goes over to her brother-in-law's laptop and looks at one of the places they've found on the letting agent's website and, after a brief conversation, she agrees to go and have her shower while her brother-in-law arranges a viewing.

I smile. Her brother sees me, and tells her that I did so, and she smiles back, and I feel, for the first time in I-don't-know-how-long like I could be – if only a little bit – back home.

Think about another married couple, a husband and wife, still in bed. They know that their children are looking for a flat to rent.

250

They do not wish to admit it yet – not to their children, not to each other, not to themselves, and so they stay in bed and watch a metalworking contest's deeply predictable grand final on the TV, and they do not go downstairs. They will admit it in time, and yet still tell themselves and one another that it is temporary and 'a cry for attention'. The father, with a gentle smile, will offer help with the deposit and the move, and 'just pop by' with homemade dinners a lot. The mother will simply wait for them to 'see sense', and she will leave their rooms as they are – ready for when that time comes.

The husband is still too consumed by relief to think about anything else. His is the relief of a smoker finally able to light up after a long haul flight or of the exhausted when a persistent alarm finally falls silent. It's the relief of someone who has found their keys after the third good rummage in their bag. The kind of relief that hits one with a rush of happy blood. He is still too caught up in that bliss. He is whole again, he thinks, whole again at last. He has found his other half.

And his wife knows that.

And, she knows that she is not her husband's other half, not even after all these years. And she knows that she cannot give him the same ultimatum that her children did, because she knows what the answer would be, and it would break her heart.

I linger at her bedroom door. When Charity goes, I will follow. I loved Brenda once, but I do not stay for her. She knows this, too. She sees me, meets eyes with me, and she nods, in acknowledgement. It's almost friendly. Such a shame. We could have had a nice time even after my death, stayed friends. Too late, too late.

She smiles a little at me. It's a sad smile, but there is also a relief to it. Almost as if she feels peace on my behalf.

Am I at peace? No. Not yet. I am not yet home. And the wrong meted out upon me and my little family has still not been righted.

It was supposed to be Brenda and Richard who died, that night. I was supposed to be alive right now, growing old with Harry, with my adult children – my daughter, my adopted son. We were supposed to usher in a merciful end to the world, together. Is that what I wanted? Is that how I will find peace? With the end of the world? Perhaps I don't have long to wait. There is a new Death. I can feel him. He is far away for now, but he will come here and he will be drawn to us.

And, once he comes, I'm not sure this fractured family will be able to stop him.

THE END

Also available

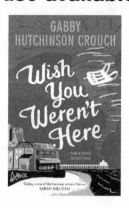

Wish You Weren't Here
(The Rooks series, Book 1)

The Rook family run a little business: ghost hunting. And things have picked up recently. Something's wrong. It's been getting noticeably worse since, ooh, 2016?

Bad spirits are abroad, and right now they're particularly around Coldbay Island, which isn't even abroad, it's only 20 miles from Skegness. The Rooks' 'quick call out' to the island picks loose a thread that begins to unravel the whole place, and the world beyond.

Is this the apocalypse? This might be the apocalypse. Who knew it would kick off in an off-season seaside resort off the Lincolnshire coast? I'll tell you who knew – Linda. She's been feeling increasingly uneasy about the whole of the East Midlands since the 90s.

OUT NOW!

Also available

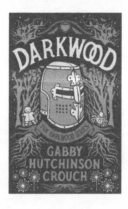

Darkwood
(Darkwood series, Book 1)

Magic is forbidden in Myrsina, along with various other abominations, such as girls doing maths.

This is bad news for Gretel Mudd, who doesn't perform magic, but does know a lot of maths. When the sinister masked Huntsmen accuse Gretel of witchcraft, she is forced to flee into the neighbouring Darkwood, where witches and monsters dwell.

There, she happens upon Buttercup, a witch who can't help turning things into gingerbread, Jack Trott, who can make plants grow at will, the White Knight with her band of dwarves and a talking spider called Trevor. These aren't the terrifying villains she's been warned about all her life. They're actually quite nice. Well… most of them.

With the Huntsmen on the warpath, Gretel must act fast to save both the Darkwood and her home village, while unravelling the rhetoric and lies that have demonised magical beings for far too long.

Take a journey into the Darkwood in this modern fairy tale that will bewitch adults and younger readers alike.

OUT NOW!

About the Author

Gabby Hutchinson Crouch (*Horrible Histories*, *Newzoids*, *The News Quiz*, *The Now Show*) has a background in satire, and with the global political climate as it is, believes that now is an important time to explore themes of authoritarianism and intolerance in comedy and fiction.

Born in Pontypool in Wales, and raised in Ilkeston, Derbyshire, Gabby moved to Canterbury at 18 to study at the University of Kent and ended up staying and having a family there.

She is the author also of the acclaimed Darkwood trilogy, a modern fairy tale series for grown-up and younger readers alike.

About the Rooks

The Rooks is a series of supernatural horror comedy adventures, about the Rook family, who run a little family business. Ghost hunting. And gracious, business has certainly picked up recently. Something's wrong. It's been getting noticeably worse since, ooh, 2016? Bad spirits are circulating…

The full series –

Wish You Weren't Here
Out of Service
Back to Business

Also by Gabby Hutchinson Crouch – the Darkwood series

Darkwood
Such Big Teeth
Glass Coffin

Acknowledgements

Thanks to Dom Lord and Abbie Headon for all their support and help. Thanks to everyone at Duckworth. Thanks to everyone who read and reviewed the Darkwood Trilogy and *Wish You Weren't Here*.

Huge thanks to Nathan, Violet and Alex for generally being a great family. No thanks at all as usual to Spooky – who is a great cat, but not particularly helpful.

These books are for the families, and for the ghosts that families carry with them. Here's to my family's ghosts. Wherever they are, I hope it's not a motorway service station.

Note from the Publisher

To receive updates on new releases in The Rooks series – plus special offers and news of other humorous fiction series to make you smile – sign up now to the Farrago mailing list at farragobooks.com/sign-up.

CPSIA information can be obtained
at www.ICGtesting.com
Printed in the USA
BVHW041050231022
650088BV00004B/100